SHOTGUN CHARLIE

"It wasn't like that, Pap. Honest." But he had no time for further thought on the subject, because Pap freed himself from the desperate grip Tawley had on the back of his vest. He blustered himself like a crazed chicken right at Charlie, in the process whipping by the wide-open stranger. Before the old man's claws connected with Charlie, his eyes went wide and he gagged out a sound Charlie hadn't ever heard from a man before. But the reason why interested him much more—Haskell's wide hands were encircled around Pap's throat.

Without thinking, Charlie went low, wedged a big arm between the two struggling bodies, and drove upward. It didn't knock the stranger's grip loose as he'd intended. Instead it appeared to have the opposite effect, and succeeded only in tightening the stranger's grip on Pap's neck. The old man's eyes bugged out like two bloodshot quail eggs and his tongue had begun to purple.

Without thinking, Charlie drove his right fist straight at the side of Grady Haskell's head and relished the cracking and shifting that he felt underneath his knuckles. The man's head snapped to the side and his grip on Pap's old neck peeled apart. But to Charlie's surprise, Haskell spun back arou

smiling.

"Now, that was a hit!

Ralph Compton

SHOTGUN CHARLIE

A Ralph Compton Novel
by Matthew P. Mayo

A SIGNET BOOK

SIGNET
Published by the Penguin Group
Penguin Group (USA) LLC, 375 Hudson Street,
New York, New York 10014

USA | Canada | UK | Ireland | Australia | New Zealand | India | South Africa | China
penguin.com
A Penguin Random House Company

First published by Signet, an imprint of New American Library,
a division of Penguin Group (USA) LLC

First Printing, June 2015

 REGISTERED TRADEMARK—MARCA REGISTRADA

ISBN 978-0-451-47238-0

Printed in the United States of America
10 9 8 7 6 5 4 3

THE IMMORTAL COWBOY

This is respectfully dedicated to the "American Cowboy." His was the saga sparked by the turmoil that followed the Civil War, and the passing of more than a century has by no means diminished the flame.

True, the old days and the old ways are but treasured memories, and the old trails have grown dim with the ravages of time, but the spirit of the cowboy lives on.

In my travels—to Texas, Oklahoma, Kansas, Nebraska, Colorado, Wyoming, New Mexico, and Arizona—I always find something that reminds me of the Old West. While I am walking these plains and mountains for the first time, there is this feeling that a part of me is eternal, that I have known these old trails before. I believe it is the undying spirit of the frontier calling me, through the mind's eye, to step back into time. What is the appeal of the Old West of the American frontier?

It has been epitomized by some as the dark and bloody period in American history. Its heroes—Crockett, Bowie, Hickok, Earp—have been reviled and criticized. Yet the Old West lives on, larger than life.

It has become a symbol of freedom, when there was always another mountain to climb and another river to cross; when a dispute between two men was settled not with expensive lawyers, but with fists, knives, or guns. Barbaric? Maybe. But some things never change. When the cowboy rode into the pages of American history, he left behind a legacy that lives within the hearts of us all.

—*Ralph Compton*

Chapter 1

The dove's throaty growls had startled him at first, made him jump right off the bed. Surely she was in pain, some sort of trouble. A bad dream at best. Then it had occurred to Charlie that no, this was a natural sound. And this was as close as he'd ever come to hearing it.

Through a thin lath-and-plaster wall mostly covered with paper—still pretty but not nearly so vivid as he was sure it had been a long time since, with tiny pink flowers, roses he thought they might be, surrounded by even tinier green leaves—Charlie finally knew the sounds for what they were. They were the sounds of a man and a woman doing what he was still a stranger to. Would be forever, he guessed.

And so big ol' Charlie Chilton, barely fifteen years old, spent the first night he had ever spent in a town, the first night he'd ever spent in a hotel, the first night he'd ever spent in a bed—an honest-to-goodness spring bed under a cotton-ticking mattress and all—and he spent it mostly awake.

He wondered as he was roused again and again from a neck-snapping slumber, if he should rap on the wall. He didn't want to invite trouble, but he needed sleep. He felt sure when he'd checked in that he was about to receive the finest night's sleep a body could get.

That the hotel was in the habit of renting out unoccupied rooms for short-term trysts was something that Charlie would not know for a long time to come. But that night's introduction had startled him. All the long days preceding his arrival to town had been one odd surprise after another, saddening and shocking and worrisome. And so this last one, despite his earnest hopes, proved more of the same.

This was what the world was like? Not much different from the everyday misery of life on the little rented farm with his gran. He'd hoped for so much more. As he listened to the moans and thumpings and occasional harsh barks of laughter from the men, he hoped that at least his mule, Teacup, was safe and sound and enjoying a good night's slumber in the livery.

It had cost a few coins that he knew he shouldn't have spent, but he'd never indulged in anything in his life and the money he'd earned at that last farm had burned a hole in his trouser pocket until he'd spent some.

Charlie passed some of the long, noisy night by counting out the last of it, searching his pockets over and over again, sure he'd dropped some of the money somewhere along the way. But no, when after long minutes he'd tallied the figures in his head, he had one dollar and twelve cents left. And he decided then that something had to change. He figured he'd worry about it in the morning, but morning came with little interruption from night by sleep, save for brief snatches.

He left the hotel early, when the sun was barely up. The woman's cries had continued long into the early hours, then dwindled, allowing him precious little rest. Before he left the room, his eyes had once again taken in the small lace doily, a marvel of hand-stitching the likes of which he'd never seen. He'd studied it for some time the night before, then set it aside.

It was white, with a pointed-edge pattern, round, smaller than his palm, but large enough to fit under the dainty oil lamp on the chest of drawers. When he'd lifted the lamp to peek at it, he saw tiny flowers, a dozen of them arranged in a circle. It was one of the single most pretty things he'd ever seen in his life, if you didn't count all the wonders nature had up her sleeve.

Those could hardly be topped by man, he figured—a new calf, the soft hairs on its head, how it felt when you rubbed it before the calf awoke, the long lashes on its eyes staring up at you in innocence, spring buds on an apple tree, then how they unfolded over a week or so, the little leaves getting bigger and darker and tougher as the season wore on.

They were special things, to be sure, but that little doily was a corker, maybe because it had no real purpose? Even its prettiness was hidden by the oil lamp. How many folks got to see what some woman had worked so hard to make, hidden as those little flowers were by the lamp? He appreciated them, at least.

And so as he left the room, he spied that doily and thought to himself, Why not, Charlie? Why not have something pretty in your life? After all, didn't they sort of cheat you out of your good night's sleep? And so he had slid it off the polished top of that chest of drawers and poked it quickly down into his trouser pocket with a long, callused finger, reddening about the neck, cheeks, and ears even as he did so.

By the time he reached the bottom of the long staircase in the lobby of the hotel, he felt as if his entire head might catch fire. He shuffled toward the front door and thrust a hand into his pocket. His fingers tweezered the crumpled little doily. He would set it on the counter and leave, walk right out. It was so early no one was there. He lifted it free and that was when he noticed the desk clerk, same man as the night before, in the mirror, was watching him from across the big room where he was busy sweeping the hearth of the great fireplace. How had Charlie not seen the thin, pasty-looking man when he came down the stairs?

Charlie nodded. The man watched him, didn't look particularly angry. No angrier than he'd been the night before when Charlie checked in. He'd looked confused then and looked more of the same now. Charlie pushed the doily back down into his pocket and struggled with the fancy brass knobs of the lead glass doors, worry warring with fear and guilt in his brain. Worry and guilt that he'd stolen the first thing he'd ever stolen in his life, fear that he'd soon be arrested, and slim wonder too that maybe, just maybe, he'd get away with it.

By the time he reached the livery and, with frequent glances back over his shoulder, saw no one trailing him from the hotel, he became more and more convinced that he and he alone deserved to own that doily, that it was made and meant for him to admire, to appreciate. He rode out of that town and vowed, just the same, never to return to Bakersfield. Just in case.

Little did he know that a few short years later he would be a member of an outlaw gang dead set on committing a crime that made stealing a doily the very least of life's offenses.

Chapter 2

Charlie Chilton woke in the dark and lay still, trying to remember where he was. Somewhere on the trail, somewhere out West. Far, far west of anywhere he'd ever been. There was a stream close by, and in the dark he heard its constant rush. It was an odd but welcome comfort.

It had been a week or more since he'd seen another person, which suited him fine. He'd been robbed and swindled and cheated so many times in the past few years since taking to the road that he didn't have much left worth taking. Except for Teacup, the mule.

And that, his sleep-fogged mind told him, was exactly why he was in this forest, off the trail, and had been for a few days. Teacup was poorly and Charlie knew they wouldn't be going on any farther together, so he'd made camp here. The best camp he could with what little he had. If he could see in the dark, he knew he'd see Teacup standing by the big pine, her legs locked, her bony old head leaned against the tree's mammoth trunk. At least he hoped she was still standing.

Before he awoke, he had been smack-dab in the midst of the same dream he always had when he was in a bad way. Only thing was, the dream was a good one. Or at least something he could understand, not like some of those dreams like when he was flying or when mountains turned into the heads of sleeping giants or some other such craziness. This dream was a good one. Points of it were sad, to be sure, but it was the warm feeling of the dream that made him feel as he'd not felt in a handful of years of living out on the road by himself.

It always began the same way—he was standing over Gran's grave, a fresh-packed affair that he himself had dug, then filled. It had been a lot like digging a posthole, only this time when he cracked open the bony ground he made the hole a long, narrow crater from side to side instead of top to bottom. In truth, the old woman wasn't much more than a fence post herself. Certainly no bigger around, and she'd had the personality to match. Stubborn too.

He couldn't pretend his upbringing by her had ever been easy, or particularly pleasant. She'd been a stringy old thing with a sour attitude and a resentment toward him that had nibbled away at him the entire fourteen years he'd been under her care—if it could be called that.

His father had been her son, the old woman he'd only ever known as Gran. He knew she had a proper given name; everyone had one. But so far as he could tell, there was little to no proof of it anywhere about the place.

Charlie had never gone into her private little bedroom in the three-room shack he'd lived in his entire life. The day she died, he entered that room for the first time in his life. In fact, he reckoned he should have gone on in earlier in the day, as she was still as a stick when he found her. He reckoned she'd died in the night.

He was surprised when he didn't loose one tear on her behalf. He figured, despite the fact that she'd been a sour old thing all his days, that he would at least feel something about the passing on of this person, the only relative he'd ever known. But he hadn't. Instead he felt that same creeping feeling of having lived through her slow-simmering, near-constant anger.

So why was it that whenever he recalled that burial scene in that blasted little dream that wouldn't leave him alone, it always ended up the same way—him feeling some sort of happiness? No, happiness wasn't quite the right word for it. More like a satisfied feeling. That somehow everything would work out all right.

It had been what, five, six years since that day when he buried the old woman? Then he'd loaded what few possessions he had on the old mule, Teacup, and headed on up that long dirt track to places unknown. He still recalled, with a knot in his throat and a twinge in his eye, the wide-open feeling that sort of washed over him, like a sudden summer shower on a hot-as-heck afternoon. The sort that feels good right when it happens, but you know you might pay for it quickly because such showers usually meant a choking-hot afternoon was soon to follow.

But right then, when he'd stopped at the end of the long lane that led to the little dirt farm where he'd spent his whole fourteen years, it was still raining, still fresh, still cool, still promising. The hot, sweltering feeling, the uncomfortable edge hadn't set in yet. He knew he'd miss the place, but only because that was all he'd ever known.

He hadn't even gone to a school. The one time he'd ever hinted at wanting to go, Gran had simply said no. "What you need schooling for when you already know all you need to take care of this here farm?" Then she'd given him that sour look that made him jelly inside. She'd turned back to complaining about how he was so big he should have been drowned at birth like an unwanted puppy instead of costing her all her life's fortunes just to keep him in meals.

Charlie reckoned she had been a decent cook. There was never enough of it on the table to suit him, but what was there was always tasty.

And so he'd turned away from the little farm forever, a farm he learned hadn't even belonged to her—she had merely been a tenant. He'd read that in what few papers he'd found in her things. He didn't know what would become of the place, but he'd buried her beside his papa, her son and Charlie's father. The man he'd been told by a few visitors over the years he greatly resembled in size and mannerisms. He had wished every day of his life that he'd been able to know the man. But his father had died when Charlie was but three.

Charlie had dim, vague memories of the man, a big, smiling face looking down at him, reaching to stroke his hair, the weight of a big hand on his head, the rough fingers of a workingman. The same hands he inherited, working the same fields behind the same mule that his father had been trudging along behind when he'd simply dropped in the field one day.

This much he knew because the old woman had blamed Charlie for her son's death. He'd heard it said to him from her so often that he had never really questioned it, had assumed he'd somehow killed his father.

He felt a kinship with that old plodding mule. He'd taken to calling her Teacup because he liked the sound of the word. He'd heard it said in the little mercantile one day when he was a boy, on one of the few visits to town his gran had ever allowed him.

A woman in a fancy dress and a tall blue hat with purple feathers on it had said the word to the bald man behind the counter. He'd attended to her even though Gran had been in there first. Gran had sputtered all the way home about it in the wagon. She'd even turned to Charlie and said he was to blame.

The claim hadn't shocked him. If he'd thought about it he would have guessed she would come around to arrive at that discovery sooner or later. In her eyes, everything in life was Charlie's fault. Well, not everything. Only the bad things. He'd never in his life been responsible for anything good that had happened.

And so, all those years later, after leaving the little farm and its two sad graves, Charlie Chilton had roamed, not expecting much from himself, not knowing much more than the dulling, ceaseless ache of farm labor, plodding along beside Teacup until her own demise, quietly in the night, along a burbling valley brook a good many thousand miles, territories, and states to the west of where he'd grown up.

When light finally had come that morning, he somehow knew what he'd find before he rose, his thin blanket dropping to the hard earth on which he'd slept. Teacup was gone, laid out cold and quiet beneath the big tree. He reckoned when he awoke in the night that he should have gone to her, but what could a fellow like him do to stop the final claim that old age makes?

He wept long and openly over that mule's passing more so than he did over his gran's. He'd never ridden the mule in all those years he'd known her, never even thought of doing so. She was a companion, had always been so, not a critter to carry him.

He'd been doing a poor job at prospecting for gold, but he had acquired a pick, a shovel, and a pan. And with the pick and shovel he'd done his level best to bury the old, uncomplaining girl. It had taken him all day to make a dent in the hard root-knotted ground deep enough to roll her into—with much grunting and levering with a stout length of log.

When he was finished, he caught his breath, said a few words over her, then with as much dignity as he could offer old Teacup, covered her with dirt and topped that with rocks, a good many of them as big as or bigger than his head. Soon the jumble was a sizable cairn that he felt certain would keep critters from disrupting Teacup's resting place.

Charlie felt a twinge of guilt over the big mounded pile, knew her body could feed plenty of critters looking for a toothsome treat, but he twinged even more inside when he thought of his old friend's body savaged by wolves or bears or lions. He wasn't even sure what territory or state he was in, not sure if any or all of those beasts lived there, but that didn't matter. To him, they were all possibilities that didn't sit well in his mind and left him feeling uneasy.

"Let them find their own food," he wheezed as he rolled another boulder on top of the pile, for good measure.

By the time he was finished, he was exhausted, his hands were bloodied, and one of his thumbnails had been half pulled off when he jammed it too hard between two rocks, scrabbling to find purchase.

Cradling his wounded, throbbing hands in his lap, Charlie Chilton dozed off, dropping like one of those same stones deep into a pit of dark slumber, snoring like a bull grizz. When he finally awoke, it was to find himself wet through.

It was nearly dark and had apparently been raining for some time. It continued drizzling a solid, sluicing rhythm the rest of that day, on through the night, and for three days following. It soaked him and his meager belongings straight through. He was numb and cold and blue-lipped. It wasn't until early the next morning that it occurred to him that something wasn't right. He felt odd, sort of numb all over.

When the shivers began, trembling his substantial frame as if someone were shaking him from behind, he knew it was a sickness. He'd always been in good health, something he valued because his gran had frequently terrified him with sob-filled tales of how his father had died.

"Worked himself to death," she'd howled. "And with no never mind paid to how his poor mother would fare in the world. I swear he wanted to kill himself. As soon as he come down with those chills and fevers, I knew he was a goner. I swear he done it to spite me. Then he stuck me with you!" She'd jam a little bony finger hard into his arm or chest or cheek and growl another few minutes. She'd tell him that as sure as she was a saint to put up with such cruelty, Charlie would end up like his father and leave her alone in the cold, cruel world.

And now here I am, he thought. Riddled with a sickness that like as not killed my daddy, and me without a soul around to help keep me alive.

It was this long, tight line of thinking that plagued Charlie enough that, despite the racking dry coughs that had begun to shake him alternately with the sudden shivers, he managed to gain his feet and try to kindle a fire.

But the relentless sheets of cold gray rain were more than he could battle. In the end, he managed little more than a cold, wet camp right beside the stone cairn he'd constructed for his dead friend. He stayed there for the better part of a week. Each day that passed felt worse than the one before.

After a number of days, he tried once more to stand, to make a fire, to get a drink, to do anything that felt normal. But none of anything felt normal anymore. All he ended up mustering out of himself were a few tired sighs, grunts, and wheezes. Finally he gave up and leaned back against the rock pile again.

"I expect I am to die right here and it probably won't take all that long either." He wasn't sure if he spoke that or whispered it or imagined it. But that, along with a familiar image of what he always imagined his dead father had looked like, came to him then. It was a smiling face, much like his own, but more handsome, less thick-cheeked, and with a kindly glow.

But that was soon slapped down by the hovering, scowling face of his gran, waiting for what she'd predicted would always happen. He'd end up proving her right. That tag end of a thought burrowed into his mind and left him slipping into another layer of sickness, angry and saddened.

Chapter 3

"You see what I see, boys?"

Charlie heard the voice before he saw whoever it was it had come from.

"No? How can you say no, Simp? You got collard greens for brains? Oh, that's right, I expect you do!"

The burst of jagged laughter that followed the odd remarks succeeded in pulling Charlie's eyes open. He jerked back with a start and whapped his head on a rock. The pain of it, hot and throbbing, helped him focus his eyes as he reached up without thinking. The laughter that his painful action conjured swiveled his head and locked his eyes on what he hoped weren't what passed for angels in heaven.

There before Charlie stood a group of four or five men, all on horseback, ringed before him. Back behind the men stood what looked to be a couple of pack animals, laden with crates and sacks, all lashed down with crisscrossed, well-used hemp rope.

Charlie's first thought was surprise that he hadn't heard all those men and horses coming along the path. As far as he could tell, the men, plus the pack animals, were for real and true. They looked alive enough. In fact, they looked like dozens of other hard men he'd seen over the years, always on the scout for trouble. Early in his days on the road, he'd seen a number of such men, men who treated him like an easy payday.

They'd robbed him of what little he had, or at least they had tried to. He'd always been much larger than others his age, so when Charlie grew angry, he had come to learn that others, even seemingly robust, frightening men, men whom he would consider fleeing from, all backed away from him. Fear glinted in their eyes, a look that told him they knew they had made a drastic mistake in picking on this lone traveler.

So when this haggard group of five men woke him, Charlie knew, by the way they were looking at him, that he was about to be robbed. The group of men broke, two walking their horses to one side of him, two to the other, one remaining in the center. Those to the sides slowly circled him, not taking much effort to hide the fact that they were working to get behind him.

He tried to muster up a big voice to bellow at them. He wanted to tell them they'd better look out because he was fast on his feet and twice as mean as a riled-up rattler.

He tried to let his shout rage at them, but all that came out was a big, hacking cough that doubled him over as he tried to stand, sending him flopping backward on the rock pile again.

When he came to, the same men were standing around him, and the older one who'd done the speaking earlier was bent over him. Other than the surprising kindness of the man's eyes, it looked as if he was about to finish the job that Mother Nature hadn't quite completed. The old man was missing half of his choppers so that he was gap-toothed. He sported a patchy, dull gray beard that might have had food stuck in it, and topping his lined, pocked face was a dented bowler hat, a bent silk flower, missing petals, drooping from the tatty band.

"Why, boy, you look plumb awful. You tangle with a she-lion or a boar grizz?"

"No . . . no, sir," Charlie responded before he had time to think, and there it was, his tongue running across the forest floor.

"You hear that, boys? This big young'un here has already shown a heap more sense than the rest of you put together. He knows a sir when he meets one."

The mumbles and rolled eyes from the other men told Charlie they paid the man's comment little heed. Charlie refocused as the old man bent closer. It was then that he also noticed the big skinning knife wagging from the gent's left hand.

Charlie tried to back away from him, succeeded only in worming up tighter to the rock pile. The effort tuckered him out and he sagged back again, working to breathe. There was a rank, unwashed sort of smell too that seemed to come from the old man. At least he only noticed it when the old man and the others had come around.

"Steady, boy. Steady. I ain't gonna harm you. You're all tangled in them clothes and blankets of your'n. Knotted tighter than a hatband on a banker's head. You must have done some thrashing in your deliriums. I'm aiming only to cut them loose from you a bit so you can gain your legs. Though from the looks of you I'd say you're a fair piece from standing."

His face pulled away from Charlie and he heard him speak again. Charlie worked to pull in a breath. For some reason he was finding it hard as stone to draw a decent breath.

"Boys! Two of you get over here and lend a hand, drag this fella off of them rocks and lay him out over yonder, well away from this rock pile. Dutchy and Simp, you two mush-heads build a fire back a ways from where he had one. Too close to whatever it is he's got hidden under them rocks."

Charlie had trouble following what the old man was saying, but if he heard him right, someone wasn't walking well and someone else was going to carry whoever it was. . . . He refocused on the old man. It startled him to see the face reappear, closer than before. Again, he was struck by the eyes set in such a craggy face. They seemed kindly. Something about them told Charlie here was a decent sort of fellow. Not at all what he'd looked at first to be.

"Boy, you hear me? Nod or say something if you can."

Charlie fought for another breath. Then it occurred to him that the old man might be talking to him. Maybe he should say something, just the same. Just in case. He nodded, then said, "I . . . hear . . . you."

The old man nodded again and smiled, his face inches from Charlie's. "Don't you worry. Ol' Pap Morton'll take care of you, see you right."

"What for?" said a voice close by.

Without a pause in speaking, the old man narrowed his eyes and in a grim, tighter voice said, "You get that fire blazing yet, Dutchy? Course not, you're an idiot. Numb as a . . ."

Charlie's world pinched out with the sound of an old man's reedy voice berating someone for something. For what, he didn't know, didn't care. All he knew was that he was probably dead or nearly so. Couldn't even recall how he got to this sorry state . . . about to be robbed or worse by strange, hard, dangerous men bent on doing him harm. Probably leaving him for dead—ha, that'd be a laugh, a joke on them, as he was about there anyway.

Chapter 4

"What I'm trying to tell you, if you'd let me get a word in edgewise . . ." Grady Haskell poked the long barrel of his Colt straight into the fleshy tip of the man's long nose. He pushed it, held it there for a moment, then pulled it away and looked close before smiling, then laughing. The barrel's snout left a pucker, a dimple at the end of the long nose. But the man didn't respond, didn't jerk away because he was dead. His only reaction was a flopped head that revealed a ragged neck gash that welled blood anew. The wound was not an hour old.

"You, sir, are a plumb lousy conversationalist. Any-body ever tell you that?" Grady leaned in close again, as if waiting for a response. "Hmm?"

Getting no response, he howled again, upended a hazel-colored bottle, and bubbled back a few swallows. A thin stream of the burning rye whiskey dribbling out the corner of his stubbled mouth. "Time to get me a Chinese girl, a long, hot bath, and a cee-gar. Maybe even a steak and an Irish apple or two." He belched and looked around him at the strange room. It should be strange to me, he thought. I have never before been here. And once I do what I need to here, I will take my leave and call it a day.

He fell asleep for a short time, awoke with a start, determined to kill whoever or whatever it was that had interrupted his earned slumber. He saw no one but the dead man, still slumped as he had been in sleep when Grady had come up behind him and sawed deeply into his bulging neck.

The sight reminded Grady of his long-dead grandpappy back in the Chalahoosee Ridge, back in the Great Smoky Mountains of North Carolina, where he was raised and where his kind still dwelled. Old Pappy, he had been a mean old coon, but he was generous with his knowledge of corn whiskey making. It was a skill he had worked to teach young Grady. But he and Grady had argued time and again on one point—the old man had said that a proper moonshiner must not like his product too much. Oh, he could enjoy it once the day's labors were through, but there was no call for taking a drink while on the job. And that was something Grady could not abide by.

There came a day when Grady had been entrusted to the operation of the still for an afternoon while his grandfather attended to business in town. Grady decided he'd celebrate the fact that he was nearly sixteen years of age. He'd ladled a dipperful of young, raw corn squeezings. One had led to two, and when he'd been nearly through with a third, along came old Grandpappy, who'd laid down the law, clouting young Grady hard enough to set his ears to ringing. That was when it all happened, when everything in Grady's life turned for naught. And when he made that unbreakable vow to himself never to put up with another man's wrath again, why . . . there was no going back.

He'd taken the beating, not saying much. But he'd managed a bottle of the prime stuff down the front of his bib overalls when he left. He'd finished that bottle off

that evening and decided he'd not said nearly enough to
the old man, so he headed back to ol' Grandpappy's
place, found him asleep in his chair before the potbelly
stove, head slumped to one side. He knew that whenever
he talked with the old man it was never a two-way road.
The old man always had to have the upper hand, always
had to edge him out of the conversation altogether.

That time he'd been determined ol' Grandpappy would
hear him out. So he'd done the best thing he knew to get
the old thickhead's attention—he grabbed up a ball-peen
hammer and brought it down on the old man's bean once,
twice, three times. And maybe a few more for good measure; he never could recall the exact number.

All this came back to Grady years later as he sat
drunk, looking at a different man he'd killed, trying to
hold a conversation with him, as he'd done with ol'
Grandpappy all those years before. The old man hadn't
listened, even though he didn't talk back to him, of that
he was sure. And this one was the same.

But now, when he looked at this man, he saw ol'
Grandpappy, and though the man had been a crusty sort,
he was the only one in the whole dang Haskell clan who
had ever paid him any mind, shown him any sort of kindness. And now Grady found himself missing the old man,
missing the ridge and those green, green mountains
more than he had in a lifetime's worth of Sundays.

"I tell you," he said to the stiffening corpse, "I don't
know how to get back there, to get back home to the
Chalahoosee Ridge. I've tried a number of times over
the years, but there's always something that needs my
efforts. Something that prevents me from pointing my
horse toward the southeast. . . . Hey!" Grady leaned forward, shouted again, but the dead man didn't move.

Grady Haskell went on like this, conversing with the

man he'd so recently incapacitated, for another hour before expiring himself, a sagged mass of angry killer, in the dead man's other chair.

When he awoke, some hours later, dawn's sun had begun its slow crawl skyward. Grady's head pulsed like a hammer-struck thumb with each beat of his heart. He did his best to ignore the voice inside that told him to lay off the liquor and he might well wake up feeling better one of these days. He knew the voice was probably right, but he pushed it down, did his best to tamp it and ignore it and kill it. And the best way he knew to do that was to guzzle back a few mouthfuls of gargle.

He leaned forward in the chair, caught sight of the man he'd sliced open, and groaned. That was something he didn't need to see first thing in the morning, at least not before he'd taken in some hair of the dog.

"Where is it?" His dry-blood-covered hands scrabbled on the floor by his feet. He usually had enough wits about him to cork the bottle before he dozed for the night. But his fingernails brushed glass. The bottle rolled from him and sounded lousy and hollow. Spent. He groaned again and sank back into the chair. This day had not started well and it was only going to get worse, he was sure.

"What I need," he said after a few silent moments with his eyes closed, "is a whole lot of money so I don't have to worry about such foolishness." And as he sat there, as if it were a gift, a reward for his fine new idea, his gaze fell on a half-full bottle of whiskey he'd not seen the night before. He smiled, retrieved it off the sideboard, returned to his chair, and recommenced drinking and thinking.

Grady recalled what the dead man had told him shortly before Grady had made him dead. He'd whimpered, said that what money he had was in the bank, that nobody but a fool would keep his money in his house nowadays.

The thought of it had stunned Grady, but for a moment. Imagine that—plain ol' giving your money to someone else to hold on to for you. Grady wasn't too sure about how other folks might think, but if he had more than the few coins in his pocket, he was dang sure there wasn't a person on the earth who could do a better job watching over it than his own self.

Grady had come back to his senses in time to drag his blade deep into the whimpering man's neck, mostly for being impertinent, but also for not having his money on hand when Grady needed it. Banks ... of course he'd known about them, even been in one a time or two to redeem pay chits after cattle drives—nasty work were those cattle drives. But he had never considered banks to be of use in his own life.

But the more he thought on it the next day, the more the very idea of banks made good sense. He tugged on the bottle again, licked his lips. A wide, slow smile pulled across Grady Haskell's blood-spattered face, and a low chuckle uncurled itself from deep in his throat. "Yes, sir, I do believe it's time to stab a big pig in the backside, as ol' Grandpappy used to say. Enough of this penny play."

First things first. Grady knew that all the big operators had gangs to help them pull it off. The trick would be in getting rid of them and keeping the haul himself once the job was done.

Grady didn't fancy sharing much of anything with anybody, never had the urge to do so, in fact, even as a child. But he had no worries about going through the motions of sharing. That was what planning such a job was all about, after all. Now all he had to do was find the gang. He needed a handful of dumb-as-rocks despera-does willing to do as he told them and then curl up and die when the dust settled.

Another swig off the bottle to seal the deal—at least in his own head—tamped his hangover down to a dull thudding somewhere behind his eyes. Grady stood, straightened his shirt and vest, readjusted his trousers, checked his gun belt, found his dark beaver, flat-crown hat, and saluted the dead man.

"Thanks for your hospitality, friend." He strode to the door, lifted the latch, and said, "No hard feelings, eh?"

His dry chuckle followed him out the door and con-tinued as Haskell relieved himself against the side of the little farmhouse. Yes, sir, he thought. This is turning out to be one of the best days I have had in quite some time. As he mounted up, he gave thought to the best direction he knew of to find a few men to do his bidding. But most important of all, he gave thought to which direction lay the richest town, one with a big, fat bank waiting for him. And as he wasn't all that far from California, he believed he knew where to go.

Chapter 5

The raw tang of slow-burning, wet wood tickled Charlie's nostrils, waking him. Something told him to lift his head, pop open those eyes. Problem was, that was a whole lot harder than it sounded. He tried to run his tongue around the inside of his mouth, but it felt like a raspy river rock and his lips felt as though they'd been hammered together by a burly blacksmith. Same blacksmith whose big fists were playing the Devil's own band inside Charlie's skull, enough so that he was sure it was about to split wide open anytime.

"Boy!"

A voice through water, echoing through a cavern, maybe through a split in a big rock ...

"Boy!"

Someone smacked him hard on the face. Charlie managed to crack an eye open, enough to let light in. Then came another smack, different this time.

"Boy, you hear me? You got to put some effort into this, elsewise I can't help you."

Something hit his face again, but this time it didn't feel so much like a crack to the chops as a wet something. It dragged up over his eyes and . . . he could open the other one. Now both, wider.

There was an old man—but wait, wasn't that the same old man? Leaning over him? Yes, he'd seen that face, homely as it was, somewhere before. Now he knew, it was the old man who'd come in with those riders. But what did he want?

"You . . ."

The old man smiled. "That's right. It's me. You remember?"

"Stop it."

The old man leaned closer. "How's that?" He was still smiling.

Charlie was beginning to get annoyed. Who smiled so much anyway? If this was heaven, he wasn't all that sure he was going to like it. "Stop . . ."

"Stop what?"

"Stop hitting me . . . in the face."

The old man backed up, eyes wide. "What? Hitting you?" Then his face split wide open in a smile. He turned and said something, and then Charlie heard hoo-raws and guffaws from behind the man.

"He thinks I was hitting him!" More laughter; then the old man bent low and held up a rag. "I was wiping your face down, boy. You done took a chill. Lord knows how long before we come along. By the time we found you, you was past knockin' on the door. You was taking off your hat and steppin' on through!" He turned again.

Now Charlie saw faces crowding down close.

"Ain't that right, boys?"

A chorus of men nodded, all of them looking down at Charlie with more concern than he recalled them having before. As if a bung had been pulled from an overfilled barrel, Charlie's memories of recent events flooded out. Teacup dying, plain old giving up the ghost. All that work of prying around in the rooty, bony soil to carve out a hole big enough for her to rest in . . .

Then gathering those rocks, the never-ending task of hauling stones back for her grave so no critters could have at her. Then the rains, hard, driving rains that laid him low, in and out of himself, as if he were being dunked one minute in icy streams, and then the next in a boiling scalding pot used at pig killings. Then these men had shown up. He recalled them arranged around him on horses, and he'd felt sure they were about to kill him.

"Boy, you back with us now? I think we should muckle on to you and get you to set upright. Can't be good on a man's body to have him all laid out like a corpse when he ain't one. Less'n he's sleeping. Mex and Ace, you get on over here and hoist this big boy upright so he's sitting like a man again."

Before Charlie could protest, a skinny, freckled red-headed man with a stubbled face and horrible breath grabbed him high on his right arm and a darkish, solid fellow, some years older than Charlie, did the same on his left. This man wore his long hair unbraided, not in any sort of ponytail. It hung down between his shoulder blades and was cut straight across, blue-black in color.

But the thing that stoppered the words in Charlie's mouth happened when he looked up to tell the men to leave him be. He looked right into the man's eyes and saw one blue and one nearly black. The man stared right back at Charlie for a few seconds, and then Charlie broke eye contact and looked away.

"Don't pay him no never mind, boy," said the old man. "Mex ain't much for talkin', but he'll do in a pinch all right." The old man slapped his leg. "I recall the time we was up to Lodestone. You remember that, Mex? And we skinned all them dandy gamblers? Hoo-wee, you'da thought none of them high rollers had ever seen an Injun before! And for us to throw 'em one with mismatched eyes? Hee-hee!"

The entire time the old man spoke, Charlie stared at the man's eyes. Couldn't help it. They were spooky, like no eyes he'd ever seen. He wanted to get up and away from the man as fast as his legs could carry him. But he was being muckled on to by two men, and as they dragged him upright slowly, sharp pains raked up his sides and made him gasp, and a cold sweat popped out on his forehead.

"Easy, boys. He's had a time of it." The old man leaned in. "Boy, you done broke a couple of ribs in all your thrashing and coughing."

"What's wrong with me?" said Charlie after a few minutes once they'd let him be and the wave of hot pains had ebbed.

"I expect it's pleurisy. Settled right into your lungs and proceeded to march up an' down, causing holy havoc and leaving a mess of misery behind, like Grant through Richmond."

There was a long silence, and then in a wheeze Charlie said, "I thank you, then, for all you've done. I expect I can make it all right on my own now. I don't have much, but you're welcome to it."

The old man sniffed, said, "You travelin' alone, boy? You don't mind me asking, how old are you anyway? You seem a bit on the young side, once a fella gets past your size and gets to studying you."

Charlie didn't reply, so the old man kept talking. "You

must have been traveling with one big pard, because that rock pile you built is mighty big! I reckon it must have been your twin, what with the size of it and all."

Charlie cut his eyes to the man, then looked away again.

"Oh, there I go again, stuffing my boot in my mouth. I'll never learn. Ask the boys. If there's a wrong thing to be said in any situation, you can bet yourself a good hand that Pap Morton will be the one to say it every time."

Charlie smiled weakly, then fell asleep. As he drifted off, he recollected that he couldn't tell how long it had been since the men found him. Pap had told him a few times, but Charlie still felt confused about the past. He didn't think it mattered all that much, though. Not much did.

The first thing Charlie saw when he awoke was that all the men but Pap had begun loading up as if they were ready to head on out. They were nearly finished and making last-minute adjustments, tightening cinches, gulping coffee, and checking buckles, when Charlie yawned and tried to sit up.

He didn't say anything and no one spoke to him, though he wanted to know what they were all up to. He figured it was none of his business to pry. He also figured they were headed out and going to leave him there as they had found him. Though he had to admit if that was all they were offering, he was a darn sight better off than when they'd found him. So all in all, he had no right to complain.

All the men, save for Pap Morton, mounted up. Again, no one paid Charlie any mind, so he kept his peace. But he was powerfully curious as to what they were up to.

Morton jutted his old bearded chin at Dutchy, the last man in line. "Tawley's place, a month."

Dutchy nodded, loosed a stream of chaw juice, then tugged the brim of his hat once and followed the others. In near silence the four men rode out of camp, threading through the trees until they were out of sight.

Pap watched them go, then turned to Charlie and clapped his horned old hands together, smiling. "What say we have ourselves a fry-up? I expect you're ready to eat a bear and three cubs."

Charlie smiled and nodded, not wanting to disappoint the old man. But he wasn't all that hungry. He knew he should be, hadn't had much more than warm broth and a few nibbles of hardtack soaked in black tea since he came around. As Pap bustled about the cook fire, with effort Charlie ran a hand across the tight wraps of blue-and-red flannel the old man had swathed around his chest. "You did this for me?"

"Ain't nobody else around I seen who was about to lend you a hand. And believe me, you needed it." Pap went back to nudging strips of thick, fatty bacon around in his cast-iron fry pan. The scent reached Charlie's nostrils and he felt a strange sensation, something familiar but almost forgotten to him. What was that?

"I see your nose flexing like a dog on a stink trail. You're hungry, boy. Hee-hee, I can tell. Any second now that gut of your'n will be growling like a angry lion."

Charlie looked down at his much-thinned belly, and his eyebrows rose as it began to make sounds he hadn't heard in a long time. "I reckon you're right."

"See? Ol' Pap knows. When it comes to vittles, Pap knows a thing or three!" The old man fairly danced around the fire ring like an Indian doing a war dance, sliding pans and clanking the coffeepot and howling because he blistered a finger.

*   *   *

"Say, Pap, what was that you said a few days back about skinning them gamblers, on the riverboat, I think it was?"

They rode in silence for a few moments, and then Pap said. "Oh, you heard that, did you? I'd thought maybe you was still half out of your bean to recall that." He looked at Charlie and smiled. "I talk a whole lot."

For another long stretch of moments, there was not much more said than that. Then Pap said, "I hope you won't think badly of us, Charlie Chilton, but I will let you in on a secret. I ask you not to judge, if'n you can help it, though. We're what you might call living as we can, taking advantage of situations as they arise, peeling a little bit for ourselves from wads where that little bit won't much be missed." He flicked a long, bony finger toward Charlie, his face drawn into a gray mask of seriousness. "Mind you, we ain't no common garden-variety thieves."

"But you are thieves?" Charlie's sudden response surprised even himself.

"Well, no. That is to say . . . not really. At least not so much like that. Here, how you like old Nub?"

Charlie reached down, patted the neck of the big horse he was riding. "Oh, he's a fine one, he is. I still feel odd about riding a beast, though."

"You mean to say you never rode that old mule you buried back there?" Pap's eyebrows rose high in disbelief.

"Naw, fella like me ain't got no call to go riding an old girl like Teacup. She was . . . well, she was my friend."

They rode in silence for a few minutes; then Pap said, "Charlie, you are without a doubt one of the kindest souls this old coyote has ever met. How come you to be so nice anyway? Most folks I know have a streak of rank running right through them a good foot wide."

"Well, I reckon I don't know." Charlie fidgeted, his big legs hanging down either side of the equally large horse as they plodded along the shaded roadway. They were following whatever course Pap had in mind, seemingly in no hurry at all.

Charlie had been happy to ride bareback, but Pap had insisted he use a spare saddle the boys had scrounged up from somewhere and had lashed to their gear pile. It had proven to be a comfortable ride, despite his initial misgivings about riding another animal. And best of all, Nub didn't seem to mind being stuck with Charlie on his back.

"I'm not one to pry," said Pap, rubbing his chin. "But I'll go ahead and ask you something, and if you don't care to answer, well, know that I won't be offended in the least. Okay, then?"

"Aw, Pap. I ain't got no secrets. Ask me anything."

"Okay, then, I will. Where you from? What's your story? I'm a curious sort, and I like to know the folks I'm riding the trail with, if you get me."

So Charlie told him. Told him all about his gran, the farm, Teacup, his childhood, what he knew of his daddy. . . . He talked on and on while the horses carried them slowly on up the trail to where, Charlie had no idea, nor did he particularly care. He was pleased to have companionship, especially with someone who didn't seem to want anything from him, except for him to natter on like an old hen. After a while he stopped, reddened, and looked away.

"Well," said Pap, after fashion, "seems to me you've led a busy life, Charlie Chilton. I hope me and the boys don't bore you none."

Charlie looked up, eyes wide, only to find Pap winking at him.

Far ahead, bars of sunlight sifted through the tall ponderosa pines and lit the trail as if they were in a church and a thousand candles were glowing.

"Now, ain't that pretty?" said Pap.

Charlie could only nod and smile.

Chapter 6

The first bullet plowed a furrow, unearthing a trench of fresh-splintered mahogany six inches long and half an inch deep. The slug finally lodged, a hot, spent devilish thing, out of sight in the bar top. But no one noticed.

The second bullet had already done what it was born to do—it stopped a living thing from ever moving forward again. That thing was one Rupert McGinley, town fireman, avid reader of books, amateur gunsmith, and on this particular day, a man not blessed with the best of luck.

Spelling his barkeep pal, John Otis, whom he was visiting on this not-very-busy Saturday morning, so Otis might visit Mae's Dining Emporium for a bite before the long, busy day grew that way, McGinley had little time to regret his decision before the bullet drove through his left cheek, through his brain, and caromed off his skull, angling downward with considerably less force, before exiting his head where his hairline stopped and the back of his neck began.

No one knew if he died right away or if he somehow managed to see the man who'd felled him. Likely all he saw were the boots the stranger wore, stovepipes with dog ears at the tops for tugging on, filmed with trail dust, the cracked heels caked with dung. They were like a thousand other pairs of boots that had stomped in and out of the Blue Bird Bar over the years.

But these boots belonged to Grady Haskell, a man known by an increasing number of people from Old Mexico to Oregon, and not a one of them recalled the meetings with Haskell favorably. The ones who survived them, that is.

If anyone other than Rupert McGinley had been in the Blue Bird that dark Saturday morning, they might have wondered why Haskell had shot the local fellow, known by all as a decent sort, reliable when friends knocked for help, steady in his work, uncomplaining, and true.

McGinley had turned smiling eyes on the stranger and asked what he might do for him, already reaching for a coffee mug, it being assumed by the man that the early hour meant the stranger might be more interested in a wake-up than the numbing effects of liquor.

They might well have wondered all this, but they too would have been shot. For Haskell took great pains never to leave known witnesses breathing. At least that was what he'd heard about himself in small towns and large, wherever he'd visited quietly, where people thought they knew him but didn't realize they were talking to the man of flesh himself, and not just the man of rumor.

"That's not the sort of help I was looking for," said Haskell as he glanced down at the oozing head of McGinley. He knew that soon a crowd would close in, attracted by the god-awful noise revolvers made. But there was nothing for it. He had to have the innards of that cashbox, and the fastest way was a bullet.

Grady liked the way sudden, sharp actions had of

blazing right through all the expected yammering and chitter-chatter. All he wanted was the money, maybe a free drink, and then . . . gone. He'd get that this morning too, but in the form of the still-locked cashbox and a nearly full bottle of Crow Dog rye.

Yes, voices drew closer, clumping along the narrow sprung-plank boardwalk out front. But Haskell was already out the same door he'd entered. Through the narrow storage room, then the alley to his waiting horse, the fidgety roan. If he had known what the beast would be like, he would have opted for a different one. But he had to admit the horse had bottom. He'd tested it three times since leaving Oregon and heading southward.

Each barroom raid had resulted in less money than he had expected, but enough to get him to the next town. The one thing he always tried to avoid was hard work for someone else. Heck, he didn't even like to spend much effort on his own behalf. Nothing more galling than sweating when he didn't have to.

By the time shouts from the alley reached him, he was already more than half a mile out of town toward a cluster of rocky gray spires visible to the southwest, jutting from the lodgepole pines like low storm clouds.

Haskell snorted down a laugh. "Rubes, every one of them," he said to the horse. "They'll be coming and we'll be gone. They always wait a little too long. They see the blood and they know they're next. They let themselves think of their wives, the little ones, their good town lives, how hard their trips out here were.

"They let those comforting thoughts settle in and then, of course, it's too late to give chase, to do much of anything but quiver and cry and mourn. Those few seconds plant the doubt, the fear." Haskell smiled. That's really what I do, he thought. I am a farmer of these fools, and their fears are my crops. He let out a snort. "I am a poet, horse. And don't let nobody tell you different!"

The metal cashbox, stuffed in one saddlebag, but too long to let him work the buckle properly, bounced in rhythm with the harried horse's efforts. Its coiny contents clanked, alternately pleasing and annoying Haskell. He'd hoped for a heftier box, but hadn't had the time to wait another day for the money from Saturday night's affairs. Besides, he reasoned, there was no guarantee that the lummox of a bartender—different from the man he'd laid low, wouldn't have taken the cash home or to the town bank.

What he wouldn't give for all the money in a rich town's bank. . . . With that fulsome, comforting thought settling over his brain like a thick, drizzle-filled gray cloud, Grady Haskell booted the wide-eyed roan to a greater lunging pace and popped the cork from the mouth of the bottle of rye. He smiled as he guzzled what he regarded as a well-earned drink. But nowhere near as tasty as that first sip of champagne was going to be from that first bottle of many he was going to buy once he pilfered clean his first big, bursting bank.

Only thing he needed was a handful of rubes willing to do all the things he didn't have enough hands for. Elsewise he'd do the entire thing himself. But there was nothing saying he had to end up splitting the loot with them. No, sir, they would serve a purpose, as all the others had done, as the man back at that one-horse-town saloon had done, served a purpose. And then Grady had done him a favor by relieving him of having to think about his part in it all.

Grady howled once more as his horse galloped hard

over the low hills far to the south of the little town. He swigged the rye and enjoyed the sound of the coins clanking and rattling in the box. Soon, he thought. Soon I will need packhorses to haul it all.

Chapter 7

"Well, I'll tell you, Charlie. Tawley's place is sort of hard to define. I can tell you what you can do there and what you can't do there. What you can do is a fairly limited list, but what you can't do there is an even shorter list."

"I reckon I don't understand that, Pap." Charlie winced as Nub stepped wrong, looking to avoid a wrist-thick branch that would've tripped him up. "Whoa, now."

Pap rubbed his chin in consideration. "Let's see. I'd say that Hawley's is equal parts education, salvation, and damnation. That is to say that at least last time I was through this way, part of the day on Sunday it was used as a church—not that there was many folks who'd attend. Tawley and his woman and some little half-breed that was left with them a while back. Little girl, I think it was. Couldn't speak, nor hear. Odd case, that was.

"Now you mention it, I do recall hearing some time ago that Tawley's woman up and left him. Lucky for him, I'd say. A homelier critter you'd have to work hard to find—she had more hair on her face than I do—and lumps and warts and whatnot. But Lordy, she could cook, I'll give her that. Yep, I heard that she up and left him. Now, who told me that? Couldn't have been one of the boys. They don't much care for palaver, though I am partial to it of an evening." He looked over at Charlie, saw the young man was chuckling and wincing and holding his sides all at once.

"What's so all-fired humorous, youngster? I will say it does me good to see you know how to smile. I thought for sure that mule you'd buried back there had taken that with her."

"Oh," said Charlie, rubbing his sides and doing his best not to laugh anymore. "It's that you started out talking about one thing, then kept going with another notion, then another."

"Oh," said Pap. "Where was it I was supposed to go, if you don't mind telling me?"

"You started out telling me about that fella Tawley. And how his place was sort of difficult to pin down."

"Yep, so it is. Then I commenced to telling you about the man himself. And one thing led to another. Can't tell about a man without telling about his woman, eh?"

"I reckon you're right."

"You already said as much."

Charlie felt as though he looked dumber than ever. He felt his face redden again. It was getting to be a habit.

"Them other things, let's see, there's the fact that the same woman tried to teach anyone who came by the basics of schooling. That's the education part of what I was saying about Tawley's place. Matter of fact, I took one of her readin' classes, but I'll be jiggered if I can do much more than decipher a plain old word here and there, maybe read my own name. But it got me this far, eh, boy?"

"Yes, sir."

"Well, makes no never mind. You'll see Tawley and his

place soon enough. I hope the boys managed to do what I asked of them. They should be there, waiting on us." He turned to Charlie as he nudged his own gray horse into a lope. "With any luck Tawley'll have a venison haunch roasting over a fire!"

Chapter 8

"Pap? You say your name is Pap?" The unknown man pushed himself away from the rough plank bar top, turned to face Pap and Charlie.

"I knowed me a fella by the name of Pap once. Of course, he was a real pap, ol' Grandpappy, he was. And I doubt very much, knowing him as I did, that you would make much of a patch on his backside. On the other hand, could be I'm being cranky and cruel. Could be I should get to know you first before I make such bold proclamations."

Pap didn't know what to make of this bold-talking stranger. In short enough order he regained his voice and bellowed not at this new jackal, but at his men, "Ain't a one of you all going to do a thing except stand there and drink and look stupid? I swear, why I ever took to dragging you fools around is a thing I will never in all my years fathom."

The most sign of offense or shame any of them could muster was a bit of reddening in the ears. None of them met his stare. The stranger broke the silence, cutting off Pap Morton before the old man began to cackle again, this time in his direction.

"Who's that big goober there?" said the stranger, nodding at Charlie. "I see he's one of them big, dumb ones."

He walked forward toward Charlie, talking and raising his voice. "I say, I see you are one of them dumb ones. Soft in the thinker?" He rapped his finger to the side of his head. "You get kicked in the head by a ornery mule as a boy? That what happened?"

The stranger looked to either side of himself, where Ace, Mex, Dutchy, and Simp were arrayed, two to a side, flanking him at the bar. He leaned back, thumbing the half-filled beer mug and smiling at his own wit.

There was a brief silence; then Charlie said, "No, sir."

"How's that?" said the stranger, his brow knitted. "What did you say to me?"

Charlie cleared his voice. "No, sir. I said, I ain't never been kicked by a mule."

"Oh, well, now, that's good to hear. Mighty good to hear, ain't it, boys?"

The four men flanking him still looked at their boots and mumbled.

"Come on, Charlie. These folks are too good for us, I guess." Pap headed down to the far end of the bar and rapped his knuckles on the bar top. Where's Tawley at? You back there, boy?" Pap smiled at Charlie. "You'll like Tawley. He's a—"

"He's a lousy bartender is what he is." Again, it was the stranger. "But I reckon he'll be out soon to fill our glasses. I sent him back there to fix us up some food. I asked about that fat little squaw he's got kicking around back there, but he told me she ain't for sale. I told him I don't want to buy the dang cow, just want to milk her for a while, you know?"

The stranger thought this was a funny thing, because he laughed all by himself longer than any man Charlie had ever seen do such a thing. Then the man stopped and Charlie felt the air in the room tighten somehow, grow colder and clammy.

After a few minutes a short, fat man grunted and nudged aside a filthy, frayed canvas tarpaulin nailed up that served as a door between what Charlie assumed was the kitchen area. The man held before him a plank on which sat the remnants of a round loaf of bread that had been not so much sliced as clawed apart. Charlie spied a hunk of cheese beside it, the yellow of which resembled thick crumbs in the man's beard.

The fat man's hands were as begrimed as the canvas that slapped back into place behind him. His head was little more than a protuberance from atop his soft, round shoulders. All in all, Charlie decided the man resembled an egg topped with a ring of hair so greasy it looked wet. Circling the very air above him, like a living halo, a tangle of flies buzzed and dipped, alternating between the heights of the man's head and the food on the plank he carried.

The man regarded warily the tray of food he carried as if it might fight back, and didn't look up until he was halfway down the long plank bar. He set the food on the counter before Grady and the others, then looked to his right, probably sensing someone else had entered. A smile cracked the fat, sweaty face. "Pap Morton! As I live and breathe, been a long time, old friend!" He shuffled toward Pap and Charlie's end of the bar as Pap responded in kind.

"You've looked better, you old cur—"

Grady's voice barked, cutting through the sudden hopefulness.

"This is what you got for us? You call this food?" Haskell jammed the end of the serving board with his hand and sent it caroming off the bar top behind Tawley.

Though Charlie admitted that the food hadn't looked all that appetizing, this stranger's rudeness was something he'd not ever seen in a man before.

"Here, now," said Pap, slamming a bony fist on the bar top hard enough to jiggle a cracked saucer with the nub of a tallow candle setting in it. "I've had about all I'm going to take from you, mister. My boys here are obviously smitten with you, but I'll be jiggered if I am. You're rude, you're a loudmouth, and you're acting like everybody in this here room owes you something."

The stranger, instead of bellowing like a scalded cat as Charlie had expected he would, grinned high and wide, barked a laugh, and slapped the bar himself. Then he said, "Finally, glad to see someone here with a set of man's best friends. I thought for sure I'd found the wrong group!"

The sudden change in the stranger's attitude stunned everyone into silence for a moment. Then Pap broke the silence. "What are you on about, mister? You looking to pick a fight, I'll oblige you and glad of it. Been a while since I mixed it up with a jackass."

Pap pushed back from the bar and with trembling hands and an outthrust bottom jaw supporting a dancing bottom lip, he fidgeted with the buttons on his shirt's cuffs.

"Relax, old man. Name's Grady Haskell, and I was funning you, as I said. Long and short of it is, I am looking for a handful of men for a job. I wasn't none too convinced of it when I come upon these four slow-witted gents trying to nab goods from a mule skinner's freight wagon. Man didn't see them, but I did."

"You the law, Grady Haskell?" said Pap, not slowing down his unbuttoning one bit.

"Me? The Law? Nah, but that's about as funny a thing as I've heard in a long while."

"You best start making sense, mister, 'cause I'm about to button up those eyes of your'n, fatten your homely lips, and make you wish you wasn't born."

With that, Pap shoved by Charlie and launched his old chicken-bone body straight at the unsuspecting Haskell. Charlie made a grab for the old rooster, but too late, and ended up feeling the back of Pap's leather vest slip through his fingertips.

All Charlie would recall of the next few minutes were a blur of scarred, bloody knuckles on grimy hands, bellowed oaths shouted by grunts as those begrimed fists slammed into flesh. All around him the melee built to a rage. Dutchy and Mex, Ace and Simp all dove in, throwing elbows, raising knees, and driving their scarred fists at one another, at Charlie, at Pap, at the stranger—didn't seem to matter to them if they were friends or foes.

Finally Charlie figured there was enough reason to help Pap and his boys as there was to fight against that foulmouthed rascal who made less sense to Charlie every time he opened his mouth.

His sides still hurt him mightily. He guessed that must be those broken ribs Pap was all bothered about. But it felt good to stretch out. Unfortunately his first punch met not with the leering face of the stranger, but with the same spot on Dutchy's head, who had managed somehow to pop up between the two of them, like a rabbit out of a hole, as Charlie swung.

Dutchy went down with an "Oof!" like a sack of ground meal at Charlie's feet.

"Thanks, friend," wheezed a still-smiling stranger, staring at Charlie.

"What was that?" shouted Pap, windmilling at anyone in sight, but angling toward the loudmouthed stranger. His bony chicken limbs and big knuckles had already clipped each of his men, and now that glint in his eye told Charlie that he was next.

"It wasn't like that, Pap. Honest." But he had no time for further thought on the subject, because Pap freed himself from the desperate grip Tawley had on the back of his vest. He blustered himself like a crazed chicken right at Charlie, in the process whipping by the wide-open stranger. Before the old man's claws connected with Charlie, his eyes went wide and he gagged out a sound Charlie hadn't ever heard from a man before. But the reason why interested him much more—Haskell's wide hands were encircled around Pap's throat.

Without thinking, Charlie went low, wedged a big arm between the two struggling bodies, and drove upward. It didn't knock the stranger's grip loose as he'd intended. Instead it appeared to have the opposite effect, and succeeded only in tightening the stranger's grip on Pap's neck. The old man's eyes bugged out like two bloodshot quail eggs and his tongue had begun to purple.

Without thinking, Charlie drove his right fist straight at the side of Grady Haskell's head and relished the cracking and shifting that he felt underneath his knuckles. The man's head snapped to the side and his grip on Pap's old neck peeled apart. But to Charlie's surprise, Haskell spun back around and stared right at Charlie, smiling.

"Now, that was a hit!" he said, running his tongue around the inside of his mouth, then spitting a clot of blood on the floor.

Charlie bent to help Pap, who was rising from where he'd dropped to his knees. "You leave offa me. Keep yer big mitts to yourself." He shouted this, but it took him a few seconds to get it out. And as he did, the room filled with a thundering boom. Charlie brought his hands to his hears reflexively and winced as pain bloomed in hot jags throughout his rib cage.

Blue-gray smoke filled the room and as the roar diminished it was replaced with ringing silence.

"There, by jove! You stop your fighting right now or I'll touch off the second barrel. And these shells don't come cheap!" It was Tawley and he looked fit to be tied.

"Tawley," said Pap, massaging his neck. He looked upward as the smoke parted, revealing a ragged slumped hole in the roof's random thick layers of branch and daub and thatch. "You touch off another and this tender old place is liable to come down around our ears!" He cackled then, but the laugh turned into a coughing fit.

"You all right, Pap?" said Tawley.

The old man merely nodded. "No thanks to the pair of them." He looked at Charlie and the stranger named Grady Haskell.

"Now, look here, Pap," said Charlie, wanting in no way to get lumped in with the big-mouthed stranger.

"He ain't with me. Charlie boy can hit, but he's too big, too soft, and too blamed young to throw in with the likes of me, old man." Haskell smiled. "No offense boy. As I say, you can lace with that big ham hand of yours, but those four sad cases over there are more to my liking."

"Your liking?" Pap looked at his boys, Ace, Simp, Mex, and Dutchy, who were hanging back by the bar. They'd thrown punches, as Charlie had seen, but they didn't seem to have regarded the dustup as anything more than a bit of blowing off steam, a fun way to pass a few minutes.

Pap stared at the men back by the bar. "What in heck are you papooses doing? Holding up the walls? By gum, if I had me an ounce more of gumption I'd let you all have it to the high heavens and back. Ain't never seen a more worthless or ungrateful gang than the likes of you all."

While Pap sputtered on, berating the four weak men, Charlie glanced at Haskell once again. He saw the man smiling, enjoying the spectacle of Pap's anger. Charlie saw in the stranger's eyes the glint of something he'd never seen in another person's eyes before. And he knew what it was—it was evil and rage and jealousy, all balled up in the man's eyes, in his mind.

Most of all, it was, Charlie decided, a murderous mind and a killing look, a killing urge that Grady Haskell represented. Charlie was quite sure, no matter what the man said, that if he hadn't stopped him, Haskell would have strangled Pap to death, would have finished what he'd begun. This was no kiddies' game to Haskell.

But now the man appeared to act as if it was all a joke, all in good fun, and that they were the best of friends. None of this made any sense to Charlie. And why weren't Pap's boys doing something to lend a hand?

Chapter 9

The cells were dark. Marshal Dodd Wickham toed the unlocked door of one, and a thin squeak filled the gloomy back room. He sighed, felt for a cigarillo in his left breast pocket through the black-and-gray-striped worsted wool coat beneath his fingertips. They were there. He slid one out, bit the end, chewed it, and let the little cigar hang between his lips. He didn't light it, but stood that way for a few more moments in silence, the fingers of one bony hand clawed loosely in the squares formed by the strapping of the cage.

"A cage for men," he said quietly to the gloomy room. He sighed again. No much call for locking men up nowadays. His smile was a grim thing—done your job too well for too long, Dodd, he told himself. He slammed the door slightly as he turned from the cell and walked to the front of the jail. The cell door clanged once behind him.

He stood in the middle of the front room. It faced the street and was laid out like all the other law dog offices throughout the territories in the north, south, east, west he'd been in throughout his too-long career as a lawman. Marshal Dodd Wickham took it all in one more time.

Same potbelly stove, grown cold, same gray-fleck

enamel coffeepot on top, half-filled with stale coffee. When was the last time he'd made it here in the office? Used to be he could drink that bold gargle all day long and deep into the night, then roust the sheets with a pretty puta, sleep it all off, and wake the next day to a fresh sunrise filled with promise.

"Where did it all go, Dodd?"

The room didn't answer. And that was another thing. He'd begun talking to himself more and more of late, and if he knew anything about old people, it was that they lost whatever edge they might have had in their prime. They started to let things creep into their daily lives that they never would have years or sometimes months before. Like talking to themselves, wearing soiled clothes so long they took on a sheen, slick with the grime of life.

No, sir, nothing good could come of talking to yourself. And yet what would it matter in another week? The town in all its mighty wisdom—no, no, that was not fair. Leave that thought be for now. No sense dredging that up again. He dragged a long wooden match across the leather desk blotter as he'd done a thousand times before, let the match burn down to the wood, then set fire to the end of the cigarillo.

He shook out the flaming stick and puffed on the cigar. No, it wasn't the town who was to blame, but the town council, headed by McCafferty and his suck-up son-in-law.

The marshal had shown up at the council's request for what he had been told would be a harmless informational meeting about the growing town's needs. He'd thought they were going to talk about that newfangled sewer system McCafferty had been banging his drum about forever. But he was in for a surprise.

"It occurs to the council," the big blowhard had said

when he'd walked in, "that you might want to begin, um, enjoying your life more than you have these past few years. It occurs to the council that you—"

And that was when Wickham had stopped them, slammed his silver-knobbed walking stick on the council's new, long, polished mahogany meeting table.

"Apparently," Wickham had said, eyeing each of the grubbing bastards individually, "the town of Bakersfield and its 'leaders' have grown right comfortable in the role of moneymaking business community. Any of you soft-handed women-boys give a lick of a thought as to why this town's come to be regarded as such a friendly place for business people to come to? Hmm? Don't think for a second I don't know what you're up to. Better yet, don't even think."

Well, that had riled them up in good shape. They'd begun to gargle and gabble like a flock of outraged hens. Wickham had taken one last look at them all—he'd been right; chubby-faced fools, the lot of them—then snatched his walking stick off the table, noting with no small degree of pleasure that he'd rammed a solid gouge half a bullet long in their fine new piece of furniture—and headed for the door. They'd tried to stop him, the more spineless of them even having hurled out weak begging sounds. But it was McCafferty who'd finally paused Wickham, his hand on the brass doorknob.

"Don't you dare turn your back on me when I am talking to you! You are an employee of this town, of us, of me, you . . . old man!"

That had done it. Dodd Wickham spun back around, pointed the business end of his custom walking stick— the weighted silver handle—straight at the pig of a man, at his fat face with its deep-set piggy eyes that stared at him in fear and rage all at once.

"You little whelp. I was a grown man laying low vile vermin when you were still soiling your short pants and suckling on a sugar teat! You ever speak to me that way again and you'll wish you'd grown up different. And as for the question of my employment, now that I finally see without varnish what we're dealing with here, I'd say I'm about finished with you and yours. And about time too."

And that time he had stalked out, not slamming the door as he'd intended, but letting them all wince in anticipation of it.

Chapter 10

By the time Grady Haskell arrived in Bakersfield, it was nearly dark. He followed the main course down into town, a long affair brimming with pretty women, dapper-dressed men, cursed children, and horses, carts, wagons, buggies, and the odd stray cur threading through the people and horses' legs.

"Hey, fella." Grady beckoned to a passing fellow in a suit. The man stopped and regarded him. "Your town got a bank?"

"You are not from here, I take it." The man looked Grady up and down as if assessing the purchase of a hunting dog and finding it lacked any redeeming qualities.

Before the man walked out of hearing range, Grady said, "And thank the Good Lord above for that!" Instead of taking offense to the dandy's comment, Grady found it amusing. Maybe it was the town, being in such a fine place full of promise. Maybe it was because he still had enough money in his coin purse for a room in a decent hotel, with plenty enough left over for drinks and food and a poke or two with a choice dove.

Yes, sir, Grady felt certain this would be the town

where all his dreams might well come true. Only thing he needed was a gang of dull-witted helpers who would do his bidding when they got out and away, all of them thinking happy thoughts about what all they were going to do with their money. Why, Grady would help them make that decision—by plugging them in the heads or dragging his skinning knife across their throats or . . . any ol' thing that needed doing. Long as he ended up with the whole haul, Grady didn't much care how many people he gutted in order to do it.

Chapter 11

In their camp under the cottonwoods, dusk dragged down like always, like someone pulling a blanket from one horizon to another, darkening the end of the day. Charlie liked this time of day the best. He'd studied on it some while they rode—it was one of his favorite topics to think on when there was nothing else going on but the steady *bump, bump, bump* of the horses' hooves on the trail, *spang*ing off rimrock or soft thuds on a piney forest floor.

He'd come to the decision earlier that day, in that long, drawn, fly-buzzed wad of time after their noon meal and before their night's rest. He'd been looking forward, as he always did, to settling down for the night and listening to Pap's stories. Seems he had a barn full of them in his head, enough so that he had one or two new ones each night.

It never occurred to Charlie that the old man might be making them up as they rode each day. It also never occurred to Charlie to ask Pap where it was they were headed. He had quickly realized that Pap was a man he could trust. He'd saved his life, after all. Might be that the others weren't all that bad too. After all, Pap had pretty much taken them all under his wing at one time or another, hadn't he?

That was another point Charlie had mulled over these past few days of riding. He was glad as heck they'd gotten shed of that Grady Haskell. He still wasn't sure why the others had taken to him so, but they'd made rare comments about how he'd be a valuable addition to their group. Pap had acted as if they'd dumped scalding water over his head, and before long they'd hushed up over the matter.

And that was what Charlie was thinking when he sighed and slid down to take a seat on the log a couple of feet from Pap. He'd offered Dutchy a hand with the stew, but the man had only shaken his head.

"Pap."

The old man looked over, nodded. "Boy."

For some reason, when Pap called him that, Charlie didn't bristle. Compared to the rest of them, he was a boy. He'd not admitted to any of them that he was, near as he could figure, almost seventeen years old, a little more or a little less. Not that it mattered. But he didn't want them to know yet. It felt like a young age, younger than they thought he might be.

Maybe he'd tell Pap one of these days. But not yet. He was secretly afraid the old man might dump him off at the nearest town, make him take up at an orphanage or some such thing. It was a threat his gran had made long ago and it still plagued him in the small, dark hours when all was still and the world seemed a hard place.

"You got any notion why that Haskell fella up and took off on us like he done?"

Pap looked at him again, cracked a smile. "Why? You missin' him already?"

"Oh no, Pap. I was only tryin' to make some chatter, is all."

"Yeah, but there's more to it and you know it, boy." Pap leaned close. "It was good to see his backside headed on outta camp. But I fear it's not long before we are unfortunate enough to feel him darkening our campfire ring again."

"Why do you say that, Pap?" He already knew the answer but hoped he was wrong. Charlie eyed the other men keeping to themselves across the fire. He knew they were unable to hear him and Pap, but odds were they could guess what they were chatting about.

Pap saw him. "Them boys seem to think Haskell's got something to offer them."

"What'd they say?" said Charlie, feeling his face redden, knowing the others were regarding him with cold looks. So that was why they'd been silent. Here it was, a split?

"No, can't be," he mumbled, toeing the soft-packed pine needles at his feet. He made a dam of them, nudged a stick like a ship through it.

Pap sighed. "Charlie, I knowed it for some time, long before you come along. I never figured they'd really get their heads turned. And maybe I'm wrong. Been known to happen." He paused, waited for Charlie to look at him, then winked. "A time or two, though, that's all."

"Well, I hope you are, 'cause that Haskell ain't no good." Charlie didn't want it to sound so childish, but he knew it did. The last thing he wanted was to seem like a kid in front of Pap.

"Pap."

Charlie and Pap looked up to see Mex standing before them. Charlie hadn't even heard him walk up. Those

moccasins made him move like a ghost. That, and the
Indian in him. Charlie didn't know why they called him
Mex if he was Indian, but he sort of admired the man,
what little time he'd spent around him. He always
seemed to be one step ahead of everyone else, knew
what needed doing, and went on ahead and did it. Charlie liked the idea of that, tried to pick up such habits. He
wanted to be useful to Pap.

"What's on your mind, Mex?"

For the first time in the short time since Charlie had
joined up with Pap and the boys, he saw Mex's normally
serious face wrinkle up a bit, sort of as if he was afraid of
Pap, afraid of what he was going to say. Charlie felt embarrassed, started to get up, but Pap rapped him on the
arm with the back of his old knobby hand. "Stick tight,
Charlie. We're all of a like mind here, right, Mex?"

Mex cut his eyes to Charlie, then back to Pap. "Ace,
Dutchy, Simp, and me, we been talking." He cleared his
throat. Charlie couldn't help looking up quickly at him.
Mex's miscolored eyes were fearful; that was the word.
Now, that, thought Charlie, is something.

"What he's trying to say is that you've, let's see, you've
outlived your usefulness, old man."

Out from the shadows beyond the fire stepped
Grady Haskell, his brown wool coat spread wide and
draped over the cherry-handled butts of his revolvers.
Perched atop them, his palms rested, his fingers curling
and uncurling, patting the guns as if they were little
kept dogs.

His pocked face wore the same sneer that Charlie had
first seen on the man's face, the same one he wore when
he whipped back up from the punch Charlie had landed
on his head in the fistfight weeks before.

"Didn't think we'd been shed of you, Haskell." Pap's

narrowed eyes said it all. He looked to Charlie as if he wanted to kill the man.

"You're smarter than you look, old man."

"That's enough of that," said Dutchy.

"Oh, you can muster up the courage to tell me off but not to tell him you're planning on making real money?"

Pap looked from Haskell to Dutchy. "So that's what this is all about, eh? Might've known." He beckoned the other two over. "You boys tired of counting your ribs yet?" None of them made a sound, except for Haskell. He snorted a laugh.

"Can't say as I blame you. Way we been surviving these past few seasons is right tough on a body. I was twenty years younger it'd be different. But I ain't and it ain't." Pap stood, strode over to Mex, looked close at him, then to the other three. "You know that if'n you throw in with him . . . the fool here"—he regarded Haskell as if he were a wormy road apple—"you'll end up dead sooner than you should."

Charlie thought for certain Haskell would draw down on Pap for that remark, but Haskell kept that sneering smirk cut in right under that bristly mustache of his. Charlie wanted to pile his fist hard into that face, and vowed he would eventually. Bide your time, he told himself. That was the key. He felt sure Pap would agree, maybe even say the same thing.

"He'll paint a pretty picture for you, but you mark my words, you'll end up with a whole hatful of nothing."

"Like we got now, eh, Pap?"

It was Ace.

Charlie wanted to say something, defend Pap in some way, but something told him he would be speaking out of turn, that there was more to these men's histories with each other than he knew.

Pap straightened to his full thin height, about to Charlie's chest, and pulled in a deep draft of air. But instead of shouting Ace down, he only let the air leak out of himself. To Charlie he looked like an old, empty flour sack. Pap turned away, waved a hand at them all as if he were shooing flies. "Do whatever it is you feel you got to do. You will anyway."

He shuffled off into the near dark. Charlie watched him go. So did everybody else. For long moments no one said anything. Then Haskell broke the silence. "He's bitter. Old folks tend to get that way. I tell you what," he said, his tone softening. "I finish figuring up the tallies on the take we'll be making and we'll cut the old man in for something. Only right, after all. I thought I was going to have to traipse all over the countryside and back to find a decent bunch of partners. But he did that work for me."

He smiled at the somber group, his tone a soft, sly thing. "You all are making the right choice, I tell you that. The job I have planned for us will bring enough in for each of us so we won't have to worry about money for a long time to come. You hear that?"

Charlie looked at the faces of Pap's boys. They didn't quite meet Haskell's gaze, but he could tell they were all excited. He wanted to tell them that it was money, that nothing like it could replace a good-hearted old man like Pap. Didn't they know him even better than he did? He wanted to tell them that, but he stood there by the log and did his best to avoid Haskell's gaze.

Even though he wanted to punch the man, button up his big mouth for all the things he said about Pap, he was afraid of the stranger. Afraid that he'd be swayed by him too, somehow. Like that snake in the story that fella had told him about back when he first took to the road. Something about a man who blew on a flute and this snake came up out of a basket, did some sort of dance. But you had to be careful because if you stared at the snake's eyes, it could put you in what the fella had called a trance. Make you do funny things that you would never remember.

Haskell had what Charlie imagined were eyes like that snake's eyes. Dangerous and deadly. And persuasive. He had to keep his own brain about him, not fall into a bad trap that he'd never be able to climb back out of.

"I'm going to find Pap," said Charlie.

"You don't want to hear about what we have planned, Charlie?" Haskell's voice was softer, kinder again. Charlie didn't look at him, kept his back to him, but shrugged. Maybe he could listen in, tell Pap what the plan was. Maybe together they could turn the boys against Haskell. Might be the best way to make them all see that Pap was the one they should be paying attention to, not Grady Haskell.

"I'll take that as a yes, then," said Haskell. He expertly rolled himself a quirley, channeling the brown-flecked paper, tapping in rough-cut shag tobacco, then twisting it all together, licking it up lengthwise, thumbing a lucifer. Charlie cut his eyes back to the log, kept his thumbs hooked in his trouser pockets. Be a cold day before he'd let Haskell catch him staring at him.

The man drew in a lungful of smoke, blew it out in a long, slow cloud, then sucked in through his nose and spat. "You all have been living on the ragged edge of the old man's weak-sister plans for a long, long time now. Am I right?"

But he didn't wait for a response. "All this time you been risking prison or worse, right? So why not do the same thing, but get real money for it, not food or tobacco money? My word, boys! You been played for a fool for far too long. Like you been asleep, but sort of training for this deal I got coming along. Heck, you all been barely keeping mind and body together. Why not make it all worthwhile, you know? Time to go for a big haul, boys. And the best of all? Ain't no one needs to get hurt."

Haskell weaved in among them like a snake, glancing at them, but he wore no smirk on that face. No, it was gone, replaced with a serious, stone face topped with concerned eyebrows, that quirley bouncing between his lips, smoke threading out from the opposite side of his mouth, trailing from his flexed nostrils.

The men were all his, that much Haskell knew. Even the big boy. He wasn't so dumb as he let on. And big too. Might be he'd be useful in ways Haskell hadn't foreseen. Maybe he'd be a decoy of some sort. Haskell nodded and studied them each as he paced slowly back and forth before them, explaining his master plan, not the details yet. But the big picture, as the high rollers called it. Now was the time for hooking these fish. Get them flopping on the bank and they'd do whatever he wanted them to.

Time enough later for the details. He smiled, blew out more smoke, and rubbed his hands together. "Now comes the best part, boys." He looked at them each in turn again. "The money . . ."

Yep, he had them.

Chapter 12

Since riling up the town council, Marshal Dodd Wickham had spent too much time stalking the streets of Bakersfield, ramming that walking stick hard into the boardwalks, the flagged sidewalks, and the hard-packed pan with all the vengeance and righteous rage he could muster. Not that it did a lick of good—no one in the town seemed to care a whit that he was headed for the door.

Marshal Dodd Wickham prided himself on the fact that he rarely, in all his days, sulked and brooded over himself. It had indeed been a long time since he felt sorry for himself. But if ever such a mood was justified, he figured it was now. But he'd be jiggered if he'd let those town council fools frazzle him and run him out of town, his town as much as theirs, like a common gambler whose luck had long since run out.

He'd serve out the term as he'd intended, and as he'd said he'd do. He was, after all, a man of his word, a man of his honor. But come the next morning, he was bound and determined to be packed and ready to mount up. Well, maybe not climb into the saddle so much as boil up a good bit of dust as his buggy rolled on out of town.

And it would be one cold day in the Devil's playground before he'd mosey on back to Bakersfield, rest assured.

It was these and other such potent thoughts that drove Marshal Dodd Wickham to regard every child, woman, man, dog, cat, snake, and skunk with a hardened eye and not a smidge of a smile on his lined, leathery cheeks. Oh, he'd still do the job he hired on for, but—and though he chastised himself for it—Wickham secretly hoped there might be a spate of crimes after he wheeled on out of town.

"Marshal!"

The voice pulled him from his reverie. He stood at the corner of Wallace's Emporium and his old friend Gimpy's Dry Goods Warehouse. Down the alley a couple of young rascals were harassing a tomcat. Was a time not long before when he would have halfheartedly told the boys to back off, give the cat his space. But now he watched them.

"Marshal Wickham. Ho there, it's me, Bert Tollinson."

Wickham sighed. "Yeah, Bert." Blasted banker. He guessed what the man wanted. Something about the bank. The fat banker was always on him about hiring deputies to help patrol the streets surrounding the bank whenever he had payroll shipments coming in. So far Wickham had put him off. And he didn't see any reason to change course now.

Bert Tollinson blustered up alongside the marshal. "Morning, Dodd."

"Bert." Wickham pulled his gaze from the kids.

The porcine banker looked down the alley, shouted, "Hey, you two kids, leave off that critter! You should know better than that." He looked at the marshal. "I'm surprised at you, Dodd. You ought to know better than to let them boys torment that cat so."

"Seems to me a whole lot of people know what's good for me and what isn't. A whole lot of people lately want to tell me my business."

The fat man's jowls drooped and his bushy eyebrows rose. "Oh no, I didn't mean anything of the sort, Dodd. Just that . . ." He waited for Wickham to interrupt him like always, to tell him to forget it, no worries. It was a joke. He wasn't offended.

But Wickham didn't. He stood waiting for the fat banker to bluster to a stop. And then waited some more before finally saying, "What can I do for you, Bert?"

"Well, Dodd. I . . . uh . . ." He puffed up a bit more, thumbed the lapels of his black boiled-wool suit coat. "As you know, I, that is to say my bank, regularly receives shipments of payroll, refined ore, and other, uh, assets on the third weekend of each month."

"Yes, Bert, I seem to recall you telling me that a time or two before."

"Well, that's only because I should be concerned about the safety of that which has been left in my care, don't you agree?"

"Sure, Bert. Sure."

"Well?"

"Well, what?" But Wickham knew exactly what the fat man wanted.

"I'll need your assurance that nothing will happen to my holdings. To my patrons' investments in my business." Now Tollinson stuck out his lower jaw, as if to emphasize the weight his words deserved.

"Bert, you ever wonder why your bank has never been robbed while I've been top law in this town?"

"No, but I would like to keep it that way."

Wickham pushed off the side of the building and rammed the hard tip of his walking stick down on the wood as he began walking away. He stopped, turned, and said, "Then you had best hire yourself a new marshal, Tollinson. Because my contract ends Friday of next week and if my calendar's correct, that's still a full week before your payroll train rolls into town."

"But! But . . . Marshal Wickham! You can't do this to me! To the town! What will we do?"

"Can't do what? Leave you high and dry? Do what you and your fancy town council did to me? Sure I can. And I aim to. You watch."

"But . . ."

"Good day to you . . . Mr. Tollinson." The marshal offered the bulbous banker a hat-brim salute and clunked off down the sidewalk.

The fat banker stood staring at the tall, thin lawman's long, black claw hammer coat, wishing with every step that the stubborn old rooster would slip on a pile of road apples and break his neck. A more infuriating man he'd never met.

Chapter 13

Charlie rattled the tin plates and cups in the streambed, scouring them with a paw full of sand to help dislodge any stuck bits. His thoughts turned once more to the old man not far away. Pap was sitting alone, whittling a big stick into a smaller stick. Not a good sign, in Charlie's estimation.

He poured two tin cups with steaming coffee and ambled on over to the older man. "I'd known you was going to make shavings, I would have waited till now to make that campfire."

The old man didn't meet Charlie's eyes. He reached up with an old clawlike hand and accepted the hot cup. "Obliged."

He sipped noisily, then set it on the ground beside his left foot.

Charlie tried again. "Mind if I set down here, Pap?"

"Suit yourself."

Charlie sat on the log, wondering what in the heck was going on with Pap—besides the obvious problem with the boys. Charlie had a feeling Pap wanted to tell him something but didn't know how. Charlie tried again. "Something on your mind, Pap?" It was bold of him to say it that way, he knew, but something wasn't right and Charlie didn't like the tension he felt rippling off the old man.

Finally Pap cleared his throat and spat a green wad into the curls of pine at his feet. "You know I ain't never told you nor anyone else what to do, Charlie."

"Yes, sir," said Charlie, a little relieved that at least Pap was in a speaking mood.

"And I ain't about to start now." The old man looked at him, wagged the stick with emphasis as he spoke.

"No, sir."

Pap looked square at him now. "But I wouldn't blame you if you was to head on out of here, you got me?"

It took a few seconds for the old man's words to sink in. "What? Pap, you know I ain't leaving you. Besides, if this is about Haskell, well, ol' Grady ain't so bad."

Pap made a snorting sound. "I'm too dang old, Charlie, for you to be lying to me."

Charlie grinned. "Aw, I ain't lying to you, Pap. I reckon this whole thing's got a bit out of hand." Charlie's eyes brightened. "Hey." He nudged Pap on the arm. "What say I go talk to him? Tell him we ain't keen on the notion of doing in Bakersfield what he's laid out. Might be he'd—"

Pap stood up with more speed than Charlie had seen the man ever display. He thrust a knobby finger at Charlie. "Boy, you don't read me right." Pap's mouth was set in a hard line, his wet eyes blazed in red rims, and his chin trembled. "It's not that I want you to like that no-account Grady Haskell, nor that I want you to speak to him for me—anybody does that it'll be me, Pap Morton, and no one else."

"But, Pap, I didn't—"

"Hush your mouth, Charlie Chilton. And you listen

good. I don't plain want you around no more. You got me? I had enough of you suckling like a newborn! Grow up and git gone. I got enough worry about without a big galoot like you dragging his feet through everything I try to do."

It was rare in Charlie's life, especially given the past couple of years, that Charlie could be surprised, but the old man's words caught him unawares. "But you can't mean that, Pap."

"I do mean it," he said, but he'd turned away, and his voice cracked.

"But what'd I do, Pap? Tell me what I done wrong and I'll do it over again, but right this time. You'll see. I . . . I don't understand, Pap."

Morton turned his back on the large fellow. "Git gone, Charlie Chilton."

"But, Pap, I—"

"Git!" Pap wheeled on him, holding his knife out as if he were about to drive the tip into the big middle of the young man.

Instead of waiting for Charlie to walk away, Pap Morton stalked off, muttering and shaking his head.

"What'd I do, Pap?"

Already too far away for him to be heard by the big young man, Pap Morton said, under wet eyes, "Nothing, Charlie boy. You didn't do a thing wrong. You done it all right. Just too dang late."

Charlie heard none of it as he watched the old man who had, in such a short time, become so like a father to him.

Chapter 14

That night, Charlie lay rolled in his blanket well away from the rest of the fellows, a confused hulk of a young man turning over and over again in his mind what it was he had done to incur such sudden anger from Pap. After hours of fruitless mental groping, the only conclusion he came to was to regretfully heed Pap Morton's advice.

Judging from the hard snores of Simp, Mex, Ace, and Dutchy—he had no idea where Grady was, nor did he much care—Charlie doubted his leaving would be noticed. He made only slight rustlings as he gathered his meager bits of gear, which consisted of a few extra pieces of clothing, his old, much-repaired saddlebags containing holey socks, a tin cup, a few odds and ends of cooking implements with which he had been able to cobble together a campfire meal, and scraps of leather and twine he always found useful to have on hand for repairs. He dithered for a long time beside Nub, the broad, tall workhorse Charlie had ridden since Pap and the boys came along.

Should he ride out on Nub? Pap had said several times to him that the horse was his. But was it really? Did that mean he'd given the horse to Charlie as a gift?

One friend to another? A few hours before he most surely would have said yes. But now . . . now he was mostly unsure. If he'd ever been Pap's friend, he wasn't any longer. In fact, the more he mulled on it there in the dark, the more he realized that Pap had been serious— Charlie wasn't wanted. He was probably unwanted the entire time he'd been with them. And for it, he blamed Grady Haskell. That man's appearance had changed everything.

As if he'd been bidden to appear by Charlie's very thoughts, Grady's voice, rough as broadcloth dragged over rusted iron, frogged in a hoarse whisper out of the dark behind him.

"You got yourself what the learned folks call a conundrum, eh, Charlie boy?" Then he laughed, long and low and slow, a snaky sound, half whisper and half branch rustled through brush.

"Who's that?" said Charlie in a hushed tone as he spun, narrowing his eyes into the dark. There was the man, not five, six feet behind him, arms crossed as if he were hugging himself.

"You know, Charlie," said Haskell, "I get me the impression you're sneaking off somewhere, and in the night too."

There was enough moon glow cracking through the branches high above that Charlie saw steam from the man's mouth rise into the cool air. He hadn't noticed it was a cool evening. Too preoccupied with thoughts of other things, other concerns.

"What are you worming around here for, Haskell?"

"Well, now . . ." Haskell's eyebrows rose and he rocked back on his heels. "Sounds to me like Charlie boy has a hankering for an argument. What you doing out here in the night, boy? You got something hid away that belongs to someone else? You been . . . pilfering, Charlie boy?"

That last bit tugged a big old smile out on the foul man's face. Charlie ground his back teeth together, his jaw muscles bunching. "I ain't never stole a thing. . . ." But Charlie stopped. It wasn't true. That pretty little doily . . . He looked again at Haskell. The man was smiling, nodding. Could he know about that? How?

"Oh, Charlie boy, you are a thief. I can see it in your eyes. Always knew it, from the moment I laid eyes on you. I told myself, 'Grady, he's one of us.' Oh, you might act the big, tough man who is too good to associate with the likes of the rest of us thieves, but no, sir, Charlie boy, make no mistake, you are a thief like the rest."

Charlie shook his head. "Ain't true," he said. But he couldn't meet the man's gaze. Even in the near dark, he felt that accusing glare. Somehow Grady Haskell had to know all about him swiping that little doily.

"You about to steal a horse, now, wasn't you?"

Charlie's big, stubbled lantern jaw thrust outward. "No, I wasn't neither. In fact, I was saying my good-byes."

"Good-byes? Why, Charlie boy, now that my eyes have adjusted to the dark, I see that you are indeed lugging a bundle in one of those big grabbers you call a hand. Could be you're going on a trip, Charlie boy? Alone and in the middle of the night?"

"Could be. At any rate, it ain't none of your business." With that Charlie glanced once more at Nub, bade him a silent farewell with a look and a nod, and began scissoring his big legs on the trail southward, the direction they'd come from two days before. The town Haskell had told them of had turned out to be Bakersfield, and it lay to the north half a dozen miles. Charlie had no intention of heading there.

That would only result in him bumping into Pap and

the boys once again, probably on the trail. Considering all that Pap had said to him earlier in the night, there was no way he was ever going to annoy that old man again.

From behind him, Charlie heard footsteps, knew that Haskell was up to something. The footsteps increased, gained on him. With sudden speed, Charlie bent low, feinted to the right, pivoting on his left foot. He tossed his gear to the ground and set his stance, but of Haskell there was no sign.

He swung back to the right . . . nothing. Then felt a cold, hard ring of steel dimple into his left cheekbone.

"Don't move no more, Charlie boy. Else I'll be forced to squeeze on this trigger and that's a promise."

"What do you want from me, Haskell?" Charlie's breath came in shallow stutters. He'd had guns pulled on him before, but never had one pressed tight to his face like this. He didn't like the feeling.

"Not so much what I want, Charlie boy, as it is a question of what it is I need. And I need you to stick around, not let those other goobers see you rabbiting off into the night right before our big day. Else they might get to thinking that you knew something they didn't, something about how it could all go wrong. You got me, Charlie boy?"

"You saying it is going to go wrong, Haskell?" Sweat stippled Charlie's round face, but he asked the question because he wanted to know the answer. He also wanted to buy himself time to think how he might get away from this crazy man. If what Haskell had said about not wanting the others to know he was leaving was true, it probably meant that Haskell wouldn't shoot him and risk waking the others.

But how sure was he? Did he feel confident enough

to risk a mistake? "You ain't about to shoot me, Haskell." The question was bold enough, but Charlie hated the way his voice quaked, like that of a scared child.

"Smart lad, Charlie boy. You're one right smart laddie. But I do have me a right sharp skinning knife too, now, don't I? You seen it. I know you have. And what's more, what if I was to tell you that it was right handy, right close by, in fact?"

Charlie swallowed, made a sound that showed fear. He hated that. Hated this man, knife and gun or no.

Haskell continued. "I heard everything you and the old man said tonight."

Charlie's face fell. He could do nothing to suppress his surprise.

"Oh yes, Charlie boy. You and Pap were yammering on and on and I heard it all. Not that it did me much good, but it did let me know that even if the old man hates you I don't. In fact, I could use you in a key position come the morning, Charlie boy. What do you say?"

Everything Grady Haskell had whispered low to him set Charlie's teeth together tight once again. Haskell had a way of doing that to a body, he reckoned. But no matter the man's demands, Charlie knew with a man like Haskell it would be one foul deed piled on another. And before long that would only lead to one thing. Quick death by bullet or rope.

Much as it pained him to think about it, he expected bad things were going to happen to Pap and the boys, and sooner rather than later. Might be something in that, some connection like a stuck thread, between how Pap had treated him and what Haskell had said, but Charlie would think on it later.

Right now he had to do something about Haskell. And with no more thought than that, Charlie ducked, spun, and whipped his left arm upward, knocking the gun away. No thunderous explosion cracked the night, no more sounds rose from the two men than grunts and the slamming of Charlie's big ham fist as it drove in the near dark at Haskell's leering face. Or where he hoped Haskell's face was.

Somehow he connected with it, felt the satisfying snap of jaw coming together hard with jaw, heard a muffled shriek as Grady Haskell's head whipped from him. In the dark Charlie thought he might have seen the dull glint of a blade angling away. But it didn't matter, for he was already backing away from Haskell, saw the shadowed form of the man crouched in the darkness several feet from him.

Charlie had no weapon other than his own sheath knife, and he rested one shaking hand atop the hilt. With his other he groped in the dark by his feet for his gear, felt it with his boot, and snatched at it, caught it up by the rough rope loops he'd made.

He heard his own breath rasping in and out, heard the same coming from Haskell. The man was still crouched low but didn't appear to be making any movements that might be him lifting his revolver, not that Charlie was waiting around to be shot.

As soon as his fingers closed around the handles of his gear, he stepped backward fast, keeping the black hunched form in sight, until it blended with the dark.

When it seemed there was nothing more than darkness there, and when he was about to turn and hotfoot it southward, a groan rose from Haskell, now a good twenty yards back. Then he heard the man cough, pull a breath, and spit, sending something no doubt bloody and phlegmy to the ground. It was a grim sound that twinged Charlie a moment, knowing he'd caused it. Then he recalled the gun, the hint of a knife, and wished he had doubled his efforts and pummeled the man into hard submission.

The most unexpected and curious sound of all came next—long, slow laughter, loud enough to heckle Charlie on down the trail. It worked, and Charlie swore he heard it for far longer than he expected he should, chasing his ears, driving him southward into the night.

Chapter 15

"Where's Charlie at?" It was Dutch, and he was inquiring as to Charlie Chilton's whereabouts for good reason. Until they'd happened upon the big galoot of a boy, ol' Dutchy had been the outfit's cook, being the newest member to that point. The task had galled him to no end, and for two years he had professed his hatred of the culinary arts loudly and to whoever might listen. Come breakfast or suppertime he groused long and hard about the various indignities and infirmities he was sure would plague him any minute all because he was forced to engage in what he referred to as "woman's work."

So when Dutchy awoke, earlier than the others, as was still his habit, to find no sign of Charlie, at first he was not concerned. Then as he wandered back from watering the roots of a nearby pine, he grew curious. And when half a minute's worth of searching revealed neither hide nor hair of Chilton, he became panicked, and then enraged. For he knew what this meant—sure as snow was white, he would be stuck once again with the womanly work.

He'd begun voicing his concern about Big Charlie's lack of whereabouts, louder with each passing second.

The rest of the boys awoke, grumbling and running their tongues over fuzzy teeth.

Pap was the only one to remain silent. Well, Pap and that new fella, Grady Haskell, the bossy one with the big ideas about getting rich and all.

Pap roamed the camp walked far and wide, checked the horses, which was something that Dutchy had failed to do, and came back. Standing alone and unusually silent, Pap toed a sooty rock protruding from the fire ring.

"Dutchy, I expect you best get the water on for coffee. I'm partial to hot coffee when I wake up, and Charlie seemed to be the only one who knew a thing about it." He looked at Dutchy, then at the others in turn, but ignored Haskell.

But Grady spoke, cutting in with a grin and that early-morning croaking voice of his, something that barely evened out after that man had hammered back a couple of quirleys, one after the next. Dutchy noticed the man had a swelled-up jaw that sported shades of purple.

"Now, there, Pap. I'd say your fair-haired boy done run out on you." Haskell grinned and set fire to his first cigarette of the day, pulling in a deep draft of smoke, holding it there a second or two before expelling it in a long blue plume, like smoke from a steam train's stack as it labored up a long push.

"Naw," said Pap. "Nothing of the sort." He was smiling. "I'd say he let you down, Haskell. From the looks of things he also give you a wallopin' on that homely mug of yours. That boy has more sense than I give him credit for. In fact, he has more sense than the rest of us all together."

"How you figure that, boss?" said Simp, stretching his suspenders up over his shoulders and yawning.

But it was Haskell who answered, cutting off the old man before he had a chance to give a worked-up answer.

"What he means, Simp, is that him and Charlie boy sat up long into the night chattering away like camp jays, figuring on ways to beat me at my own game. Ain't that right, Pap? You're all set to deal with that bank your own self, ain't you? And for your information, I walked into a tree last night while watering a bush. Walked into a big ol' dumb tree."

Dutchy, Simp, Ace, and Mex all stared between Haskell and Pap. This was more amusement than they'd had in a long time.

Pap broke the spell with a smirk. "You know so all-fired much about what me and the boy was up to, you'd do best not to lie to us all." He leaned forward, pinned Haskell with a steely gaze. "But then again I expect lying is something that you can't help, being the lowlife you are."

"Out with it, old man. What's your angle?" Haskell strutted toward Pap, who set his feet and held his ground. Though he did look to Dutchy as if he had suddenly grown very old and very small.

He was at least a head shorter than Haskell and his chest, without all the layers of shirt and vest and coat he wore all day, looked sunken beneath his pink, timeworn long-handles.

"You want to test me, Haskell, you come right ahead. I know what I know. And I know you're a bad seed. Anyone with enough sense God give a goose can see that. But that don't mean I won't go along with you fools tomorrow. It's obvious I can't save you all from yourselves, so I'll do what I can to save innocent folks from you. That's about what I've been up to for years now."

Chapter 16

By the time the six men were saddled and picking their way down into town from the campsite twelve miles northwest to the bustling burg of Bakersfield, their spirits had buoyed. All except for the old man's. Pap Morton sat his mount straight, as if he were once again riding into battle—like the war, he thought. No, not quite that bad. At least not yet anyway. Maybe the day would get worse and worse. Maybe, maybe, maybe ...

And before he knew it, Dutchy was nudging him. "We made it to town, Pap." The man's voice was low, but excited. "And man, Grady was right. You looky there, Pap. Now, that's a town like I ain't seen in a long time. If I was rich I'd consider locking up all my precious dollars in a bank vault in a town such as this. Like as not I'll have use of such in a few hours anyway." He guffawed. "Once I have my share, that is."

He winked and rode off, leaving Pap shaking his head.

Off to the side of the road leading in, an out-of-place thresher warred for space with an abandoned wagon that looked as if it had been scavenged for parts until there wasn't much else left to pry off the old thing.

"About what I feel like," muttered Pap. "Boys use me

and then move on. Well, good luck and good riddance. The only one ever mattered, I had to run off." He sighed.

Up ahead, Grady began speaking. "We get into town, I want you all to do exactly as I laid it out for you. You got me? Ace, Mex, you two head on over to the Lucky Dollar Saloon, tie up out front, but don't go in, you got me? Last thing I need is to deal with a couple of drunks." He smiled broadly and winked. "Time enough for that business when we've conducted our transaction. When it's time, you come on over to the bank, lead your mounts there, tie up."

"You got it, boss." Ace's eyes widened as he realized what he'd said. He cut his glance quickly to Pap, but the man was still lagging behind.

But Grady heard it, and he smiled. He liked the sound of it. Someone calling him "boss." That had happened before, earlier in the week. If he recalled correctly, it was the one they called Simp. It was an entirely appropriate name, given the man's dumb nature.

He was not impressed with any of the men, but he felt sure they'd do what he told them to. He'd gone over it time and time again in hopes that it would stick. He felt confident that he'd hit the right combination of explanation and ordering without sounding too much like a cavalry boss.

Pap watched from the street, trying to figure an angle, some way he might be able to stop the foolish proceedings. They were really going to do it, really going to rob that bank. It was easily one of the grandest structures Pap had ever seen. In fact, his first thought on arriving in Bakersfield, when he saw the brick edifice of the bank jutting in all direction, angles and roof points and arches and column, was one of awe.

He'd never seen so much brick in one place. He even made the mistake of saying so aloud, and wouldn't you know, Grady Haskell had to be riding up alongside him. They both slowed, staring hard at each other. Another moment of unvarnished hatred exchanged.

"And I'm fixing to take it apart, brick by brick, very soon." Haskell didn't take his eyes from Pap as he said it.

"Don't do this thing, man! You're a fool if you think you can get away with it."

Haskell had laughed at him, then ridden up ahead once again, to take the lead.

"My word," Pap said, thumbing his grizzled chin. He had to admit that neither he nor his men had been much impressed with Haskell's so-called plan to rob the bank. With it boiled down to its raw parts, there wasn't much to it, in fact. They were going to bluster on in there, wave guns, and snatch what money they could.

He had to admit that Haskell was a natural leader of some sort. He had a way of convincing folks around him that they had to listen to him, had to trust him. But Pap saw something else too. Saw that the man was an idiot and not someone who had brains enough to plan a job the size of this one.

But he had no luck in convincing the boys that Haskell's plan was little more than a whole lot of talk about how much money they were all going to get, equal parts, in fact. Including Haskell, which Pap doubted to high heaven, but he gave up trying to convince those fools that their new leader, an even bigger fool, would turn out to be anything but fair.

He watched Dutchy, Simp, and Haskell swagger on through the tall, heavy oak-and-glass double front doors of the bank. Nothing like being obvious, eh, boys? Pap shook his head.

The plan was more than a joke. Either Haskell is a genius and I don't see it, thought Pap, or he's even more of a fool than I give him credit for. Pap swung down from his mount, gave thought briefly to the boy, Big Charlie, as he unwrapped the lead rope of the horse he'd been leading behind, Nub, the one he'd expected Charlie to take with him. "Should have been more forceful with the boy, told him he'd earned the horse. Dang fool kid's too polite for his own britches."

He had lain awake much of the night, and between snatches of sleep had heard Charlie rise, gather his meager gear, and head on out of camp. He'd heard the voice of Haskell too, berating Charlie, badgering him in some way about whatever it was he felt he needed to. Pap had almost risen then, almost butted in, but he'd stayed put, laid out like a dead man in his cold blanket, regretting having given Charlie such a tongue-lashing earlier.

Had to be a way to make it right. He'd lain there for hours and it wasn't until they'd been riding to Bakersfield that Pap Morton had come up with the perfect idea. So simple he wondered why it hadn't come to mind yet. But there you go, he thought. The best ideas are like that, aren't they?

He'd provision up in Bakersfield, then leave those boys to their own thickheaded devices. Next, he'd head on out of town, return southward, which was where he thought he saw sign back at the camp of Charlie's direction. Eventually he'd find the boy—he was hard to miss—and together they'd travel, find that little valley they both spoke of. Build up that homestead and spend the rest of his days swapping lies with the boy. Pap smiled at the notion.

Simple and sudden. And setting there on a fence post right before him all the time, grinning like that monkey he'd seen at that traveling circus show years back. Made him want to know more about the world. If there were such creatures as monkeys out there, why not other, more fanciful critters? Who knew what might be out there, living in the trees and rivers of strange, far-off lands?

He'd gotten into such conversations with Charlie in their brief time traveling together. He'd felt a good kinship with the boy, as if he were the son he'd never had.

In the past he'd tried to strike up such conversations, what he liked to think of as deep, thoughtful ruminations on life and the world, with the other boys. But none of them, save Dutchy when he'd been in his cups, had much interest in speculating about much of anything beyond whiskey, women, and getting rich.

Pap looped the reins on the hitch rail and looked out at the street. He reckoned it wasn't nine yet, by his inner clock. Still have time to do something about this, Pap, he told himself.

Pap pushed out away from the stamping, fidgeting pair of mounts and looked up the street for any sign of a law dog's office. Normally he'd not go very far at all out of his way for a lawman. He'd spent far too many years looking to get away, then keep away from them.

But knowing what was about to take place and knowing he'd been a fool for far too long where Haskell was concerned, Pap figured it was high time he made amends, even at the risk of getting his boys in trouble. He had to do it, had to get the law involved lest innocent folks get hurt or worse.

He stepped up onto the boardwalk with a creak and a pop in his joints. "Never was a man more tired or old feeling than I am today," he said aloud. A woman passing by not two feet from him clutched her drawstring purse tighter to her chest, her thin form draped in what looked to be a heavy wool cape. Pap noticed the deep blue of the fabric complemented her narrowed eyes.

"Ma'am," he said, touching his hat brim. "Getting right chilly, ain't it?"

She nodded, kept walking.

"Uh, ma'am? I wonder if you could tell me where I might find the law. Marshal, maybe? Or a constable?"

Her eyes widened and she shook her head, kept on walking.

"Well, Morton. That went well. Considering you about frightened the poor rabbit out of her boots." He rubbed a bony hand across his whiskers. "Likely I shoulda shaved."

The late-season chill seemed to crawl under his coat, claw its way beneath his vest, made him feel as though he were being slowly frozen to death. As though it might take months. That was about what the winters were like too. He liked the high country most any time of year, but especially to gaze upon it in winter, all bedecked with snow, now, that was a sight. But these past few years it had been a whole lot more work than it ever was to get going in the morning, to keep warm all day. Heck, he was even cold in summer in the high country.

Pap sighed and clumped along the boardwalk, looking for a friendly face he might ask of the whereabouts of the law in Bakersfield. Once he committed to a thing, he didn't like to back off it. Haskell's plan had been a harebrained thing from the start. Pap had only gone along so he might convince the man or more likely his boys to scrap it altogether and get away from the fool. He'd secretly been hoping that they'd discover on their own what a bad seed Haskell really was. But that hadn't happened, and now that the planned day of the bank robbery was on them, it seemed there was nothing for it but to rat them out. He'd take the consequences for himself too, come what may.

Pap wasn't sure if there was paper on him in California, but if he had to guess he'd say it was likely. He found himself well along the boardwalk, getting more anxious by the minute. He reckoned, as unpredictable as Haskell was, that he might open the ball any second instead of waiting for nine o'clock, the time Haskell had told them he would kick off the robbery.

LOFTON'S DRY GOODS was painted on the small sign tacked to the right of the glass-pane door. The sign itself had been painted by someone who knew their craft. And the decorations of dresses and hats set up in the windows looked like headless people. Always struck Pap odd that women might want to see a particular store-bought outfit even though it was draped on a dress dummy.

He reached for the glass doorknob, paused, pulled off his hat, and ran a hand over his wiry thatch of gray hair. He caught quick sight of himself in the glass door and shook his head. Didn't do a lick of good. In fact, he thought he looked better with the hat on, but he'd be jiggered if he could bring himself to enter a shop, and especially a women's finery store, with a hat on his head. But he had no time to waste — he had a niggling feeling that something was going to happen soon at the bank.

"Hello?" he said too soon as the brass bells rang and rattled above the door.

A woman looked up from behind the counter, pince-nez forking the end of her slender nose. She was a long-faced old girl, hair pulled back in a bun, forming a topknot that made her look even taller than she was. She wore a dark dress, maybe burgundy, with puffy sleeves. Pap couldn't be sure of the color, as the store itself was dimly lit.

"Yes? May I help you?" Her eyes settled on Pap and they narrowed.

He decided right then that while she might be a handsome thing in certain ways, there was little possibility he'd ever make any inroads with her or any women of her kind. Class and status and station meant all to such women, and he carried none of those things in any amount. So it was little problem for Pap to ignore her arched eyebrows and cut to the quick of the matter.

"I'm looking for the law in this town. I . . . uh."

Her eyebrows arched even higher, like dark wings of a raven. Looked as if they might take flight any second.

"Yes, you were saying?"

"I . . . uh, well, I need the marshal, ma'am."

"Oh, really? What is it you've done?"

"Oh no, ma'am. I . . ." He spun his hat in his hands, gnawed his lower lip, stretched his lips over his teeth. Nothing. Couldn't remember a thing he was going to say. Been that way his entire life around the ladies. "Confound it, ma'am, I . . . I ain't done nothing yet. I mean, nothing's been done yet."

"Then this is purportedly for a crime you expect to commit?"

Pap looked up, eyes blazing and chin set. "Now, looky here!" He was set to light into her, but caught the beginnings of a smile on her face.

"Calm down, sir. I'm having a little fun with you. I've never been called 'ma'am' so many times in my life. It's amusing, maybe even flattering."

Uh-oh, he thought. Here's a pretty kettle of fish I didn't see settin' there before me. "I'm looking for—"

"Yes, an officer of the law. As you said." She sighed. "It so happens that we are between lawmen. That is to say our usual town marshal has seen fit to leave service in a snit. We are high and dry, as it were."

Pap wasn't sure what she was going on about, but he took a stab at it. "You're saying your law dog, er, marshal, has up and vamoosed on you?"

"That is exactly what I'm saying, sir. Oh, he's still around, but there's no telling what condition he's in. When he's sober he's without reproach. But when he's in his cups, he's useless. And since that fool, McCafferty, that's the head of our illustrious city council, decided to all but lynch the old law dog, as you so quaintly put it— and behind closed doors at one of his silly meetings, to boot—why, there's been nothing but a steady stream of hand wringers and teetotalers howling for his head because they claim he's forsaken them." She leaned over the counter.

Pap felt inclined to do the same, though he had no idea why.

"In truth, Marshal Wickham gave them the best years of his life. Well, perhaps not of his prime, for he is now long in the tooth, as you might put it, but nonetheless he has been a long-standing asset to Bakersfield. And to be treated in such a way ..." She clucked her tongue and turned her head as if she'd caught a favorite nephew sneaking cookies.

"Ma'am, is he or ain't he around?" Pap glanced out the window. "I got a ... I need to speak at him right now."

She looked at him as if he'd suddenly belched in her presence. "What have I been telling you, sir? He's here, in town, but no longer in the employ of the town, though a good many of us still consider him most able to carry

out the duties of our lawman should the need arise. And
yet he's not here, is he? With his having given himself
over to the maniacal dreadfulness of drink, I can only
tell you that I think he's unable at present to answer
your questions, let alone offer assistance, at least in any
professional capacity."

She cocked her head to the side. The gesture reminded Pap of a little curious little bird. "What is it you
know about our town? What do you foresee happening
here, sir?"

She had him there, by golly. It was all Pap could do to
head on out of there, with those two eyes under those
beetling brows piercing his old raw hide. He backed
toward the door, afraid she was about to vault the glass
countertop and swoop down on him.

She said something to him, told him to "halt!" but
then they both remembered at the same time that the
town had no one official she might call for assistance.
Her appearance had changed so drastically in a matter
of moments he was sure she'd been replaced with an angry twin.

Pap reached the door, spun in the open entry, and
shouted, "Been a pleasure, ma'am!" He plopped his old
battered hat atop his head and hustled on out of there,
back to his waiting horses, not quite sure what to do but
knowing if anything could be done to stop the robbery,
it was up to him to do it.

Pap made it back to his horses and looked up in time
to see Mex and Ace, leading their mounts, cut quick
across the street, heading from their assigned loafing
spot near the saloon over to the bank. They darted behind a barouche and in front of a man leading a mule
and wagon with milk cans in the back.

The mule never slowed his pace, but the man, a middle-aged fellow, slowed his gait and lifted his face from staring at the hard-packed earth of the street. He watched them as they loped, hands on the butts of their revolvers, looking left and right as if they were being pursued.

What in the deuce are those two playing at? Pap had never seen them act skittish during a job. Of course any jobs they'd worked had only been small-time and, he always liked to tell himself, had not caused enough bother to anyone for them to land in any real soup.

Pap didn't think Haskell had it in him to make this one work, but by gum, if they all weren't going after it with more dedication than he'd seen them show anything other than their dinner plates, especially when Big Charlie had taken over the cooking from Dutchy.

A smile had begun to creep up on Pap's grizzled maw when two things happened almost at once—Ace and Mex swung hard through the front doors of the bank. As they disappeared within and the doors settled back into place, a muffled slamming sound—could it have been the doors?—paused Pap with one hand on Nub's rump.

He'd been ready to head to the mercantile and see what his meager poke might buy for provisions. To the Devil with the lawman. Maybe the town deserved to be robbed, run as it was by fools, at least that was how that woman at the shop had made it sound.

People were gathering, beginning to stare at the bank. And that was when Pap knew that something had gone wrong. And he knew too that if he didn't get on out of there, as a stranger in town he would be pulled into the mess with the rest of them. All of a sudden Pap regretted not taking Haskell seriously. Up until they went into the bank, he didn't think they'd really give it much of a try.

Thought they might see what a big frightening mess robbing a bank was going to be and call it quits before they'd begun.

He realized now that he was fooling himself. Realized too that they really were going after it, hammer and tong.

Pap wanted to get on his horse and get out of that town, tugging Nub behind and hightailing it. Instead he found himself moving out into the street, unsure of the sounds he was hearing, but his convictions becoming clearer with each step forward.

Those fools had opened fire. At least one of them had. And Pap knew his boys. He knew enough about Haskell too to know he didn't trust the man in any situation. He cursed himself for thinking all this would play out harmlessly.

Haskell had the look of a coldhearted killer, sure enough. Pap knew now he should have gone straight to the law, but it was Haskell's words that kept him from doing so. The rogue had said that Pap would be regarded as one of them, no matter how much of a hue and cry he put up, no matter how much he told them that he wasn't one of them. The law dogs wouldn't believe he was innocent, not a man with a long, shadowy past such as Pap's.

But now all that lost its meaning, especially when Pap heard shouts, three sharp thudding sounds followed by rising screams. And that was when Pap knew that all hell had busted far beyond loose.

Chapter 17

The old man never should have looked at him in the first place, especially not in the way he had—fixed him with those two yellowed old-man eyes, sharp and piercing despite their age. Grady Haskell entered the bank and the man had looked right at him and Grady knew that the old man had somehow known he was there to rob the place. He couldn't say how he knew; he just knew. So Grady did what he had always done in such situations—he relied on his instinct to guide him.

And that little voice inside told him to nip this old dog in the bud right quick. He complied with a fast-pace walk straight to where the old man leaned on the counter, where he'd been glaring Grady down from the second he walked in.

Grady's nicotine-yellowed fingers wrapped around the revolver's grip long enough to heft it aloft. It spun in the air. He grabbed the barrel and in one smooth movement brought the butt to bear on the old man's left temple. He'd tried to shield the deed from prying eyes, but didn't much care who saw. The ball had been opened.

He managed, through his building veil of rage, to give quick thought to whether the others had come in yet. It wouldn't do to kick up much of a fuss if the boys weren't in place.

He glanced toward the big oak-and-glass doors he'd swung on through—looking for all the world like a happy bank customer, a depositor—no, no, make that a man about to make a significant withdrawal—and he spied Mex and Ace coming in, right on time, as he'd told them. And since Simp and Dutchy had come in with him, he felt safe enough about dealing with the old man.

"When we get to town," he'd said, "you all tie your horses out front, close enough that you can walk fast to them once the commotion's behind us."

Other than for the money, he didn't really care whether they made it to their horses or not. He had told them that as a way to gauge whether they were as dumb as they looked. They hadn't let him down. Yep, they'd all nodded, we can do that, by gum.

Grady still couldn't believe he'd actually found a handful of willing and able-bodied—if not able-minded—men to go along with his plan of robbing the biggest dang bank in all of California. Or at least that was what he told himself it was. Close enough, he figured. It was big and it got regular deliveries and rarely made any shipment south of town.

And then, to verify his suspicions, he'd bedded down with that woman who'd known all about the comings and goings of the bank, its employees, every buggy or horse that rolled on by the front and back streets, and even the one side street.

"How come you know so much about the bank?" he'd asked her while he lay there building a quirley, wondering if he'd paid her too much. She hadn't been all that good, in his estimation. But maybe that was the way it was with these California girls.

Could be he had to get himself back down South, maybe even all the way back to Tennessee, before he'd find himself a real woman again. Then he remembered those two in Texas the year before and he recalled how they had surprised him at every turn. So he had revised his thinking for the time being.

"I'm a whore," she'd said, taking his cigarette from him and pulling long on it. He'd almost said something, but he was in a good mood, so he figured he'd let her get away with that business this one time.

"I never wanted to be one and I don't intend to be one forever. And I have a whole lot of hours in a day when I'm as rested as I'm going to ever be and here I am, sitting right across the side alley from a big ol' bank. You tell me what you think I'm going to do." She hadn't waited for him to respond. Instead she plowed on ahead. "I'm going to up and marry one of those bank men. Or rob the place myself. There's nothing saying a woman can't rob a bank, you know."

He sighed. Talking to her was confusing, but he liked her. She had spunk. But maybe she was too smart for her own good. "You accusing me of thinking of robbing that bank?"

She'd snorted at that, chuckled. "You think you're the first to ever think of that? I was you I'd get at it right quick before Marshal Wickham sobers up. Once he's back on the job, you won't stand a snowball's chance, you hear me?"

"Who's he? Why should I be concerned about him?"

She'd only sighed and begun tugging on her stockings. But he kept on peppering her with questions. Finally she turned back to him.

"What part of 'lawman' don't you understand? Look." She tugged her dress back down over her breasts and

sighed again. "I like you. You're . . . strange and kind of
exciting. But I don't want to know what you're thinking
of doing and I don't want any part of it. As far as I'm
concerned, anything you've said to me, and anything I've
said to you, is just that . . . talk to be forgotten, and nothing more."

"Suits me fine," said Grady. And that was the way
they'd left it. He'd not seen her since, but found it curious
that he still thought of her now and again.

After Grady clubbed the old man, he rummaged behind
the teller counter, slamming drawers and shouting orders to the other men. He'd told them he wasn't going to
call them by name, but he did the same.

"Ace! Dutchy! Get on up to the front where the money's at." The two men looked at each other, then strode
forward to the front, doing what he bade them. It also
became apparent to every customer in the bank that
they were there to rob the place.

Haskell felt that worn grip in his hand, comfortable as
a broken-in boot, and he regretted that he had only been
able to bean the old gent to keep him from squawking.
He would have preferred to shoot him, but it was too
early in the proceedings to make such noise. He'd tried
to club him out of sight, but the old man was quicker
than he looked. With the drooped mouth on that old
hangdog face of his, Grady knew he'd been about to yelp
and spill the frijoles to everyone in the place.

Chapter 18

The old man, whom Grady thought he'd laid low with that temple blow, had only sagged back against the counter. The old gent clawed at Grady's gun hand and tried to knock the weapon free. Grady growled, took a step back, and in a single familiar motion, raised the weapon, thumbed back the hammer, and squeezed the trigger, a smile blooming on his face even as the weapon barked a harsh sound and rammed its deadly fist into the old man's shoulder.

The shot caught the old warhorse of a prospector in the right shoulder, plowing a bloody canal, shredding meat and splintering bone, and spinning the veteran around on his feet as if he were engaged in a dervish dance.

"No shooting!" shouted Dutchy. "You said there'd be no shooting!"

Grady turned the gun on him. "You shut up or you're next!"

Dutchy bit down on the angry oaths building inside him.

The old man, who went by the name of Muley Timmons, and had done so since the War of Northern Aggression, had always appeared older than his years. Even when he was a child of seven or eight, his parents had watched in confusion as he would roam the dooryard of their homestead in Nebraska, hunched over as if he were ailing from a bad back, hands thrust in his trousers waistband, a look of seeming concern pulling his little boy eyebrows together.

He'd kept that perpetual overall elderly look his entire life and now that he was actually an old man at sixty-four, near as he could recall, he felt for certain that it was all over. He'd made it through the war all those years before without so much as a sniffle, though the prospect of being shot at any moment had weighed him down, as did most concerns major and minor throughout his entire life.

But feeling the sting and seeing the spraying blood—and feeling that it was his blood, after all that time—why, it made him angry, angrier still that he could do little about it as he lay there on the gleaming marble floor of the Bakersfield Bank, twitching without control.

And as Muley lay there seeing smoke, smelling its sharp edge, and hearing screams of women and outraged shouts of men, a sputtering sound rose from his throat, mixed with the gagging sound he hadn't been aware was his own voice. Then in his fuzzy vision, a long, pock-marked face bisected by an unkempt dragoonish mustache hovered into his sight line, not two feet away.

"Why, how you doing, old-timer? Look at that," said the face, leaning closer and staring at Muley's now useless, bleeding shoulder. "I done a right pretty job of that, if'n I do say so."

And then the man was gone from sight, leaving only the quavering echo of a rattling laugh. And that was all Muley Timmons knew, for he lost consciousness and then expired, as he was about to deposit another tidy little sum earned shambling about his gold claim four miles east of town.

"You all see that?" shouted Grady Haskell. "I done for that old man because he was standing in my way." He waved his brace of revolvers, smoke still dribbling from the snout of one. "Let that be a lesson to you all. We are in the process of robbing the very short pants off this here bank, and not a one of you will argue with me or me and my friends here will lay you low."

A woman to Grady's left, all tarted up in a bustle and some sort of flowery topper with a feather poking out of it, began giving voice to a scream. She looked to be carrying a few extra pounds beneath a corset that rippled as she began squawking.

Grady reacted fast, like a snake striking, and let his left hand lash out of its own will, snapping hard against the vile creature's puffy face. Enough force was delivered that her head snapped backward, surprise on her big eyes. Grady saw the whole thing as if time had slowed. The hairy back of his hand mashed into her soft features. Her nose flattened; then something inside it snapped under his knuckles, and her head whipped backward, the hat with it. She dropped, and a wet, gagging sound bubbled up from her face.

He waved his bloodied backhand at the room in general. "Any other of you all care to taste this delicious recipe, you come on over to my house and I'll dose you up with a whole heaping plateful."

As he spoke he glanced at the other men, all standing where they were supposed to be, guns drawn now— good. At least he didn't have to instruct them in that. All this was taking much longer than he'd expected. It hadn't been but a few short minutes since he walked into the bank, but already the ball was rolling faster than he had wanted.

All these thoughts played out in Haskell's mind as he snagged a young man behind the counter. The man's starched collar broke free in front and separated, giving him a comical look. As soon as he'd seen Grady bolt toward him, the young man began blubbering. Then he froze, wet himself, and weakly held up his trembling hands.

"Where's my money?" Grady barked hard into the man's left ear. The man replied with a sound equal parts whipped dog and thrashed child. Grady repeated his request and the young man raised a trembling arm aloft. He pointed toward a door at the far end of the narrow room. It had to be the bank president's office.

Grady strode for it, swung the door wide, scanned the room and saw . . . no one. Then he heard a slight scuffing sound, as though a boot toe had been dragged but an inch. And it came from behind the desk. He made for the mammoth piece of mahogany furniture, paused before it, and delivered a hearty kick to its front. The wood cracked and from behind it, he heard a pinched whimper, as if someone had clapped a hand over a sobbing mouth.

The thief smiled and edged around the desk. He leaned low, his revolver poking between the chair and the space below the desk. "There you are!"

Haskell reached in and dragged the man out by the collar. "You must be the president of this here fine bank."

The man nodded, his tiny eyes wet, his fat face bunching above his string tie.

Grady thumbed back once on the hammer and pressed the snout of the barrel into the soft man's temple. "I am about to make a significant withdrawal and I need you to open that big ol' safe of yours. Hear me?"

The man swallowed but didn't acknowledge Grady's question.

Grady cranked the hammer all the way back, to the deadly position, and said, slower, "You hear me?"

This time the fat banker nodded, a string of drool trickling from his mouth, tears leaking from his eye corners.

"Good. Now, you're going to cut a trail straight for that vault, right quick. And if you slow down, I am going to kick you in the backside. Got that?"

Once more the man nodded.

Grady released the man and kicked him in his wide rump, eliciting a whimper. "You'll have to move faster than that!" His laughter trailed the fat banker to the safe.

Grady followed close behind, sticking to his task. He trusted that Mex was doing his appointed job, keeping the other two tellers—and any other bank employees—in sight, and preventing them from hauling out bravado guns from secret spots under the counter.

Grady had said he'd get the bank's big safe opened while Ace and Dutchy made their way around back and emptied the tellers' drawers into the flour sacks Grady had provided them all with. While all this ruckus went on, Simp was posted at the door, standing to the side, peeking through the ample glass toward the outside. He kept his own double scattergun leveled low but ready to swing.

Grady had told him not to worry about being vocal should anyone on the outside look as though they suspected a disturbance within the bank. But he also told him to let in anyone who looked as though they were headed in to conduct business. It would also be Mex's job to make sure any and all within the bank emptied their pockets and watch pockets into a flour sack.

And all that looked as if it might be happening. Except for the halfhearted shouts from Simp at the door. "Hey ... boss ... people outside. They's ..."

"They're what? Speak up, you jackass!"

"Well, they're ... fixin' to come in, I'd say."

"Great—the more wallets the better." Grady's words were interspersed with the sound of hard slaps he was delivering to the bank president's jowly face. He didn't want to cut the fat man yet. He still had to open the vault door.

"Don't think I won't gut you like a fresh-caught fish, fat man, but you can make it easier on yourself by opening that big black safe! Now!"

Whack! He drove a half punch to the man's neck, but all that did was double Fatty over and make him gag. Then Simp shouted from the door, "Yeah, boss. They definitely got wind of something. They're milling out there like ducks on a pond. I expect they're waiting on the marshal."

"Simp ...," Grady growled, spittle flecking from his wide-spread, tight lips. "Stop telling me bad news!" He drove another fist to the president's head that dropped the chunky man to his knees. "I told you I want you to open that there big safe with all my money in it!"

"What?" shouted Simp from the doorway.

"Shut up, you idiot! I am talking to this here banker!"

The bank president's trembling hands eventually found the correct combination. A few metallic clicks and pops, a couple of spins on what looked to Grady like a ship's wheel, and the door slowly opened outward, tugged on by the sobbing, sweaty fat banker.

"Much obliged," said Grady, jerking the man's black boiled wool suit coat downward by the collar so it fetched up around the man's arms and rendered him unable to defend himself.

A scuffle broke out among the customers stretched facedown on the floor.

"You hush up," growled Mex. "I warn you this one time only. Then I shoot—and I do not miss."

"Nobody's going to do any shooting," shouted Haskell. "If they keep on with that foolishness, drag your skinning knife across their throats." As he rummaged in the safe, Grady winked down at the bleary-eyed, wobbly-headed bank manager. "Got to keep them rowdies down, don't we?"

"You're insane! You'll never get away with this!"

"The Devil you say! I believe I will, and what's more, I believe I about did." He dragged the fat man forward into the vault, then headed for the young teller, who howled when Haskell did the same with him.

"No! No!" the young man screamed, then simpered, sagging as if giving up.

"Oh, shut up," said Haskell as he swung the pistol butt down hard on the whining young man's pate. There was a flat, slapping sound, blood geysered up in a sudden spray, and the teller collapsed. His chin smacked the floor and his head continued to spray blood, speckling Haskell, the inside of the open vault door, and a couple of canvas sacks Haskell had been stuffing with loot.

"By gaw," shouted Haskell, dancing sideways, trying to avoid the unconscious man's blood. "It's getting so a man can't leave his house of a morning without someone bleeding all over him!" He let out a quick bark of laughter, and shouted to Dutchy to lend him a hand. "Too much dang loot here for me to truss up all on my own."

Within half a minute the pair had finished and began dragging the sacks to the front door.

"Boss," said Simp, still at his post, peeking around the doorframe through the window at the slowly gathering crowd of confused, curious townsfolk outside. "I think they're catching on to what's going on in here."

Haskell grunted as he lugged the last sack over to the door. "Well, Simp, let's not keep them waiting any longer. You and Ace each grab a couple of sacks. Keep a gun in one hand. I've tied ropes around the necks of the sacks, so lug it on up and over your shoulder."

"That is it? That is all the bank has?" Dutchy looked at the sacks with wide eyes.

"Wait till you heft them, boy. They're right heavy. Plenty of money in there to go around."

"What all else was in that big vault?"

"Papers and deeds and such. Nothing we can easily spend south of the border."

"South of the border? You never said we was going in that direction." Dutchy stared at Haskell as if the boss man had clucked like a chicken. "You said—"

"Another word, Dutchy, and I will let my revolver carve you a new eye socket. Right twixt the others."

"Oh. . . ."

Haskell waited until the other three men followed what he did. Then he hefted the last two sacks. "Now, Mex, you get all the watches, wallets, rings, and such from these sad little nest of fools?"

"Yeah, boss. Like you said. I got it tucked in my shirt, safe and sound."

Haskell wagged a hand at him. "Well, give it here."

"What?" Mex looked as if he'd been slapped. "You don't trust me?"

"Not that. I don't trust anyone. My own mother was here, I wouldn't turn my back on her. Give it here."

Mex pooched out his lower lip. "I'm not so sure I will."

"Oh, for heaven's sake, Mex, give him the damn sack

full of trinkets, if it means that much to him." Dutchy looked at Grady, his eyes narrowed. He continued talking to Mex without taking his eyes from Haskell. "He is the boss, after all. At least that's what you all have been calling him."

"Ain't got time right now to talk to you about your attitude, but we'll get down to it when we get to where we're headed." Haskell broke his gaze from Dutchy, and noticing movement to his right, he spun, clawing at his right holster. As if conjured, his right revolver appeared in his hand. Equally as fast, without thinking, Haskell cocked the hammer and shot the man who was trying to rise.

Immediately Dutchy barked at him, "What are you doing? We said no shots—and no one was to get hurt. Now you go and kill another? This has become too much . . . too much!" He began walking forward, pushing past Haskell.

"Where are you going?" said Haskell, ignoring Simp's frenzied entreaties from the doorway.

"Oh boy . . . they're coming up the steps. That shot definitely told them something was up in here."

"Where do you think you're going?" Haskell spoke to Dutchy.

"To see if the old man needs help."

"I don't think so, Dutchy." Haskell cranked back on the hammer once more. "You take another step and I'll make sure you land right on him."

Dutchy stopped, his back to Haskell. He sighed, then said, "You're the boss." He looked down at the motionless old man. The force of the shot had slammed him back against the floor, and now a puddle of dark red blood thickened and widened around him. From the vault, a man's voice moaned.

The three people still lined up on their bellies in the front of the room snuffled and tried not to attract attention to themselves. But the ringing echo of the shot seemed to pull fear from them. Mex knew it was raw, rank fear because he felt it too.

"Now let's get going before that rabble out there coaxes a few shots from my revolvers." Haskell moved toward the door, stopped, and glanced at Dutchy, who was adjusting his sacks over his left shoulder. "Unless you have something to say about it, Dutchy?"

Dutchy glared at Grady but said nothing.

"Thought so. Now let's git gone. And remember what I told you. Ain't no splitting up, none of that foolishness. You all stick close by me and we'll have 'em licked." He glanced downward. "I tell you any more and I'll have to plug these plump town turkeys on the floor."

That set off a fresh round of sobs and muffled squeals from them.

"Simp," said Haskell, chuckling at the effect his words had on the people on the floor, "you swing that door wide and head on out to your horse, no fooling around. Straight to it. Same goes for the rest of you."

"What if someone follows us, boss?" Simp said, worry pulling his eyebrows tight.

"Oh, I got a plan for that. You never mind. Now let's go!

"You all on the floor, count to a hundred, slow as a hard winter, before you raise your heads. Else I'll be forced to open up on you like I done for the old man."

A fresh round of squeals from the people on the floor, then whispered counting, all at differing intervals, brought a smile to Haskell's face as he pounded on out the doors following Simp, Ace, Mex, and Dutchy.

True to his word, their horses had not been interfered

with in the least. He'd told them that no one would think oddly of strangers' horses standing at the hitch rail out in front of the bank, especially on a workday morning. At the most they'd looked like drovers headed into town to cash their pay chits.

"Where's Pap?" shouted Ace as he leaped off the boardwalk.

"Who cares?" said Haskell, looking around at the folks looking at them. He was pleased to note it was but a few folks who'd taken an interest in them. But he could see realization dawning on their faces, of mounting understanding. Their previously impregnable fortress of a bank had finally been breached. And all they could think to do was stare at the small group of brazen thieves.

The five men wasted no time in mounting up, adjusting the well-tied sacks once more, this time draped around their necks. Faster than the others, Haskell danced his horse ahead. He drew a revolver, aimed it in the general direction of the puzzled onlookers, no more than ten, perhaps a dozen people. But already heads were poking out of nearby shop doorways, and other people were cautiously advancing toward the end of the street anchored by the impressive bank building.

"You kind folks don't need to come any closer. Want to let you know we have relieved your impressive bank here of various deposited funds that are needed elsewhere. You might say we are relocating them."

A few men, the truth dawning on them, advanced, anger marking their eyes, jaws set hard. Only one of them wore a visible sidearm. He looked like a dandy to Haskell.

"You come any closer, mister, and there's going to be a mess in the street."

"Come on, boss," said Simp. "You talk too much."

Haskell ignored him, jerked his reins hard to the left and straight at the throng of people. "Follow me, boys!" As he carved a path for them through the growing crowd, he cranked off two shots over the townsfolks' heads, the bullets heading toward the fronts of buildings lining the main street. Screams mingled with the sound of shouts and the thumping, drumming of hoofbeats.

Dead ahead of him stood a little girl in a blue dress, a bonnet flopped back on her shoulders. But Haskell didn't see her. His horse knocked her to the ground, and shouts bubbled up from the crowd, from others witnessing the scene from afar.

Mex, whose horse was last in line, saw what happened to the girl. He slowed his horse, a clot of regret lodged in his throat. "No!" he shouted, but his voice was drowned out by shouts from the enraged crowd.

Haskell rammed his horse hard with his spurs, carving deeper through the fast-approaching crowd. The sounds of rage and fear rising higher, screams at something, he knew not what, began to drown out the other sounds. All was beginning to haze in his sight, like when he'd done for his old grandpappy, like so many others since then.

When it came right down to it, there was only one man whom he cared to blame should all this planning go to seed with no fruit born from it. And that man was fast approaching, off to his left, covering ground with his bony old man's legs. Pap Morton came at him fast, anger pulling his face into a tight mask, his old stubble-covered mouth shouting oaths, he was sure. And Haskell knew the old dog was going to do his best to lay him low.

As he saw the old man reach for his own sidearm, Haskell swung his right arm around, already having slipped his revolver into its sheath. In a swift, practiced movement, he lifted free his single-barrel coach gun, a lightweight single-shot shotgun he liked to have on his person for close-in work. Just like this.

Haskell didn't even have time to smile as he thumbed the hammer. He swung the shotgun up, wedging the butt under his shoulder. The old man came up fast, cranking back on his own hammer. Grady let him have it, right in the chest, and the force of the blast lifted the thin old chicken of a man up off his feet, sent him sprawling a good ten feet back against the street.

Pap Morton lay twitching in the dust, blood seeping outward from what seemed a hundred holes in his old but oft-mended red-and-green flannel shirt.

That felt good, thought Haskell as he regarded the still-stunned crowed. They began surging forward toward him. He waved the smoking shotgun at them, clawed free a revolver, and cranked off a shot over their heads, then more into the mass of them. They shrieked and howled and someone dropped and oh, wasn't it as it should be? He could not help bellowing a laugh at the morning sky.

Then as he began whipping the horse into a renewed frenzy, he glanced back at Pap and saw Big Charlie Chilton running toward the old man. From a dozen yards away, the big bumbling boy shouted and waved his massive arms, rage and terror and fear all writ large on his equally large face.

Oh, thought Grady Haskell, this day just keeps getting better!

Mex felt an arm clawing at him, looked down into the eyes of a man angrier than any man he'd seen in a long time. Then another, and two women, all angry, so angry . . . They slapped and grabbed at his legs, dragging at him, at his horse as the big beast danced, wild-eyed and foaming, neighing and thrashing. Mex felt himself being pulled from his saddle, losing the battle, the sacks of cash feeling as though they weighed more than anything he'd ever carried.

Mex held tight to the saddle horn with his left hand, his knuckles popping and tightening on the worn leather knob. Almost without thought his right hand snatched at his Colt. He pulled it from the holster and swung it blindly, madly, downward at the attackers, not intending to do anything but get them away from him. He was following an animal urge to free himself from them, not even aware of the fact that his thumb had begun cranking back on the hammer, all the way, to the deadly position.

Another jostle, another tug, and his finger jerked against the trigger. The sound hushed the crowd for the briefest of moments. In that slice of time, as Mex jammed his spurs hard into his horse's gut, a man who seconds before had been dragging hard on his leg, staggered backward and dropped against two of his fellow townsmen, a smoking ragged hole, puckered red and black, carved into his white-and-blue-striped shirt.

As Mex raked his horse hard with his spurs, he glanced back, his heart filling his throat, and saw the man he'd shot staring at him, eyes beginning to glass over, blood gouting from his slack mouth.

And then other hands grabbed at him, caught him unaware, and before he had time to react, he slipped free from his saddle. The last thing he saw was a rain of fists and clawing hands and howling, rage-filled faces, eyes wide and wild, all driving down at him. The pain they delivered to him was intense and quick, and then blackness overtook him.

Chapter 19

For a few hours after leaving the camp, Charlie had trudged along in the dark, half paying attention to the trail, though he did step off a time or two. As he walked he pondered on the events of the preceding few hours. How on earth was he supposed to figure out what it was Pap had wanted? Was he truly angry with Charlie? To his mind, Charlie hadn't done anything to offend the old man.

But in keeping with Pap's wishes, he walked on. But with each step that led him slowly from the only fellow who'd ever really felt like a friend, a father sort of figure to him, Charlie's thinking turned to the old man's reasoning, and it occurred to him that maybe Pap was doing nothing more than protecting him. It became clear that Pap didn't want Charlie to get mixed up in Grady's big heist. Heck, Charlie didn't want any of the boys to be part of it. But the boys were grown men, as Pap had told him. And if they chose to throw in with a no-account like Grady Haskell, then so be it.

But the part Charlie couldn't fathom was the way Ace, Mex, Simp, and Dutchy so easily hitched up with Haskell, ignoring all that Pap had done for them. He reckoned wading through life with Pap leading them wasn't the same as making a whole wad all at once.

He could see the appeal, he guessed, but Charlie didn't hold with thievery. He knew what effort went into earning a dollar, and all those dollars that they were going to steal had to be earned by someone. Now that he thought on it, he was a little surprised that Pap would go along with such notions at all.

Something scuffed gravel off to his right, under a scarp of rock, though it was difficult to tell exactly what it was, given the clouded moon. Charlie paused, listened, his head cocked toward the sound, one hand on the hilt of his knife. There it was again, low down toward the ground, but quick and slight. Charlie relaxed. Likely it was a snake or some other night critter hunting.

For a few moments he had dim thoughts that it might be Grady tracking him, especially now that he was well away from the camp. Haskell was the sort to sneak up on a man and lay him low, shoot him in the back, stab him, or worse, then leave him there for the varmints to fight over. Charlie shuddered at the gruesome thought he might end up as wolf bait or a grizzly's meal. At that, his stomach growled, a low, long mournful sound. It reminded Charlie he'd only picked at his own supper, and now he was paying for that. He swigged at the water in his water bottle, resisted the urge to drain it, unfamiliar as he was to the countryside and what opportunities for drinking water it might offer.

The going was slow, as the moon refused to do much more than peek for seconds at a time from behind its dark cloudy scrim.

The more he thought about Grady Haskell, the more Charlie grew agitated with himself. There was no way on earth Haskell could be talked out of his plans to rob the bank, and now that Charlie was out from under Pap's stony gaze, a creeping guilt worked its way up Charlie's spine, its cold claws digging in and refusing to leave him be.

Should he have done more to stop the crazy plan? Maybe so. Could he have done anything, other than probably get himself shot? Maybe, maybe not.

Charlie dithered like that for long minutes, and only when he had begun to doubt his initial reason for leaving the camp did he realize he had stopped in the trail. When it did occur to him, he scratched his lengthening beard stubble on his big, wide jaw, sighed inwardly once more, and turned around.

He calculated that he might make it back to the campsite by daybreak, and he knew the boys would have ridden to Bakersfield by then. They'd only been camped a few miles out. His advantage was that he would be traveling at a fast walk when they were still sleeping. Beyond that he had no real idea how fast he'd get there, though he doubted he'd catch up to them before they made it to town. Hopefully he wouldn't be too far behind. He might make it in time . . . to do something. What, he had no notion yet.

Something had compelled him to turn, that clawing in his gut that wasn't hunger. It was what he'd heard someone call a little voice. Or maybe it should have been in his head. He didn't much know or care, but he did know that when he'd followed it in the past, he'd been glad he had, for the most part. But this time? Would he even make it to the town in time?

"Can't hurt to try, Charlie," he said aloud, hitching up his trousers, readjusting the gear bag he'd slung over his shoulder, and picking up and putting down those big legs at double speed.

*   *   *

The return trip back toward the campsite took Charlie less time than he thought, though he'd not guessed correctly the number of hours until daylight. He blamed the low clouds and hiding moon. By the time the spot where he and Grady had tussled came into view up ahead, Charlie realized he could see most everything clearly enough to make out what might be the distinctive shapes of men and horses. But of those he found none.

He walked on and soon the campsite itself revealed itself from out of the trees. Charlie paused on the outer edge looking in. No sign of the horses, no bedrolls, no nothing.

"Hello the camp," he called softly, his eyes skittering about the little clearing and into the trees beyond. No response. He repeated himself, a pinch louder this time, but heard nothing. The camp was bare, the only life a thin curl of smoke rising from the otherwise cold fire. Charlie kneeled, palmed the inside face of a few of the rocks that made up the campfire ring. They still offered slight warmth. He stood and glanced around the quiet site again. The men hadn't been gone long.

Pap must not have been the last out of the site, he reasoned. The old man was particular about making sure a cook fire was good and out before moving on.

"It's dry out here in the West, Charlie," Pap had told him months before. "Drier'n a cork. Always douse your fire, then douse it some more. At least till she's good and cold. And if you don't have water, make water, right on it. Won't harm nothing."

And with that, the old man had unbuttoned his fly and urinated on what Charlie had assumed were dead cold ashes and coals. But it steamed and Pap had nodded and winked. "You see? Take care of the natural world, Charlie, and she'll take care of you."

Recalling that little lesson brought a smile to Charlie's face. And as he had precious little water in his canteen to spare, he glanced around, still saw no one, and mimicked Pap's method. The last of the warm coals were soon doused.

He continued on toward town, hoping Haskell's plan of taking their time once they got to town hadn't changed. Grady had thought that if they didn't appear hurried they might not attract as much attention. Charlie wasn't sure what the thief had based that logic on. But Charlie had silently disagreed. It seemed to him that the more time they spent there, the more people would remember them. But he hadn't offered his thoughts on the subject because he hadn't wanted to help Haskell in any way.

Charlie stopped now and again to check hoofprints, saw several piles of road apples from the horses, and, as with the campfire, held his hand over them to see if they might offer telltale warmth. They did. Good, that meant the boys weren't that far ahead.

He came up on the outer edge of town sooner than he expected. He'd seen a handful of squat shapes up ahead to his left, and as he drew closer he realized they were shacks. They became more frequent, some taller, more impressive, until the road was flanked with houses, businesses, a few men who gave him looks.

The road forked once, and a man in a black suit and bowler hat rushed by him. He wanted to ask which way to the bank, but held his tongue. No mention of a bank by a stranger in town could be a good thing.

He knew he was getting closer to the center of town, the location of the bank, at least according to Haskell, because he saw more people out and about, not surprising given that it was a workday and not the Sabbath. But he noticed something else too about these people. They were in a hurry. Just to get to work? Maybe so, but many of them looked alarmed, flustered. And they all seemed to be headed toward the same spot—right where he was headed.

"Hey, mister," he said. "What's happening here?"

The man to whom Charlie spoke looked him quickly up and down. "Some commotion down at the bank. I dunno." He stopped, looked Charlie up and down. "Strangers, they say. Like yourself."

But Charlie was already pushing past him. The closer he drew to what he guessed would be a growing throng before him, the louder the shouts grew. Before he turned a corner, his boots hammering hard on the wooden boardwalk fronting a line of shops, a mix of false-front buildings and low-line adobe structures with low-hung ramadas, he heard a shot, followed by screams and frenzied shouts.

He tossed his gear to the boardwalk, where it hit, then tumbled off the edge. But Charlie didn't care; he was beelining for the growing crowds. There were two, one to his right, one left. Bristling from the throng at the right, a horse rose above the people, lunging and spinning, neighing and thrashing. Charlie had appeared in time to see what looked a whole lot like Mex being dragged from his mount, mismatched eyes beyond wide, black hair splayed outward, a silent scream formed on his big mustache-topped mouth.

Charlie was set to bolt into the fray to help his friend, but the throng to his left drew his attention, and what he saw there made him stop, big head shaking. No, no, no, this can't be.

He couldn't imagine that what he was seeing what actually happening. Right there before him, time seemed to slow almost to a stop, all the bristling sounds and sharp smells of horse, gunpowder, the shrieks and angry shouts of the other crowd all dissipated, pinched out. Charlie felt as though he couldn't take another step, as if he were waist-deep in river muck, as if boulders were tied to his boots.

There before him, as if he'd bloomed into view, Grady Haskell sat his horse larger-than-life, a gnash-toothed grin spread across his pocked face, a revolver in one hand. In the other he'd drawn that single-shell shotgun of his, the snout of the barrel smoking. The recipient of the shot was a crumpled mess on the street not but a few feet from the stamping hooves of Haskell's horse. The crowd surged forward, but Haskell swung around on them, still smiling, bulging money sacks flopping across the saddle horn before him. He cranked back on the revolver's hammer and sent a shot slicing over the heads of the crowd.

With the speed of a snapped finger, time sped up, sound rushed in, smells blossomed, and Big Charlie Chilton found himself shoving townsfolk away from him, flinging angry people left and right as he drove through them like a plow cleaving packed earth.

"Pap!" he bellowed. "Pap!"

Still a few strides from the crumpled form, Charlie drove forward at top speed, dropped to his knees on the cobbled street. He lifted the curled form into his lap and yes, it was Pap, no mistake. A mass of shredded cloth—shirt, vest, coat—gathered in a bunch in Charlie's beseeching fist. But the old man's chest had taken the full brunt of the shotgun blast.

"Pap!"

The old man's head lolled, his eyelids fluttering open. "Charlie?"

His breath was a weak, raspy thing. Charlie wasn't even sure he'd heard it.

"Don't pay him no never mind, you big oaf!"

Charlie looked up to see Haskell still there before him, his horse dancing even as the hesitant people moved closer. Charlie wanted to lunge at him, but he didn't dare upset Pap, who was still breathing and still staring up at him.

The crowd rushed at Haskell, who was gigging his horse around in a circle. He looked down once more at Charlie, who returned the vicious glare. Then Haskell squeezed another round right into the crowd, then another. More screams rose, and howls of pain and rage filled the air.

Haskell appeared to be enjoying the show. As a last gesture, as he wheeled his horse around to head on out of town, to follow the thundering retreat of Ace, Simp, and Dutch, Haskell threw the shotgun hard at Charlie.

Charlie saw it coming in enough time to instinctively fling an arm up. The shotgun slammed into it, smacking the bone. Charlie ignored the pain, tried to struggle to his feet, but Pap let out a shudder and a moan. "Pap, it's all right now. I'm here. Ol' Charlie's here."

By the time Charlie tore his gaze from Pap, Haskell was nothing but a long, howling laugh trailing behind his thundering form, kicking up a thin cloud of dust as a few townsmen cranked off haphazard shots at his retreating back, his sweat-soaked brown hat bouncing across his shoulder blades from the stampede strap about his neck.

The only thing Charlie wanted to do now was track him down and kill him with his own bare, brawny hands.

The only thing the townsfolk of Bakersfield wanted to do was kill the people responsible for robbing their town, killing or wounding a number of their fellows, and creating a scene the likes of which they'd never seen.

And the only one left alive, since they had already set to hard, gang work on the howling form of Mex and had, as far as they could tell, killed him, was the big man on his knees in the street, cradling the old stranger. All they saw were strangers who hadn't been in their peaceful town before all this mess took place. And right then, strangers were the only people who needed to be blamed.

But Charlie wasn't paying attention to them. He was too busy pleading with Pap. The old man was still with him, smiling up at him, even as blood slowly welled up in a thin line between his lips, leaked out the side of his mouth.

Charlie bent low over Pap's face, kept his right ear close to Pap's mouth, whispered close and urgently into the old man's ear. "Pap, don't you leave me now. I got big plans for us. I . . . I figured out a way for us to have that place we talked of so often. You know, that place in the mountains where we're going to keep stock, grow that garden—biggest one you ever did see. It's going to be a big old spread where we can keep chickens, place tucked back in the mountains where we ain't never going to be bothered, you wait and see. . . . Pap? Pap?"

Charlie pulled back, looked at Pap. The old man's eyes were still open, filming with a death glaze, staring at him, a wide smile on his bloody lips. His silly dented bowler hat sat a few feet away, the bent silk flower more crumpled than ever.

Charlie swallowed, nodded, a lone tear rolled down his face, balanced on the end of his nose. "I reckon you heard me all right." The tear dropped, hit Pap's cheek.

Then the crowd set upon Charlie with a howling vengeance.

Chapter 20

"Gentlemen, I expect you know why I convened this meeting." Horace McCafferty stood at the head of the long table in the council chamber. The rotund man thumbed the lapels of his amply cut frock coat and jutted his chin, though it was so round no one noticed. He regarded each of the men in turn.

"Oh, get on with it, Horace. We got bigger things to deal with than you today."

The fat man winced. "I am merely trying to perpetuate the air of dignity and respect that befits this institution we have erected."

"Institution?" Gimble, the editor of the *Bakersfield Gazette*, snorted and shifted his cigar to the other side of his mouth. "Horace, there's nothing to convene. We need to get this dang show on the road. We have a bank full of people handled so savagely that they might never recover. One man, old Muley Timmons, was shot, clubbed, and then, sadly, expired of his wounds. God rest his old soul. Good man. Then there was our fellow on the council, Tollinson, the banker, and his subordinate, the Matthews boy, a good lad. Both of them treated rough enough that we might never get the full story of what happened out of them. And we have a giant of a man imprisoned for crimes we can't in all likelihood pin on him."

"Why not?" shouted Stewbins, a normally docile man whose outburst and slammed fist on the tabletop paused them all for a long moment. "Why can't we just let the crowds have him and be done with it?"

Gimble, the newspaperman, took a breath, rubbed his eyes. "That would be anarchy, Mel. And you know as well as I that we can't allow that to happen here in Bakersfield."

"And why not? Worked out with that Indian-looking bank-robbing, killing thief they laid low."

Gimble ignored him and continued with his litany of affronts. "As Mel Stewbins so kindly reminded us, we have had one of the robbers savaged apart at the hands of our otherwise gentle townsfolk. We have a stranger, an old man, gunned down in the street. Marcus Cottrell was shot dead by the man who was savaged. A couple of other folks were wounded." He rubbed his eyes, as much from the long list of affronts as from the blue smoke drifting into them. He sighed and continued. "And perhaps saddest of all, little Minnie Petersen was trampled by one of the thieves' horses—the same man who appeared to be the boss of the thieving gang, same man who shot the old stranger, same man who was likely connected somehow with them all. Poor Minnie may or may not live. We don't know yet. If she does, well, I pity her family. And if she should leave us, well, my response will be the same." He shook his head, regarded his folded hands on the table before him.

The assembled men nodded in mutual commiseration.

He continued. "And that's not taking into account the as-yet-unknown tally of money the thieves made off with. The Indian, or Mexican, or whatever he was, had a tidy sum on him, and there were four other bank robbers seen to ride out of town, with roughly the same number of bags draped about their persons and on their saddles. Given this scant information, we can draw a rough conclusion as to how much money was stolen from the bank."

"The big fella in the jail, he has to be part of the gang," said Stewbins. "He seems a fool, but I think there's more going on in his bean than he lets on. I think we can wear him down before we hang him."

"What do you think you'll get from him?" said the newspaperman. "Some folks said he was shot at. Others said he was a shooter. Still others claim he was the one with the shotgun, the one who shot the old man. Then he felt badly about it and held the man until he died."

"Yes, and I heard that he was all those things and more!" McCafferty, still standing, thumbed his lapels all the harder. "I heard that he held the old man down and strangled him until he died in his arms. Can you imagine? And to think we have these brutes running rampant in our town. It's almost too much to bear."

"Regardless," said Gimble, "we have to keep him locked up until we can get the law in here to deal with him."

"What law? We don't even have a constable anymore. He up and quit, then crawled inside a bottle. He should be strung up too for leaving us so high and dry."

"Look, Horace, I know how you all feel about the man in the prison. And I can't say I wholly disagree with you, but if we let our citizens run vigilante roughshod over everybody who commits a crime in these parts, why, it won't be long before anyone who happens to look askance at Widow Dunphy will be strung up in a tree with their own braces. And what will we have then?"

"We'll have a town safer than it is now!" Stewbins scowled and slammed his fist to the tabletop again. Drinking glasses shook and rattled.

"No," said Gimble, eyes closed and sighing. "We'll have a town no one in their right mind would come to invest in. We'll have a town with much promise but with no hope of ever growing larger, and the very real prospect of the town shrinking and dying on the vine, drying up. And that means no more business and that means no more profits."

That was the one sentence Gimble had uttered that managed to shut them all up for long moments. Finally McCafferty, visibly shaken by the disastrous prospect, said, "Well, what do you suggest we do about it, then?" His tone was still antagonistic, as though he knew the obvious answer but wanted Gimble to spell it out for him.

Gimble happily obliged. "We are in a dicey situation, gentlemen. We must retain order in Bakersfield. To do that we must squelch any action remotely smacking of vigilantism. For that is a black eye this town will not be able to sustain for all the reasons I mentioned."

"So?"

"So we need to act in a unified way to get law and order back on the docket here in Bakersfield. And the best way to do that is to get the best lawman we can afford. Fortunately he still lives here in town. Though I hear he's readying to move from here. We must get Marshal Dodd Wickham back on the job. We must beg him if need be. I really see no other option."

McCafferty snorted, shook his head, but offered no verbal opposition. The other four nodded slowly.

Gimble said, "Now, it's one thing for us to sit here and make a list of all the things we'd like to have happen. It's another thing entirely for them to come true."

"What are you saying?"

"I'm saying that I don't think Wickham will accept. If I was him I'd be leery of working with us. We didn't exactly treat him kindly in this very room a few weeks back."

Another long silence, in which several of the men shuffled papers, and one of them dug around in his mouth with a fingernail, dislodging a hunk of his breakfast from his teeth.

"Who's going to be the one to go humble himself before the old man?"

No one said anything. Finally Gimble sighed. "I'll go, then. Can't be all that bad, right? Besides, I used to be chummy with the man."

They all knew it was hokum, as no one had ever really been friendly with the marshal. Which was the way he wanted it, apparently. But this time would be different. It had to be.

"Maybe we can get Mamie Lofton to talk to him. She seems sweet on him, after all."

"Mamie Lofton? Really? Well, don't that beat all?"

"I'm sure he's heard all about the mess so far. But one of us has to make the effort to visit him. Maybe earlier in the day is better. Rumor has it he's pretty well into the bottle by the end of the day."

"You'd think he'd feel guilty about all this, wouldn't you?"

"Nah," said McCafferty, thumbing his lapels, looking

bleary-eyed at the tabletop, at the spot Wickham had so recently dented on the otherwise fine, smooth surface. "He's a crusty old cur with a heart of stone. Ain't no way he cares. Not about any of us anyway. Not about Bakersfield."

Chapter 21

"Marshal?" *Bang, bang, bang!* Mamie Lofton's knuckles rapped hard on the weathered wood of the front door. "Marshal! You may as well come to the door. I know for a fact you are home and ignoring me. We can't have it both ways in life. You understand? You either come to the door and hear what I have to say or I will be forced to smack a rock through that perfect window right beside the door. And don't think I won't do it, Marshal. And get a move on, will you? I left my shop closed and I can ill afford to lose sales because of some old drunkard."

Presently she heard a shuffling-clumping sound from inside. It grew closer. She rapped on the door again and it swung open to reveal a wet-eyed old man in his stocking feet and a tight-set mouth.

"What do you want, ma'am?"

"Ma'am? Everything we've . . . participated in together and you call me 'ma'am'?" Mamie outthrust an arm and pushed right past the astonished man.

"But . . ."

"But nothing."

"I . . . don't have much say in the matter, do I?"

"Not this time, Marshal."

"Nor anytime, as I recall," he mumbled as he closed the door behind her.

"Don't think I didn't hear that," she said, turning around as she strode manfully down the hall.

Marshal Dodd Wickham's house was a rental, something that though he did not own, he had managed to find nonetheless quite comfortable as an abode for the many years he had been Bakersfield's chief lawman. It consisted of two bedrooms upstairs, a kitchen and dining room downstairs toward the back of the house, and a formal sitting room to the front. It was a small house as such went in Bakersfield, but it suited his needs nicely. It was just far enough from his former office that it required a brisk walk each morning to get there.

He'd been about to leave this place, had intended to, but he'd allowed his baser demons, rascals he'd not allowed to rise to the surface of his stalwart personality, to escape. They came about in the form of drink. A number of bottles of fine whiskey, most empty, stood neatly aligned on an otherwise bare sideboard.

"My stars, Dodd," said Mamie Lofton, calling him by his given name for the first time since arriving. She surveyed the room, her purse handles looped in the crook of one arm, her gloved hands poised, fingers thrust upward as if she were about to perform surgery.

"While I respect a body's requirement's for privacy—I know of what I speak, having been enjoying spinsterhood for a good many years now—I can also recognize when a body has ventured far beyond the parameters of what is acceptable in and out of society. And you, sir"—she dragged open the heavy drapes to allow full sunlight to invade the somber room—"have self-indulged in such silly little notions for far too long."

"What do you want, Mamie? I am a busy man." Wickham gestured limply at the two open valises askew atop the dining table visible through the doorway leading to the next room.

They sported jumbles of clothing, papers, a stack of books, several of which had tumbled to the floor, bringing with them articles of the aforementioned clothing and papers. A derby hat stood upended and balancing dangerously close to the edge of the table.

"It appears to me as if you've made very little progress in the way of, as you put it—let me see if I remember how you voiced it that day a few weeks ago after the council meeting in which you claim you were disposed of. . . ." She rubbed her chin and glanced at the pressed-tin ceiling theatrically. "Oh yes, you were about to embark on a 'revenge leaving' the likes of which this town would not forget for some time. Isn't that about the gist of it?"

The old man sighed. "Mamie, I realize that you and I have had some high old times together. Heck, you've been a lovely respite for me in this otherwise increasingly soulless town. I hope I have been able to repay in some small way the favors you have . . . bestowed on me."

"Save your idle chatter, Dodd. I'm not here as a woman scorned. I realize that I don't have enough of a hold on you to keep you here, tied by some silly romantic heartstrings twaddle. And for the record, though time spent with you has always been most pleasurable, I hope you'll not take this the wrong way, but I am always glad to return to my own abode."

He looked at a half-filled bottle of whiskey on the sideboard, sitting enticingly smack-dab between the two of them. She saw his eyes dart to it, saw his tongue run over his lips, and looked at the bottle herself.

"Oh, for heaven's sake, Dodd. You look like hell. Pour yourself two fingers and pay attention to me. I daresay you're going to need it."

He paused in reaching for a small drinking glass. "What's that supposed to mean?"

"No, not until you've had your libation."

He followed through, and though he tried not to guzzle the ample drink, he was unsuccessful. "Out with it, then. What matter of such weighty import called you here, Mamie?" He smiled and sidled a step closer to her.

"Easy, now, Dodd. I would ask you to take a seat, but I know you are a man and as such are not prone to taking suggestions, let alone orders, from a woman. So I'll tell you."

"Out with it, already, Mamie. My word, you have a way of dragging out the inevitable far beyond the point of reason."

She grimaced, pulled her purse tight to her chest. "Your lack of presence in office as marshal of Bakersfield has resulted this very morning in the deaths of a number of people."

"How's that?" said Dodd, steadying himself with a hand on the back of a chair.

The dressmaker explained the events of that very morning, elaborating on what had happened to the little girl, Minnie Petersen.

"As far as I know, the city council, albeit without Tollinson, the banker, convened a special session—that's what they've called it—and are about to send an emissary to ask you to resume your old job. I should say you could write your own meal ticket."

But Wickham had not heard that last bit. He sagged against the back of the chair that now was truly holding him upright. He also lost all the color in his face and his grizzled, unshaven cheeks took on a drawn, shadowed cast. "Will the little girl, the Petersen girl . . . will she make it?"

Mamie Lofton regarded him with the first soft look she had given him the entire visit. "She passed on about an hour ago, Dodd."

It was too much to bear. That was all he could think. Too much to bear. He sagged with a groan, barely found the seat of the chair, and slumped into it.

"I know you'll blame yourself, and you may think it harsh of me to say so, but to a certain extent, you are to blame, Dodd."

He looked up, ashen, at her. "What about my deputy, Randy Scoville? Where was he and his chums? They couldn't wait to get rid of me. They should have been on the job!"

"Well, they were and they weren't. Scoville was clear out of town at his sister's place because he trusted the Tompkins twins to do his deputying for him."

Wickham shook his head, his indignation already claimed by a wash of regret.

"It's not too late, Dodd, to make amends."

He looked up at her again. "How's that? Seems as though a whole lot of bad has already been done."

"Yes, but those thieving killers are long gone. Scoville and his two simps, plus a handful of others from town, formed a posse and took off after them, but that will likely prove fruitless. Scoville's barely brighter than the twins."

The old man reached for the bottle, but Mamie snatched it from the shelf. "You would be a whole lot more useful if you were relatively sober, don't you agree?"

"What would you like me to do? It seems no matter

what I turn my hand to, it comes up foul." He stared at her a long moment, tears welling in his rheumy eyes.

Finally she broke eye contact with a click of disgust from her tongue. She slammed the bottle down before him, the amber liquid jostling in the bottle. "There, then, if that's what you want so badly. Take it and slink on inside it. It's the easy way, the most logical thing in the world for a drunkard to do."

"I'm no drunk—"

"Save your words for someone who will care, Dodd Wickham. For that someone is not me." With that, Mamie Lofton spun away, her bootheels clacking hard down the hallway.

Wickham listened to the front door slam so hard he half thought the leaded panes would collapse and fall to the floor. But they didn't. His gaze rested on the bottle before him. It was the only thing he could rely on anymore. Apparently not Mamie. And certainly not on himself.

Chapter 22

Later that afternoon, Gimble and McCafferty from the city council bustled their way toward Dodd Wickham's residence, arguing about everything. They turned the street at Rosewood and Pine and smacked right into Dodd Wickham himself.

"Marshal, what . . . a pleasure to see you out and about."

"There's nothing pleasurable about this day, nor any of the incidents it has brought to Bakersfield."

The old lawman made to push by them, but McCafferty blocked his path with a halfhearted gesture. Wickham drove his walking stick upward, slammed into the man's forearm. He groaned and winced, cradling his freshly wounded limb.

Gimble said, "Marshal, I see you're still wearing your badge."

"Course I am. Never was sworn out of office. Had to give you jackanapes time to cool your heels."

"No, no, no, don't misunderstand me, Marshal," said the newspaperman. "I am, that is to say, we are pleased to see you're wearing your star. Aren't we, McCafferty?" He looked at his companion with the wounded arm, a fat, seething man who looked ready to hurl his fat body forward at the marshal. But he bit his tongue and rubbed his sleeve.

"Why are you so all-fired happy to see me?" Wickham glared at the pair.

Gimble stuttered, "You, uh, apparently have heard about the unfortunate events of earlier today."

"Yes, I have."

McCafferty blustered in, cutting off Gimble, who was about to speak. "Then I'm sure you'll agree the best plan of action is for Bakersfield, a town on the verge of becoming one of the most viable commercial centers in California, is to—"

"Save your hogwash, Horace. I'm going to see that whoever did this swings . . . lawfully . . . for their crimes. And then I'm going to get away from this place once and for all. After I resign my post." He leaned in toward them both, forcing them to lean back with wide eyes. "But before then, I intend to do whatever is necessary to make sure that little girl's family, and everyone else who was savaged by those louts, finds some sliver of relief knowing the law—and not a bunch of yahoo vigilantes— was on their side."

"Well, you've got your work cut out for you, Marshal," said the still-wincing McCafferty. "Because as we speak there's a pile of townsfolk fixing to string up that big ol' boy they caught from the gang." He smiled, looked around. "In fact, I'd be surprised if you were able to get there in time to do much more than watch the killer's body empty itself and dribble his last meal down his pants leg and off the toe of his boot."

The fat man smiled as the normally unflappable old lawman's face turned whiter. Without a word, Wickham departed, thunking that walking stick down the street at a rapid pace.

Chapter 23

Marshal Dodd Wickham was surprised to see that Deputy Randy Scoville had ridden back into Bakersfield. From the looks of the ragged, haggard men behind him, the posse was made up of a much-abused, spent clot of trail-soft townsmen unused to exertion of any sort. It was all too obvious by the desperate looks on their faces that they knew they were trailing a gang of hard men, robbers and thieves who proved they didn't mind killing to save their skins and keep their ill-gotten money.

Wickham angled across the street, headed toward the straggling group. "Randy, what in tarnation happened to you all?"

The deputy, in the midst of dismounting from his paint, spun his perpetual scowl on the marshal. He eyed him up and down. "I see you decided to pin on your badge again. You sober or do I have to keep carrying the load around here?"

Wickham decided to let that pass. The boy had obviously had a bad time of it. And he was a poor excuse for a calm and collected person at the best of times, let alone when a situation arose. Why Wickham ever let himself be saddled with the fool boy—nephew of a city councilor—

was a point that had daily set the marshal's old teeth to grinding, for three years now. He'd hoped the boy would have mellowed, grown into the job, taken it more seriously when he needed to and less so when he was too gun-happy. But none of that had happened. He'd only become more annoying.

Word had even leaked back to the marshal, from various folks about town, how Scoville had begun hinting that a pouch of cash on a monthly basis might help decrease the odds of a business getting hit by thieves. The marshal had dressed the boy down right on Main Street over that one. Not surprisingly, the dumb kid hadn't denied it. He'd smirked, shrugged, then walked off, leaving the marshal standing alone on the street with a handful of nothing but balled fist.

And now he'd come back from leading a posse of ill-equipped fools after bad men. And from the looks of things, it hadn't gone well. In addition to a grazed Scoville, Wickham could see at least two men bleeding, one from the side, one a shoulder wound. And as the horses danced, skittering from the rough, angry handling they were receiving at the hands of the men, he could now see a body draped over a horse. Not something he had expected to see. They'd gotten close, then. Maybe he could glean some information before visiting the prisoner.

"Where'd you meet up with them?" he asked.

Scoville didn't look at him, busied himself with staring at someone to his right. Finally he answered, "Up by Delaney's old claim. They was holed up, waiting."

"How many?"

"I don't know! Four, five of them? Maybe even ten! What the heck does it matter now? We didn't land a lick and we got all shot to pieces!" His rage carried through his voice, quavering it and shaking the young man's head and hands.

Scoville slid the rest of the way down from his horse, jerked his head back over his shoulder, then turned back to the marshal. "You caused this, old man! You had your head on straight, been doing your job, you'd have prevented this mess. Now look!" He pointed his face more screwed than ever, his dark eyes glinting between anger and tears. "One of the Tompkins twins, draped yonder over that horse. You see that?"

"You made them posse members?" Wickham squinted from the body to the deputy.

Scoville hustled in tight to Wickham, standing close enough that his spittle flecked the marshal's face. "You dang right I did. It was my decision and I made it."

Scoville had a point, but he'd only take so much from the boy. Wickham nodded. "Then you'll have to live with it." He returned the hard stare. "And it won't ever get any easier on your mind, boy. Now stop yammering at me and get those men and yourself on over to Doc Whipple's." He nodded toward the deputy's grazed upper arm. "Don't dawdle."

"You ain't my boss no more."

That was it. Wickham turned on him, poked a long finger in the deputy's face, and said, "I can appreciate that you're all riled up. I was too, first time I was shot, and shot at, had a friend and a deputy killed, and all because of me. But unless you tell me you're quitting the job, then I am indeed still your boss. Like it or leave it."

The two men stared, nearly nose-to-nose, right there in the street. Finally a long, drawn-out groan from behind the young deputy broke the standoff. The marshal turned on his heel and headed toward the jail. From behind him, Scoville shouted, "You best see to that killer in the cell, Marshal, 'cause we'll be coming for him. He's a killer and he ain't going to get away with it! The whole town feels that way!"

The marshal stopped smack-dab in the middle of the crossroads that formed the heart of the downtown. He turned, faced the deputy, planted his fists on his narrow hips, coattails flung back. Wickham spoke in a loud, withering, commanding voice that seemed to echo up and down the streets leading to him, like echoes pulsing in and out of deep desert canyons.

"Any man or woman who dares to raise a hand against the prisoner while he's in my care will receive short, hard justice from me. I will not tolerate murder. Nor will I allow murderers in my custody to evade justice. Let me be plain. Justice will be done. And there will be a judge along soon to see to the fact." His bellowed words carried, echoed, faded.

No one said anything, but the dozens of people on the street all regarded him with anger and awe, fear and confusion. He knew his point had been made well enough. They would comply with his wishes but only for as long as the prisoner was in his custody. Anything beyond that and he was sure that death would come fast for the prisoner.

Now to meet the one prisoner the townsfolk had managed to capture alive.

Chapter 24

It was a sharp, thunking, whacking sound that yanked Charlie awake, as if the big ol' hand of God had grabbed him by the shirtfront, dozens of church bells pealing in righteous discord all around. He sat up. No hands had grabbed him; no big brass bells were sounding. What was it, then? There, there it was again, a clanking, banging sound. Less ominous than bells, to be sure. But still an odd sound.

Charlie looked around. Where was he? Dark, near black; he could barely see a hand held before him. And it hurt like the dickens to raise that hand. His arms pained him something fierce. Like when Pap found him and . . . and then it hit him. All at once. Pap, shot dead in the street by that no-account, murdering fiend, Grady Haskell. Didn't any of that matter when Haskell was hoodwinking the lot of them? Why hadn't he seen through the man's sham ways?

There in the dark, despite the pain, Charlie gritted his teeth and vowed, somewhere, somehow, he'd get his revenge. He didn't care what anybody said about turning the other cheek. A good man was dead, another few were probably also killed, judging by the way the townsfolk had set to on Charlie there in the street, he thought.

And me, standing there with a shotgun at my feet. My word, they all but thought I'd done the deed. That's what they were howling about, wasn't it?

Charlie shook his head, trying to remember, but the throbbing in his head set in hard and fast, and the rest of it came back to him. The townsfolk had wanted his hide. They'd all but ripped old Pap apart, tugging him away from Charlie. He tested his feet against the floor, winced as a needle of pain angled up through his knee. No way was he going to let a little thrashing he took get in the way of his mission, his sworn duty.

And then the rest of the story wormed its way through his fuzzy head. He was not in any place where he could do a thing about it. Haskell might as well be a million miles away, because Charlie realized he was in a jail cell. He wasn't sure he'd ever been in one before, and it was only now filtering back to him in bits and pieces as to how he'd landed here.

He looked around, his eyes adjusted now to the near-dark gloom. There were the steel straps of the cell, woven together like a huge basket. There was no window, at least not in this cell. He reached up slowly, rubbed a stiff hand across the back of his neck. It was stiff too, worst he'd ever felt. He concentrated—the last thing he remembered happening had been taking a nasty knock to the bean. He'd turned his head in time to catch something that felt a whole lot like a log slamming into the soft spot above his left ear.

As that last slice of information came to him, he realized he could easily have been strung up high, if not torn apart the way poor Mex had been by that wild horde of townies.

Not that he could blame them, but he was mighty glad he hadn't awoken dead.

There it was, a clacking, thwacking sound. In the half minute or so since he'd come back to the land of the living, he thought he'd heard it three, maybe four times. What in the deuce was it? Whatever it is, thought Charlie, it's getting closer.

And then the loudest and closest noise sounded a few yards away, a grating, sliding sound—a key in a lock, that was what it was—and then soft light angled in slow, widening as a heavy door squawked open on its steel hinges.

It opened fully, thudding into a stone wall behind. In the doorway stood the outline of a man, not a big man, but tall enough. He had his hands on his hips, a short-brim low-crown hat, looked as if he had longish hair jutting out from under the hat, worn like a plainsman, he'd learned, for sun protection more so than for purposes of vanity.

"Well, son," said the man after standing there a minute or two. He advanced into the short corridor. *Clack, thwack*—it was a walking stick that had been making the sound, set down and picked up again with each step the man took. He walked closer and Charlie saw more of the man. He was an older fellow, black hat, black suit, neatly trimmed silvery mustaches, the longish hair, as he'd suspected. Not a big man, but with the walking stick now planted as if it might take root through the stone flags of the floor, and with a sharp, piercing gaze that even in the dark cells of what Charlie assumed was the basement of the building, those eyes looked right at him, right into him.

"Well, well, well," repeated the man. "Looks to me like you've landed yourself in a pond filled with snapping turtles and poisonous snakes."

Not sure how to respond to that comment, nor if he

even could respond, Charlie kept quiet and regarded the man a little longer.

The man stepped closer. *Whack! Clack!* He ground the tip of the walking stick into the floor. His voice matched the distance perfectly between them—only a few feet now. Charlie pushed up off the cot, stood with no small amount of pain, and made his way to the strap cage wall between them. The old man didn't flinch.

It was then that Charlie noticed that the soft light that angled in from behind where the man had come touched the face of a worn, polished silver star on the his left lapel. Here was the law.

"Yes, sir," said Charlie, though it sounded more as if he were gargling rocks and spitting sand. He coughed, swallowed, tried again. "Yes, sir, I reckon it looks that way."

The lawman regarded him for another few long moments. "You got a name, boy?"

"Charlie. Name's Charlie."

"Well, Charlie, you don't look like a child killer."

"What?" The word ripped up out of Charlie's mouth. "Mister, I don't know what you think you know, but I ain't never killed nobody in my life. Least of all a child. But I aim to make amends for that real soon." He cut his eyes downward, a moment's rage filling him as he envisioned the leering face of Grady Haskell. "Haskell, I mean, not a child."

"Who's Haskell?"

Charlie looked up at the marshal. He almost responded, almost told the old lawman that Grady Haskell was the worst of the worst, almost said so. But he didn't. Because in that last second, he reckoned that the marshal, being a lawman and all, would likely get to Haskell before Charlie. And that would ruin everything. Charlie still wasn't sure how he was going to get out of jail and get to Haskell, but he was darn sure going to give it a go.

"Boy," said the old man. "You don't need to play tight-lipped with me. I'm the law in these parts, such as it is, and I can tell you that this jail's locked tighter than a bull's backside. Especially to you."

"What's that supposed to mean?" said Charlie, though he knew full well what the man meant. He was doomed to die in this hole.

Instead of an explanation, the marshal sighed. "You know what they're calling you, boy?"

"No, uh-uh." Charlie shook his head, not really caring what anyone much thought of him.

"They're calling you 'the Shotgun Killer.'"

That brought Charlie's gaze up again. "Why?"

"Because the entire town saw you totin' that old single-shell, barn-door blaster, that's why. And a man lay dead at your feet, an old man, from what I hear, an old man who'd been shredded to death by that same shotgun. They say you picked up that shotgun, tried to make a run for it. That's why."

Charlie gripped the strap iron tight, his aching muscles screaming, his bloodied knuckles whitening. "I told you I ain't never killed anyone. I've never even shot anyone! They saw me holding the shotgun because . . . because he threw it at me. I was angry, he was riding off, and Pap was there dead by his hand. They couldn't have seen me fire that gun, because I never did."

"You don't need to have fired it. To the folks who saw you with it, standing there hefting it, it was enough to damn you."

"I was angry, I told you. That's all there was to it."

"Angry, why?"

"Because he killed my friend, that's why. Because I

should have been there. Because none of this shoulda happened, that's why!"

"Who killed your friend? Haskell? He the one you're so all-fired to protect?"

Charlie ground his teeth together. "Mister, the day I protect him is the day you can hang me from the highest tree." He rattled the rugged cage for emphasis, then turned away to face the dark gloom of the cell in disgust.

The lawman pooched his lips. "I can see you're upset, Charlie." His voice wasn't as cold and hard as it had been. "Anything you can tell me about the rascals who caused all this will help. You know that, don't you?"

Charlie said nothing, just stood there in his cell with his big, broad back to the marshal.

"Anything I can get you, Charlie? I expect we got ourselves a little time before the vigilantes come down around our ears."

Charlie was silent a moment more, then cleared his voice and faced the marshal once again. "What I'd like more than anything is for my good friend, Pap, to be buried like a Christian. You know the man I mean."

"I understand, Charlie. From what I can tell he wasn't much a part of the proceedings, now, was he?"

"No, sir, no, he wasn't. I believe he was trying to stop those ol' boys from doing their dirty deed."

"I'm willing to do my best for your friend, Charlie. I know you don't know me from Adam, but I'm here to tell you my word's my bond. But as with any deal in life, I do something for you and you got to do something for me, you understand me." It wasn't a question. It was a statement. A fact.

"I got no problem with that. But I can't imagine I have too much to offer. In case you ain't noticed, I'm in jail. Even when I wasn't, I don't have two pennies to rub together."

The man slammed the end of his walking stick hard to the stone-flagged floor. "Confound it, boy! I'm not talking about money! What kind of lawman you take me for? I'm talking about the spot those thieving friends of yours are headed for, better yet if you know where they're planning on holing up.

"Where would they have got to? I expect I'll have to track them myself. It's a cinch Scoville doesn't have the sense God gave a goose. The only way he'll pick up a trail is if he stumbles on it, blind luck on his side, and nothing but."

"Truth is, Marshal, I don't rightly know where the boys are headed." Even as he said it, Charlie realized that wasn't the truth. He knew, deep in his hollowed-out chest, where they were headed. At least the general direction anyway. In all his hours of instruction and prep, some of which Charlie had to admit he'd been impressed with, Haskell had told them all a few times where they were headed.

Said if any of them should get turned around or separated from the others after the job, they were to head for the miner's cabin, high in the Sierras, past the abandoned mine camp of Tickle, of all names. Haskell said it was a good week's ride north till you hit the foothills, find a rocky knob called the Needle, a tall rocky spire shaped like a church steeple, jutting up to the northeast side of the trail, can't miss it. An old abandoned freighting line ran through there on up to Tickle.

From there, Haskell had said, it wouldn't be but a short haul at best past Tickle, where a body might find an old miner's shack in a gulch north of a grove of pines by a stream as pretty as you'd be likely to find anywhere.

Haskell said they'd meet at that cabin, and that anyone who didn't show up had better be dead by the hands of the posse they were sure to send after them, or else he would, sure as the Devil was in the details, track them down himself and peel their skin off as you would a prize goose.

Not a pretty picture, but there it was, and the statement wasn't something that surprised him much. Haskell was always spouting off about all manner of dire things he was going to do to people once he got hold of their unfortunate necks, should they cross him.

"From that look on your face, Charlie, I'd say you know more than you're telling me." He leaned back into the dark behind him, dragged over an old wooden chair, the woven seat sagged and frayed. He sat with a sigh, held the stick before him, both his hands resting on top. It was then Charlie noticed the old man wasn't wearing any guns. Odd.

"Charlie," said Wickham, "I can see in your eyes you're a conflicted man. Got a lot going on in your mind. That's good. I respect a man who will do some thinking now and again. Heaven knows there aren't many of us left. But I'm here to tell you that a man would have to be plumb crazy to escape, especially much before oh, say one, one thirty in the morning."

He leaned back in the chair, coughed, then leaned forward again. "But I tell you, one of my own father's favorite phrases always was 'If there's a will, there's a way.' I have come to agree that sentiment is a fair assessment of the entrepreneurial spirit in the United States of America. Why, I'd venture to guess that if there was a man in a cell, say, for the sake of conversation, that he was in there because of a robbery gone wrong, if he was left holding the bag . . . if he was taking all the blame on his own broad shoulders ... but he was also filled with the mighty urge to avenge the death of his friend, who also died in that botched mess of a job ... why, I'd guess he might find himself a way to make good his escape from that cell, somehow, because that urge for revenge can be so strong it blots out all other thoughts in a man's mind. I know only too well how such a thing can prey on a man's brain."

Charlie sat down on the edge of the cot with a groan. The old man was trying to tell him something, sure as shootin', but he was so dog-tired he could barely makes sense of it. Still, something told him he needed to pay attention.

Wickham leaned forward a little, an almost smile playing on his mouth. "Let me tell you a story, Charlie. You like stories, don't you, Charlie?"

Charlie shrugged. Tired and as angry and sad and confused as he was, he could listen to a chicken cluck and he'd be as happy.

The shrug was as good as a shouted cheer to Wickham. "Once was a man who thought he knew all sort of things. And in truth, he was a pretty bright fellow. But one day he ended up in jail, oddly enough, for a crime he said he had nothing to do with. Imagine that." He chuckled, then resumed. The sound of his laughs came to Charlie as dry paper rustling.

"Charlie, you got to listen to me now. I'm getting to the good part."

Charlie nodded. "Okay, okay."

"The prison this man was locked up in was so rough, so tight, so well built that no one was ever able to escape. Might say it was one of the best built in the whole of the West. I should know, because I worked there as a young man."

"You did?"

"Yep, but you never mind where because I'm not about to tell you." He smiled, then continued his story. "Long story short—no easy task, given my nature—this fellow, he up and decides one day that his desire to prove he was innocent and didn't deserve to be incarcerated was so great that he said to himself, 'I can end up staying in this cell, muddle-headed, not thinking straight, and dying like a mouse. Or I can take my life in my own two hands and get on out of here.' And that, Charlie, is what that man did. He made his escape."

"He did? What happened to him?"

"Last I heard he ended up having a harder time than he thought proving his innocence. Heck, maybe he was guilty all along, I don't rightly know. But I did hear he ended up a wealthy rancher down in South America somewhere."

Charlie nodded, rubbed a big hand over his jaw. "Seems to me you're trying awfully hard to tell me something most lawmen wouldn't want to be telling a prisoner, Marshal. Don't that strike you as a little odd?"

"Not at all, Charlie, not at all. I'm adding color to a dark situation. Take my meanderings for what they're worth. Do what you will with them." He stood and dragged the chair back to the dark corner. "Oh, I almost forgot. I have a sack of food for you out here. Nothing fancy, but I don't like my prisoners to wither on the vine in here. An apple, half a loaf of bread, hunk of cheese, a flask of water. It's out in the office, on my desk. That's where most everything I forget about ends up. It's the Devil getting old, Charlie. But it beats the alternatives, eh?" He winked and headed up the hallway. "I'll be right back."

Now that the marshal had mentioned food, Charlie

felt peckish. Could be why he was having trouble concentrating. True to his word, the old man came back, canvas sack in one hand, the walking stick clacking and tapping in the other. Looked as though he walked well enough, so Charlie wasn't sure why he needed the stick, but he reckoned that was a thought for another time.

"Now, Charlie, I'm going to have to ask you to turn around and head to the back of the cell so I can open this door without fear of you rushing me. You got me?"

"Oh yes, sir." Charlie made his way to the far end of the cell. Two strides were all it took. He faced the wall. Then heard the cell door's clock being keyed, the tumblers clicking, and then the door swung open. He heard the soft sound of the man's boots on the floor, the sack being laid on the cot—and Charlie gave quick thought to doing exactly what the old man had told him not to. Maybe that was what he wanted him to do?

But then the moment passed. He herd the cell door slam shut once again.

"Okay, then, Charlie. Have yourself a snack. Sorry I can't do a thing about those bruises and scrapes you took at the hands of the crowd. I reckon you'll heal up. You look tough enough. I'll bid you good night, then, Charlie. And mull over everything we've talked about. If nothing else, it'll make for good fodder for sleep."

"Thanks, Marshal. I will. And good night, sir."

The old man stopped, turned, and said, "Well, and a good night to you too, Charlie." He chuckled as he walked on up the short hallway. Charlie heard the doors clang into place. The iron and wood and stone echoes sounded for long moments, filling the cold space of the cells. Charlie didn't know what to make of the entire talk he'd had with the lawman, curious old sort that he was. But it hadn't been altogether unpleasant. And he had sort of promised to make sure Pap got treated right. That was something.

He sat down on the cot once again, with a groan, and rummaged in the sack of food. He found all the items in there the old man had promised. And he promptly set to work on munching the foodstuffs—a tasty portion of dark rye ripped from the half loaf, alternating with bites of the soft cheese that tasted as if it had been smoked. It was, Charlie thought, one of the most delicious things he'd ever tasted.

Of course, it wasn't until he'd devoured half of everything in the bag that he realized he'd been grunting, jamming the food into his mouth like a greedy child set loose at the candy counter. He belched quietly, looked around the otherwise empty cells, red-faced, as if the shadows might be appalled at his behavior.

As he chewed and swigged the water in the flask, he felt his head clear a bit. He was still bone-tired, but whatever cotton batting had been stuffed in his skull felt as though it was fading away. And as his head cleared he thought more and more about what the old lawman had told him.

Not much of it made sense at first, but Charlie knew he was nothing if not methodical, so he repeated the lengthy visit over and over in his head. And as he did so a few truths bubbled to the surface, until it became pretty obvious to him that the old man had been more than trying to tell him something, that there was obviously a hidden meaning behind the man's words.

The marshal wanted him to escape. Or at least try. But why would the man do that? The most obvious answer to Charlie would be that he would be lying in wait, ready to pounce on him, probably to lay him low and make himself out to be the hero before the townsfolk.

But somehow that didn't sound right to Charlie. Didn't sit right. It seemed to him that the old man was more of a straight shooter than that. Then why would he tell him to make a run for it? No, he thought. Couldn't be. But that was the line of thought that got Charlie to his feet.

He heard his knees pop, felt the stitches in his sides— felt as though he'd broken a rib or two again. And the side of his head throbbed when he walked. But he made his way to the strap-steel cell door.

He held up his hands before the steel, not yet touching it. The old man wanted him to escape so he could . . . what? Follow him? Had to be it. Had to know that Charlie knew where to find Haskell. Sure, all that talk the old man had done about avenging and getting revenge. He knew what Charlie had been thinking, hadn't he? Charlie almost smiled. Why, he'd practically told him what he was thinking without the old man asking him any real questions. He reckoned it wasn't the marshal's first day on the job.

And then what happened next did bring a smile to his big face. A wide smile, never mind that his jaw had been punched or kicked so hard it hurt like the Devil to smile. This was something worth grinning about.

Charlie gripped the steel of the door and rattled it— and the door banged loudly for as long as he rattled it. But it swung wider than it should, in fact. Because it was no longer locked.

Of course, when the old man had brought in the food sack, he'd shut the door, but had not locked it. Charlie hadn't heard the mechanism click into place.

He tugged lightly and the door swung outward a couple more inches, squawking slightly. Charlie's smile paused, froze in place, tempered now with caution. No matter the outcome, he knew he was being toyed with, for good or ill. He poked the door once with a big sausage finger. It opened farther, swung to a stop. He looked behind him, saw the last half of the food in and out of the sack on the cot. He hated to leave the door for fear it might swing shut and really lock him in there.

He pushed the door wider, winced as its squeak seemed to fill the otherwise still air in the cells, and quickly snatched the food and sack from the bed. Then he took a breath, stepped through the door, and stopped. No one shouted, no one shot at him, nothing much happened except his heart jittered more and he felt sweat bead on his lips and chin.

He walked on up the short hallway and there stood another door, the big one leading to the cells themselves. Here was the true test. If the marshal truly had arranged this escape for him, then this door would also be unlocked. If not, maybe he really was nothing more than a chatty old man who was forgetful with his keys. He had admitted, after all, that he'd been forgetful in the past, but could always find the lost item on his desk.

"Stop thinking so much, Charlie," he rumbled to himself in the dark, and grabbed the steel ring handle of the door. It turned and stuck. His heart fell. He reset his palm on the handle and gave it a good twist, then shoved it forward. The heavy, ponderous door swung open slowly.

Charlie made his way forward, saw a short stairwell headed upward to what he guessed was the marshal's office, up out of the basement to the first story, street level. It took him a few long minutes to make his way up the narrow, angled set of steps—thick hard planks, well worn in the middle, set in steel supports.

In this manner he made his way upward to the first

floor. Soon enough he found himself crouching low, the small food sack gripped in his left hand. He expected to be shot at, as he had expected moments before. But he heard no gunfire, no shouts, no rocks thrown through windows. Nothing, save for the occasional sound of a passing person on the dark street outside, the clopping of a horse whose rider was in no hurry to get to where he or she was going, the gravelly rolling of a buggy's wheels.

It was late and he heard each of these sounds but once. And footsteps, measured, perhaps hurried, crunching on the gravel outside in the street. He kept low and cast his glance about for a door that might lead to the back of the building. There, to his right, near the back corner of the room. Had to be it. He made his way over there, still keeping low, hoping it would guide him to a back alley where he might make his way out of town.

He wasn't sure what part of town he was in, but figured he would get a sense of direction once he could see the stars. And if it was cloudless, he'd take his chances. Anywhere but in the cell was the place he wanted to be.

By that time, he made it to the back door and found that it did lead to an alley. Despite the increasing cold of the autumn weather, dribbles of sweat ran down the bridge of his nose, tickled his scruffy beard. Once he committed to opening the door to the alley fully, he felt relief as the cool night air chilled him all over. Down four wide plank steps and to his right, he saw a low, jutting angle of roofline, stark against the blue-black sky. His breath plumed and he struggled to keep his breathing quiet and controlled.

Charlie felt sure his excitement was going to get him caught. Bound to be some snoopy townsfolk wandering

around. He'd already heard a few on the street, not unusual for a town of this size. He cut his eyes again to the
low roof. There was a gaping black hole beyond and . . .
the smell of horse dung and old hay. Might be the stable
for the lawmen? It was dark as the inside of a boot over
there, but he kept to the edge of the building, low, and
sidestepped toward the place.

The smells, always welcoming to a farm boy, grew
stronger, and then something moved ahead of him in the
shadows. Dang—his heart hammered like a pugilist on a
hayseed at a county fair. Whatever it was moved again as
he watched. Might mean that whoever it was wasn't
afraid of him. Might mean whoever it was didn't even
know he was there.

And then it snorted and Charlie knew it was a horse.
He squinted into the night without moving, saw the faint
outline of its back. It was saddled, tied to a rail there. But
he didn't see a soul sitting on top of it.

He rubbed his big jaw, nibbled his bottom lip. He'd
already been put in jail for murder—would horse theft
really matter? Then the horse nickered, seemed to turn
its head toward him. Charlie walked forward. Nah,
couldn't be. He leaned closer.

"Nub?" He breathed the name quietly. The horse
nickered again, tossed its head as if to say, Yes, yes, it's
me. Your old horse. Now get a move on. . . .

That was all the invitation Charlie needed. He would
normally hedge, look over every angle before making a
decision like that. But this wasn't a normal situation.
And somehow he didn't think his life would ever be normal again.

He risked it and moved out away from the building's
deeper shadow, into the moon glow, then back into
shadow as he approached the horse. He knew before he

touched the horse that it really was Nub. Pap must have brought him along for Charlie.

Nah, he reasoned. He was Pap's horse anyway, so of course Pap would have brought the horse along. Charlie shook his head at being so foolish. Odds were the law had rounded up all the horses and gear belonging to anybody associated with the robbery.

He reckoned now that Pap was gone, the horse was more his than anyone's anyway. He'd been ridden by Charlie more than by any of the other fellas in the group; that much Charlie was sure of. And while in the eyes of the law that didn't make Charlie the horse's owner, he reckoned he'd be darn close. And besides, he told himself as he reached for the saddle horn, up until a few minutes before, he'd been in a jail cell, accused of murder. How could it get worse?

"Hey, boy, hey, now," said Charlie in a low whisper, rubbing the horse's neck. He looked closer. Yep, it was the same saddle he'd used, and what was more, as his hand roved along it, he stopped, tensed when he felt was for certain his own bedroll and satchel. All snugged and cinched down tight behind the cantle. The old marshal had to be the one to have done it.

Then his hand stopped short again as it roved over the horse's back, across the seat. There was the polished butt of a long gun. His fingers played along it lower. Not a rifle, but a shotgun. Single barrel. His gut tightened. Same one that laid Pap low. Same one. Had to be. All of a sudden Charlie's instincts and cautions fluttered out whatever window might have been open in his mind. And in their place roosted the cold killing bird of revenge.

Sure, the old lawman might well be setting him up.

But he'd gotten this far, and if the ruse continued to play in Charlie's favor, there might be shells for that shotgun nested somewhere in his satchel. And if not, well, he'd cross that bridge when he came to it.

But he didn't feel all that uneasy. Something told him he could trust the old man. He untied the horse and led him around beside him. Mostly he thought he could trust the marshal because he reminded Charlie of someone . . . Pap.

"That can't be a bad thing," hissed Charlie as he swung into the saddle. He wasted no more time, but keeping low, he reined the horse left, then straight down the dark street, straight toward the direction he knew Haskell had headed. He winced with each hoofbeat, each of the horse's footfalls sounding as if they were gunshots in the quiet of the slumbering town's early-morning hours.

Far behind, Charlie's every move was watched with much interest. Interest and silent encouragement. Sitting a horse deep in the shadows of the little stable, Marshal Dodd Wickham nodded and a wide, grim smile spread across his face. When the sound of the escapee's horse dwindled to a far, steady knocking, Wickham urged his own horse, Missy, forward out of the stable. He'd forgone the use of a packhorse, instead opting to burden Missy with a modest load of well-tied bundles. They left town at a steady clip.

Marshal Wickham hadn't tied on manhunting gear in years. It felt good to be back on the trail, on a vengeance ride. He snorted, half at himself. Call it what you want to, Dodd, he told himself. But we are on a ride of revenge.

"Heck," he said aloud, in a low voice. "If this is what retired life feels like, I should have trusted my gut and

Chapter 25

The creeping cold caught Charlie unawares and jerked him upright in his saddle. "What in the blue blazes?" He said it almost out of reflex, remembered with a start that it had also been a pet phrase of Pap's. Had been. The bygoneness of the words stung like a honey bee attack. But there was nothing sweet about the memory. Especially considering all that had happened.

He'd been dreaming—there was a crowd of leering, distorted faces looking down at him, as if he were lying on his back in the street, just like Pap. And they were all chanting something the marshal had said . . . "Shotgun! Shotgun! Shotgun Killer! Shotgun Killer!" It grew louder and louder, echoing wider and deeper with each utterance, and their faces grew uglier and uglier and drew closer and closer. . . .

He ran a big hand down his face again, as if the thick, stiff fingers could wash away the badness of the past few days. But no, the motion only served to remind him of how bad off he had it. The cold snicked into him like thin-bladed knife, from a hundred directions. What was he doing out here?

His entire body ached, from his much-kicked ribs to

his near-stoved-in head. He touched a fingertip to his right eye, still half-swollen shut, the left ear, a pulpy-feeling blob of crusted blood and gum rubber. He sighed, could hardly blame the townsfolk for reacting as they did. He was a stranger, after all, and he was holding the shotgun used by Grady Haskell. . . .

Wait a minute, he thought. Who am I to be thinking this way? Before he could flip-flop back and forth, berating himself and excusing others, his horse, Nub, nickered. Charlie looked down at the back of the big beast's head. He'd momentarily forgotten him.

"Oh boy, I am a sorry one." He swung down out of the saddle, ran a hand up and down the horse's long neck.

"Ho, now, ho, now. I expect you're a tired beast, lugging me all night long." Charlie looked around. They'd gotten a far piece from Bakersfield, he reckoned. Though being unfamiliar with this region, he wasn't so sure he'd gotten far enough. Surely there would be a posse after him. Might be staring him down right now.

The thought froze him, dispelling the real cold in favor of a frigid feeling conjured by his mind. He turned his head slowly. Nah, they'd not waste time eyeballing him. They'd likely commence to shooting. The thought didn't chill him as much as he reckoned it ought to. He was cold and tired and sore and confused. But he wasn't in a cell. He was alive and out on the trail . . . hunting Pap's killer.

He narrowed his eyes and scanned his surroundings. The terrain wasn't much of a surprise to him. He was still in the low country. Judging from the early-morning sky, it had been light about an hour, no more than. The trees, a mix of scrub oaks and lodgepole pines from the looks of them, were growing in thicker, so he was still a piece from the mountains, from where he knew Grady to be.

Or hoped like the dickens he was. Didn't matter, Charlie had vowed to hunt him to the ends of the earth, and nothing was going to change that; nothing was going to make him snap that vow. Pap deserved at least that much from him.

"Well, I'm out of the saddle, old boy," he said to the horse in a low voice. "Might as well take stock of what we have, see if I can't rustle up a bite, give you a rest, eh, Nub?"

The horse had already become visibly relieved, at least temporarily, of no longer lugging the substantial burden that was Charlie's big body. Now he set to work with vigor at cropping the wispy grasses and low-lying greens, most of which were dying off, losing the battle against shorter days and cooler nights.

Charlie sniffed the cold air, one hand working the knots cinching down his gear behind the cantle. "Reckon it's going to be winter before it'll be summer again, eh, Nub?"

The horse kept on cropping the grass, nosing for something toothsome amid the browning growth.

Charlie turned his head back to his gear. What had possessed the old lawman to do this anyway? And how had he been savvy enough to get him his own gear and horse? The horse, Nub, might not be such a mystery. He was, as Pap had so indelicately put it, the only horse in the territory that could haul around Charlie's beefy carcass.

But his gear? Maybe someone had told the lawman where Charlie had stashed it. He remembered now, he'd dropped it by those stairs near that building to his right as he'd seen Pap in trouble.

Maybe someone saw him do so. Charlie didn't really care. He was hungry and thirsty. The first thing he did was plunge his hand into the small cloth sack Wickham had given him. He still had most of the apple left. "How about that?" he said as he rummaged in his gear as if he'd never seen the contents before.

As he unrolled his blanket, he found his wool jumper, a thin, hand-knitted thing he'd traded labor for at a farmhouse; must have been one, no, two years before? Just as he'd taken to the road, as he recalled.

The old woman had been happy to have the wood split. She hadn't had any money, but she did have a dead husband and a few garments that had been his. From the looks of her, she'd been wearing a good many of them herself, just to keep warm. But there had been this one, a light blue yarn, that she hadn't worn, for some reason.

"Hubert was your size," she'd said. "No, no, maybe bigger. . . ." She'd smiled then at the memory. Charlie remembered her face as she recalled her long-dead husband. They'd carved that little homestead out of the prairie. A windy place with that stand of bent poplars. Low, it was, and the trees had grown plentiful there at one time, but by the time he'd come along the trees were succumbing to their last seasons with the elements. He reckoned she'd lose the last few of the big old things that coming winter.

He'd offered to stay on and help her, but with her few chickens and the sad remnants of her garden, and that cough that doubled her over every few minutes, he'd known she hadn't wanted him around. Even if she had, he doubted he'd have been able to stay and not starve to death.

No, he reckoned, as he had walked on out of there that following morning, leading Teacup. That was the way she wanted it. She'd practically begged him to leave then. And as he had walked on out of the old place's dooryard, she called to him and shuffled out to meet him, coughing as she got to him. She held out a thick bundle of pretty blue. It had been the jumper.

"I knitted it for my Hubert as we headed out West as young folks. So full of promise then. We thought we'd have a big family, many children, you know."

Charlie recalled she'd sounded Scandinavian, maybe Swedish, though in truth he had no idea what a Swede sounded like. But that had been all she'd said, even when he protested, told her she'd need it, that she could use it through the long winter to keep warm. He'd told her it was far too important for a fella like him to use. But she'd only shaken her old head, turned away, but not before he saw she was crying.

He'd laid in a pile of wood for her, as much as he could in the few days he'd bunked with his mule in her old leaning barn. But he knew it hadn't been enough to carry her for more than a month, maybe two if she'd been careful. But something told him she might not have lasted all that long anyway. And he was sure she knew it too.

Charlie pulled the much-worn, stained, stretched, thin jumper from the bedroll and held it to his nose briefly. It smelled of the smoke of a hundred campfires, but he closed his eyes and smiled, thinking of the happy couple they must have been, the old Swedish woman and her husband. So full of promise when they were young.

He tugged it on over his much-patched, tatty denim shirt that covered his worn long-handles. He'd been glad many a nippy night that he had the warmth of the wool garment. He'd helped an orphaned wagon train child for a week a few months before he'd met up with the old woman, and the near-wild young thing had up and run off with his old winter mackinaw. It had been his one decent, useful possession, save for his Green River knife.

So he'd been doubly thankful when the old woman made a gift of the old jumper.

Now more than ever, for though it was much worn, it was warm. And the chill weather was coming in. He rummaged, found his spare wool socks, and tugged them on his hands. The apple would have to do for now. He found no other food and though he owed the old lawman much for setting him free—though maybe he was also setting him up for a mighty tumble—he secretly wished the old man had seen fit to lay in a few more supplies for him.

It had been a while since he'd snared a rabbit, but Charlie reckoned he could give it another go. Living with Pap and the boys had been easy, in certain ways. For there had been many of them and they'd all taken turns hunting for meat for "the family table," as Pap had called their nightly gab sessions around the fire. Good times they had been.

Charlie still marveled that the boys had been so taken in by Grady Haskell that they'd all but abandoned Pap for him and his promises of wealth. And now Mex was dead—and Ace, Dutchy, and Simp? What of them? He could hardly think of them as killers. Charlie didn't trust Haskell as far as he could toss the bum, but he banished thoughts from his mind. Now he had to keep moving. Put distance between himself and the posse. For he was sure there would be one.

He reckoned he only had to keep ahead of the posse enough to reach Haskell. That was all he would need—a little time. He glanced at the shotgun in the scabbard hanging from the saddle. Just a little time, that was all he would need.

"Come on, Nub. We got us a cold trail and no time to waste." He tugged the reins, and the big horse reluctantly fell in line behind the big man, both trudging northward toward the mountains, storm clouds boiling at the peaks.

The thin old man in the long black duster rubbed his gamey right leg with a leather-gloved hand and sighed. His breath rose in his face and vapored on the wind. His horse champed, bowed her head. "Missy," he said in a low voice. "Enough."

Nearly a mile behind the big young man, Marshal Dodd Wickham resisted the urge to retrieve his pocket watch and pop it open. Surely the young fool had a sense of urgency? The more time he wasted standing by his horse, the more time that Haskell character had of getting away, far into the hills, apparently, if that was where the young man was unwittingly leading Wickham. He sighed again. It had been long years since he had to posse up and head out on the trail. And even longer still since he'd reached daylight without a cup of coffee in his hand. Even a skin-blistering tin cup from a campfire. The memory of so many fine meals and cups of coffee— spiked with ample slugs of gargle—brought a smile to his grizzled gray face.

Wickham watched the big former prisoner, far up-trail and upwind of him, for a few moments more. He hoped he hadn't made a mistake. Hoped the boy knew, really knew, where to find the murderer and his gang. The money from the bank didn't much bother Wickham. The suffering of the depositors was hardly his concern. Judging from the way they treated the one they'd caught, as well as the big young man up ahead of him on the trail, the depositors would get their blood money out of Tollinson, the banker. Wickham wouldn't mind at all seeing the chunky man squirm under their fists and heels.

But what he really wanted was to find the rapscallions

who put a permanent black mark on his long career. The rogues who stamped all over his lifetime of service to communities throughout the Western territories. The filth who killed a child and more, all for the sake of pilfering a hardworking community because they were too lazy to work for a living themselves. Oh, that could not stand.

He glanced once more at the big young man up ahead, now unstrapping his bedroll. Wickham reached into an inner coat pocket and lifted free the small flask he'd brought as his trail flask, his three bottles of precious whiskey wrapped snug in his spare clothes in his saddlebags. He upended the silver flask, the scrollwork and fancy lettering that bore his own initials, D.A.W., Dodd Aloysius Wickham, in a cameo-shaped center, emblazoned on the flask.

He smiled as he swallowed, regarded the flask. It had been a gift to himself years before, as a young man when he was on a roll with law dog successes in Dodge City first, then Wyoming Territory, becoming known as something of a sure shot, someone who in hushed conversations it was said might even be a better shot than Wild Bill himself.

Dodd had liked hearing that. Knowing that had put a spring in his youthful step. But he knew it had been little more than luck, little more than average skill with a gun, coupled with sobriety on his end and lack of it on his opponents'. And that, in his long experience, was what made the difference when lead flew.

Maybe that was why he took to sampling whiskies. The finest at first, then the mediocre stuff as time wore on. And the years whistled by like lucky bullets, and the jobs the same, one after another, too many towns to count, grinding him to a fine powder of what had once been a promising young man.

He sucked in breath through one unclogged nostril — dang cold weather always clogged his nasals. Same time of year, same month, maybe even the same week each year. He slipped the flask back in his pocket and nodded slightly in approval as the young man far ahead on the trail began walking forward into the mountains. If Wickham wasn't mistaken, he fancied the boy now sported a determined drive to his long-legged step. Good, good. Sooner the better. End it all. And with a bang.

Chapter 26

Ace rounded a corner in the trail, a narrow twisting thing that had become more treacherous the closer he drew to the mountains. And there before him, on the edge of a boulder, sat Grady Haskell. "Well, I never . . . ," said the perturbed man.

"That's right, you never did, and you never will," said Haskell, toying with the ends of his leather reins, slapping them on his trouser leg, a grin cracking his stubbled face.

"Didn't expect to see you again." Ace regarded the man.

Haskell looked up, squinting and cracking a smile. "Hello, Ace. Been waiting on you."

"How's that?" said Ace, cupping a grimy hand to his right ear. "I'm afraid I didn't catch that, since all that gunfire back in Bakersfield near about ruined my hearing. Not to mention the screaming and crying and howling."

Haskell slid down off the rock face, dusted his palms against his legs. "Now, Ace," he said, strolling over. "What gave you the notion that you wouldn't never see me again?"

Ace sighed, climbed down from his horse to face the man. He flexed his jaw muscles, then spoke. "Nothing but the way you up and left us not far from town. Shouted something about how we should stick to the trail, that you'd meet up with us."

"And ain't I come through on everything I promised you so far?"

Ace shook his head. "Not hardly, Grady."

Haskell shied back as if he'd been slapped. "Now, what's that supposed to mean, Ace, old boy? I am heartily offended, I don't mind telling you."

"Then why did you up and leave us? You know we didn't really know the way to the rendezvous point. You said so yourself after you give us such sketchy directions that it would be best if we all stuck together. That way we could get to your hidey-hole and divvy up the money, then all be on our ways."

Haskell rubbed his chin, squinted. "Now that you mention it, I did say all that, didn't I? Hmm. Could be I was overly proud of my abilities to get us there."

"Well?" said Ace, poking his hat brim back off his forehead. Despite the cool of the day, standing in the sun he was beginning to feel a little heated up. Or maybe it was that he was finally seeing Haskell for what Pap and Big Charlie had seen in him. And he didn't like the notion one bit. He'd always prided himself on being a little swifter than the average fellow. But the hard truth was dawning, and it pained him.

Haskell stepped in close. "Well what, Ace?" His voice was a low, gravelly thing, his eyes suddenly more snaky than they had seemed before.

Ace couldn't let Haskell wear him down. "Well . . ." He swallowed. "Where are the other boys? You catch up with them yet?"

"Oh, the others?" said Haskell. "Nah, not yet." Still he stood scarcely two hand lengths away, his voice lower and measured. "You got a message you want me to give them for you?"

Ace swallowed again. "No . . . no need. I'll ride along with you."

Grady shook his head slowly, his eyes locked on Ace's. "No?"

Grady still shook his head. Ace did not notice that while he was being mesmerized by the killer's snaky eyes, with a move born of practiced ease, Haskell slid free a long, thin-bladed boning knife from its slit sheath along the outside seam of his trousers. It was positioned in such a way, its hilt hidden beneath his larger skinning knife's wide sheath, that most folks who met him never saw it. Certainly Ace hadn't noticed it. And that was a mistake.

The knife punctured, fast and slick as you please, through his wool outer coat, through his ratty wool vest, through his flannel shirt and long-handle undershirt, through the soft walnut-colored skin of his slightly pooched belly, and angled upward beneath his ribs. And then Ace noticed that he could no longer speak, but only for a moment before the hot flashing pain flowered upward from the deep-sunk blade.

He tried to speak, but a warm, wet feeling bubbled up inside him, filled his gorge, and a gout of blood burst from his mouth.

"What's that? Huh?" Haskell leaned closer, ground the blade deeper. "You got to speak up, Ace, old boy. I know you can talk 'cause you just got through wasting a whole bunch of words about how I didn't do this, didn't do that."

Ace's eyes widened, blood flowed down his chin,

along his shirt, vest, and coat. Behind him his horse fidgeted, nickering, and worked itself wide, the reins slipping from Ace's weakening grip.

"Oh, I see," said, Grady. "You want to know where I been. Well, that's mighty thoughtful of you. You see, I had no intention of sharing any of that bank loot with you or the boys or anyone else. And there ain't going to be anyone to save you, Ace. You're a goner. Any minute now, matter of fact. And Pap? He's gone too. And Mex? Yep, I reckon you didn't see all that that I did, seeing as how I was last to leave Bakersfield."

Ace's eyes widened impossibly then, as if what he'd heard shocked him. He was beginning to feel the clouding of death overcome him.

"No?" said Haskell. "Not enough of an explanation for you to chew on, eh?" He spun Ace around as if they were dancing, one hand on the sagging man's shoulder. Just before Ace's legs gave out, Haskell leaned him back on the same boulder he'd been sitting on moments before.

"There, now, ain't that better? Now, where was I? Oh yes, you see, when I left you all on the trail and told you to head on without me, that I'd catch up. I wasn't lying, you see. I was telling the gospel truth. Aw, forget all about that now. Fact is, here I am." He leaned close to Ace's face, touched nose tips, and said, "Nothing to say? Well, that makes for a nice change."

He backed away, pushed the dying man's chest when Ace leaned fully flat against the rock, slid the long boning knife out slowly. A slow wheeze, undercut with a grating, bubbling sound, leaked out of Ace's mouth. His eyes glazed as tears welled and then drained like tiny mountain streams, from the outer corners of his eyes. His chest slowed rising, falling. It rose once, held, then released and rose no more.

Grady Haskell stood back, hands bunched on his hips, one hand covered in gore as if it wore a scarlet glove, the boning knife still held tight in his fist. He looked for all the world as if he were admiring a work of art he had wrought.

Behind him a horse uttered nervous, throaty sounds and stepped farther away. That wrested Haskell from his reverie. He turned, saw it was Ace's mount. "Not so fast, horse. You're carrying what I need."

He hastily dragged the knife blade along Ace's lifeless pant leg, both sides of the blade. He wiped his bloody hand on the other leg, then slipped the knife into its accustomed spot as he strode to the horse, snatched the reins before the already tired beast could bolt. Then walked it to his own horse, which had stayed put, perhaps because it was used to his activities.

Grady mounted up, glanced once back at the dead man. "You know, Ace, old boy, you really ought to think twice before you commence to blaming a body for only doing what he'd intended to do in the first place."

Grady smiled, booted the horse into a trot, and said, "And besides, I kept my promise. I come back for you. Like I said I would." As he rode on up the trail, over his shoulder he said, "Now I'm off to find your friends. Keep my promises." His wry chuckle unwound and carried off on the stiff, building early-winter breeze.

Chapter 27

"I guess we'll be doing what I say all right." Deputy Randy Scoville had batted away the doctor's hand for the third time.

"But, Randy, you and the other men are in no condition to go back out there." Doc Slattery reached for the muslin wrap he'd split and tied off tight along the young firebrand's nicked upper arm, but thought better of it. The deputy was testy at the best of times, but today he was really worked up—and for good reason. One of his best chums, a man in the posse he himself had organized, had been laid low by the killers.

The deputy spun on him, rising out of the chair in the midst of the doc's bloody rag-strewn surgery. "Doc, I know you mean well, and I know you were good friends with my Grampy and Paw too, but I don't try to tell you how to doctor on a man, so you shouldn't tell me how to be a lawman."

Doc Slattery suppressed a smirk. Then he thought better of ignoring the comment and turned on the deputy, who was shrugging back into his shirt.

"You young whelp!" He smacked Scoville with a soiled implement. "You think because you wear a tin star and walk around like dung doesn't stick to your boots that that makes you a lawman? Marshal Wickham has more gumption, tenacity, veracity, and law-abiding spirit than you will ever discover in all your days. And this debacle that happened in our town proves it."

Scoville's eyes blazed. "You dare to blame what happened to the bank on me? I been trying to run down the varmints who done it!"

The doc opened his mouth, closed it and shook his head, then spun on the boy again. "You go back out there and you're sure as shootin' signing a death warrant on yet more people of Bakersfield! And who'll have to patch them up? Me, that's who. Now get gone out of my office. I have plenty to do without tongue-lashing the likes of you . . . you whelp!"

Scoville, standing hipshot at the door, regarded the old surly doctor coolly. "I reckon I'll work up another posse if I want to. Ain't nobody else man enough to do the job."

Before Doc Slattery could respond, the red-eared deputy whipped open the door, strode out, and slammed it behind him.

"Good riddance," said the doc, drawing a bottle out of his medicinals cabinet and pouring himself two fingers of amber whiskey. He figured he'd earned it, had gone without sleep for a full day's cycle, doctoring the wounded and tending the wrecked bodies of the dead. His assistants had all dropped away to various rooms to grab a few hours of rest.

He knocked back half the glass, carried the glass to the window, and parted the curtains. Down below, in the street, the lightly wounded deputy looked up and down the street, eagle-eyed, no doubt, thought Doc Slattery, scanning the citizens of Bakersfield who might be unlucky enough to be out. If they were men, the doc knew that Scoville would press them, through guilt or force, into service on the next ill-fated posse.

Doc let the curtain fall, turned from the window, and shook his head. He had to hand it to Scoville, he had his own brand of tenacity. Misguided and ultimately danger-ous, but he had that fire it took to roar raging into battle. Doc had seen it in the war and though, more often than not, it cost the holders of the fire their lives, he doubted that battles—posse track-downs included—could be suc-cessful without such men.

"Good luck, boy," said Doc. "You're going to need it." He downed the rest of the drink and set to work tidying the office before the next inevitable wave of victims was carried in.

Chapter 28

The cold of earlier that day had waned, as Charlie expected it would. But he knew that it wouldn't be long before Old Man Winter invited himself to town for a lengthy visit. And when he arrived, anywhere near mountains, even those Charlie hadn't personally visited, there was bound to be trouble. Water got hard, walking grew tough, skin froze, eyeballs puckered, and game didn't move around as much as it did in the warmer weather. What all that meant to Charlie as he surveyed the trail before him was that he was ill prepared for cold weather up in the high places, the peaks of which looked whiter with every step forward Nub and he took.

Charlie's gut growled again, loud enough that the horse nickered. "I know it, I know it. I wish you had some brilliant idea about how I can fetch down meat, as I don't have much in the way of time or tools to go after it right now." But if he didn't spend the time doing it now, he would likely become so weak from lack of food that he'd wish he'd spent the time snaring a rabbit. Exploring the contents of his nearly empty gear bag a few hours before had turned up a neatly wrapped paper parcel of jerked meat, venison, if he had to guess. He didn't much care. He'd tucked into it and devoured nearly half of it before it dawned on him that this was all he'd be getting in the way of food for some time to come. He'd chewed slowly what was in his mouth, sucking the meat and savoring the salty, peppery juices, then reluctantly swallowed it down.

It hadn't been much, but it had been darn tasty. And he was grateful to the old lawman for it. He'd wrapped the rest of it carefully back up in the paper, brown and wrinkled, then slipped it back into the bag, tucked behind what few spare articles of clothing he had. He hoped that would make it more difficult for him to get at.

Charlie could be a tough individual when he needed to be, but he was weak as water when it came to food. If he was hungry, he was a surly bear. And unfortunately for him, he was hungry most of the time. He was also big. And it took a whole lot of food for him to feel filled up.

His gut grumbled like a grizz cub again and he groaned, nudged the horse forward. They'd found a decent mountain stream that looked to be one branch from a larger river farther up. There he refilled the glass flask he'd been given by the old lawman, as well as his own old water bottle. He'd also been able to lie on his belly and wash his face in the stream, slowly, carefully so he wouldn't open up and set to bleeding again any cuts and scrapes he'd received at the hands of the townsfolk.

Oddly enough, the trail cut narrow at times, and wound steeper along a boulder-lined route that looked as if it had been formed in ancient times when there was nothing but God's critters roaming the place. Maybe it had been cut through by a mighty river, the very bottom of which he was riding through right then and there. He looked up, saw wide, tree-stippled stony chasms rising above him far to each side, imagined the place filled with a roiling green mass of water. And the fish! What sort of finned critters would be in a river like that? The thought made him shudder him, then gave him an idea.

He had an old steel fishhook in his bag somewhere; he was sure of it. All he had to do was rig it up to some sort of line . . . and then Charlie stopped that train of thought as suddenly as if it had been felled by a bullet. Nub saw it too—up ahead along the narrow, curving trail defined by a series of tumbled boulders that had all but concealed the route. They paused on the close side of the nearest of them, a massive pink-and-white outcropping overlying boulders and rubble.

And there, a dozen yards up-trail, appeared to be a man laid out on a rock's warm face as if he were in the midst of a cool-weather nap. But something about this scene didn't sit right with Charlie. Nor with Nub. The horse fidgeted and nickered. A sure sign that he was bothered by something.

A horse's instinct is not something to be trifled with, Pap had told Charlie. And though Charlie knew a whole lot about animals in general, from cows to mules to chickens, sheep, goats, the sage and earned horse sense advice Pap doled out so freely had rung true during the time he spent with Nub.

"Easy, boy, easy," Charlie soothed the horse, who'd begun to back up. Charlie held him in place, not wanting to emerge from around the big rock mass himself. Then he smelled it. A subtle shift in the cool-day breeze drifted a tangy, sickly stink to him—a thread of it, but Charlie knew what it was. The aging rankness of blood and death. As if a favorite dish had been left out in the sun, gone off.

He tugged his long-handle shirt collar up over his nose, held it there, and peered closer at the scene. No horse, nothing but a man wearing dark clothes, laid out on a dark blanket. He peered tighter, narrowed his eyes, squinted, leaned over the saddle horn, as if another few inches would make the difference in what he was seeing. But it confirmed what he'd suspected. That was no blanket. The man had bled out. Maybe gut-shot, or gut-cut? Didn't much matter now. For despite the cool temperatures Charlie saw a haze lifting and settling with the breeze. Flies, a cloud of them, feasting on the congealing mess that had been a man.

And there were only a few men he knew who could have come up this way so close ahead of him. Had to be one of the boys. Which one? He knew Mex was dead. Maybe one of the others had been hit on the way out of town and when he died the rest left him here?

No honor among thieves, wasn't that what Pap had said? He'd laughed about it in a shamefaced way, aware that Charlie didn't much agree or like the way they conducted themselves. All that seemed so long ago and so innocent compared with what they had done in Bakersfield. And seeing one of the boys dead made it even more difficult.

He hoped it wasn't Haskell, for he wanted to bleed the man out himself. Charlie looked behind himself again, as had become his adopted custom since making his hasty departure from town. He knew the hellhound posse was behind him somewhere, but how far back and how many of them, he had no idea.

For all he knew, the marshal had somehow warned them off. But for what reason? No time, no time to think on that now, Charlie, he chastised himself. Find out who this was, how he died, and if there's anything you can learn, then get going. He nudged Nub to work him forward, but the horse wouldn't go.

"Fine," rasped Charlie, sliding out of the saddle. "But

don't think you're not coming along. It's bound to happen. I ain't about to lose this argument." He tugged the reins and led the reluctant horse down the path. "Come on, now." He gave up trying to hold the shirt collar up over his nose. The smell wasn't so bad—the breeze had shifted. But the flies were not a welcome sight. And neither was seeing the man's face, a mask of pain stretched wide, misshaping his features.

Charlie led the dancing Nub wide as he could around the dead man, lashed the reins around a jag of branch busted low some time ago, no doubt by a trail traveler. "Stay put, you. I don't fancy walking the rest of this trip."

He looked down, saw who the dead man was. "Oh, Ace. Blast them, they didn't even close your eyes for you." Charlie reached a trembling hand, backed off, and tugged the shirt up again, then with twitchy fingertips tried to close Ace's eyes. It wouldn't work. He tired it a second, then a third time. Nothing.

"Dang, Ace. I am sorry, but you're going to have to stare awhile longer. I'll find something to cover your face with."

As he'd reached for Ace's face, he nudged the laidback man and found he was stiff as a plank. There was nothing like the feeling of a dead person. Nothing at all in the world, Charlie thought. There was that softness of the clothes, but even they were different, not right. And the skin of the dead, soft on the very outside, but that was all.

The rest, the underneath, was firmed up, already on its way to doing whatever it was that needed doing. And now here was another. And someday he'd end up the same way too. But not for a little while yet, he hoped. Not until . . .

Charlie couldn't bring himself to inspect the body

closer, but there was, or had been, a whole lot of blood, mostly on the front of the man. It had trailed down along his legs, down the rock on which he lay back, and finally in a sticky puddle at his feet.

There was a single line of alternating tracks, small like those of a tiny dog, hill coyote, most likely, leading away from it, one foot having touched the blood. The critter had likely worked up the nerve to inspect and when he'd gotten close had not liked what it had come up against. Charlie felt the same way.

He went back to the horse, rummaged in his bags until he found the cloth sack the marshal's food had come in. "It ain't much, Ace, but it'll have to do. He laid it over the man's eyes. Then turned, stopped with his back to the dead man.

"Dang it all, I can't leave you. No matter what you did, no man deserves to be left out here, picked over by buzzards and other such critters." Charlie was surprised, in fact, that there hadn't been sign of buzzards. Usually they had a keen sense of death, knew when it was coming and sometimes didn't wait. Maybe the cold temperatures had prevented the stink from building. Come to think on it, the man didn't smell all that bad yet. Had to be the cold, and the fact that he'd probably not been dead all that long.

Charlie looked back at the dead man. Sure he was angry with him, angry with the whole lot of them. Even, if he admitted it, with Pap, and most of all with himself for not putting up more of a fight when it came to that foul Grady Haskell. But that didn't mean he could leave the man there, baking on the rock, varmint bait. But he had no shovel, no way to dig a grave, and most of all, he had no time. He glanced at his back trail once again. Nobody.

He looked at Ace. The dead man hadn't moved. "Well, at least I'm safe with you, Ace." Charlie sighed and looked around for a solution. His eyes rested on a gap between two boulders, trailside, deep enough to wedge a man, if he was sitting upright. Charlie reckoned he could pile rocks over him, stuff them atop the boulders to fill in any holes. That would have to be good enough. It wouldn't prevent the most determined of critters, but it would have to do.

It took longer than Charlie had anticipated, mostly because he had to work extra hard to wedge Ace into the space, as he'd stiffened into an unnatural backward-arched position, sprawled as he'd been on the bloody boulder.

He'd been tempted for a few moments to flip him over, facedown, and nudge him in the space in that position, but decided he'd not want to be treated that way, so why do it to another man? Instead he worked to arrange him as best he could given the space and the position Ace had died in.

He pressed and pressed on the one last limb that needed to fit into place, and finally, afraid the bone might snap—a sound and feeling Charlie was sure he'd never forget—he left the arm as it was, angled a bit upright, as if the dead man were calling to someone on a crowded street. It would have to do. He piled rocks on rocks and stuffed them wherever he could, saving the man's head until last. The task reminded him of the cairn he'd built for Teacup.

Charlie stood atop the two boulders that flanked the corpse, straddling the gap and looking down at Ace's uncovered head. His face was bent skyward, eyes open, sunlight glinting off their dull surface, as if he were looking at Charlie for something anything, one last thought before the inevitable. Perhaps Charlie might be able to think of something?

Thoughts slipped through his mind of the conversations he'd had with the man, not a whole lot of them that were memorable, to be honest, but maybe Ace had felt that way about Charlie too. Finally he shook his head sadly, and said, "I'm so sorry it had to be like this, Ace. You stay put now and . . . um, may the Good Lord, in all his fine ways and kindnesses, keep you in the palm of his hand."

It was the only thing Charlie could recall from the few snippets of Bible talk and prayer he'd been subjected to throughout his young life. He bent and tucked in the cloth sack once again over Ace's eyes. It had fallen loose when Charlie dragged the man to his final resting place. The little muslin sack covered much of the dead man's face, save for his bristled chin. "'Bye, Ace," said Charlie as he laid rock upon rock until the man beneath was no longer visible.

He looked up and shook his head. By the position of the sun pinned in the sky like a blinding moth, fluttering shards of fiery embers, he'd spent far too long at this task. He didn't regret it, but he did mount up in quick fashion and spent the next couple of hours swiveling his head to glance at his back trail.

He'd become convinced he'd see a line of black-clad riders, bristling with all manner of guns arranged along a cliff side high above, staring him down and slowly shaking their hat-topped heads. Then they would shoulder their weapons and crank off volley after volley, perfectly timed in precision movements. Charlie knew this would happen because that was what he imagined posses did to murder suspects who had escaped from their towns' jails. Throw in the death of a handful of citizens, among them an innocent child, and you have an anger that is unmatched.

Charlie rode, urging Nub to greater speeds, difficult because of the oddly winding trail that led down, down, down, then along the vast valley floor. They cut through an old streambed that wound its way through the foothills, then slowly upward into the higher hills of the Sierras. And if those were foothills, thought Charlie, then he must be in the knees by now.

A clanging, ringing sound tensed him and he pulled Nub up short on the reins. That had to be a horseshoe striking a rock. From behind him. He was sure of it. He froze. The ponderosas were slowly winding their way upward, still thick enough that he didn't think he was as much of a target as he had been in the more open scrubland below. He slowly turned, scanning over his left shoulder, moving only his eyes. Any second now, he told himself. Any second, Charlie, and you'll see that big old posse you were daydreaming about.

But he saw nothing. Nothing save for the slowly waving treetops, sunlight on rock, rock that shadowed other rock, longer shadows as the day wore on. Nothing moved. No birds, no squirrels, no nothing. He waited a long time, many minutes, he reckoned, but still nothing moved.

He had been giving thought to making a cold camp soon, but now that he had proof and not scared guesses that he was being followed, he had to keep pressing on. Had to find that next landmark that Grady Haskell had told them about. Even if it was a trap.

It was a trap he was willing to spring if it meant getting him to that killer. He heeled Nub into a hard walk, and though he sensed the beast's fatigue, one that he was sure surpassed his own, he knew they had to keep going.

He'd hop down soon, give the horse a rest. But not yet. Not yet. They still had distance to cover.

Far below him, emerging out of the scrub and more open expanse of the semi-treed old riverbed, Marshal Wickham sat his horse confident in his camouflage, behind a stand of ponderosas clustered out of a clot of harsh rock.

His old gray face bore a tight-lipped grimace. His horse had stepped wrong and whanged a rock with a shoe. Even as he felt it happening he knew it would be but seconds before the big young man far ahead of him, but mostly within sight, would stop, would freeze, would scan his back trail. And that was what his "escaped" prisoner had done.

And Wickham knew that Charlie was now convinced he was being followed. As Wickham sat there, aching for a pull on his flask, but not daring to move and risk a shadowy movement, he thought that perhaps this wasn't such a bad turn of events after all. Maybe it was time to close in on the boy. One side of his mouth smiled and he snaked an old hand under his coat and rested it on the lip of the pocket holding the flask. Soon enough, he thought.

Chapter 29

Wickham watched the big tired man leading his big tired horse slowly upward, angling in a zigzag route toward a sag in the trees. The marshal sighed. Another canyon. But he had to hand it to the young man; he had stuck to a course seemingly without hesitation. Wickham hoped the young man knew where in the heck he was bound, because he was placing all his eggs in the boy's basket. If he was beelining—slow as molasses—in a random direction away from Bakersfield and not toward the killers' hideout, then Wickham was going to be one surly old law dog; that much he knew about himself. But something told him to keep his revolver holstered. This fella was different, not a killer, as he'd been painted in town, and maybe even a good egg. Time would tell.

But Wickham wished the big bruiser would get a head of steam built up. He knew Charlie was aware that a posse would be on his tail, even before Wickham's mount had glanced a ringer off that rock. But the boy sure wasn't moving as quick as he should.

Wickham hadn't reckoned it would take more than a couple of days to track the thieving killers. And so, in his haste to put his quickly formed plan together, he had neglected to stock the boy up with enough food, water, and gritty sustenance for the horse too. A sack of feed corn would have gone a long way to keeping that horse's feet from slow-stepping.

Wickham cursed himself. A packet of jerky? What had he been thinking? That wasn't enough to sustain a man, and such a big one as Charlie Chilton.

He'd have to show himself soon, much as he'd intended. He'd wanted to wait until he was sure Charlie had gotten close and hadn't been playing him. Call it a lawman's prerogative, but now that he was pretty certain Charlie was dealing straight, Wickham felt sure he'd have to tighten the cinch. Convince the boy they could work together on this. After all, they both wanted the same thing, though for differing reasons.

"No," he said to himself as they walked down the trail, well hidden, he knew, by the thicker stands of aspen and ponderosas. "That's not entirely true. I reckon we're after the killer, this Haskell, as the big young man had referred to him. We're after him for much the same reason: revenge. To even the score."

That was the core of the reason, beyond that he knew they each had their own axes to hone. He hoped he could prevent Charlie from getting himself in too deep with the rough boys. Wickham was a lawman; he was used to dealing with hard cases. But Charlie seemed an innocent, too young to have been seriously in league with them. If he ended up fighting with this Haskell character, he might well lose his life, and too cheaply. If on the lucky chance he didn't, then he might still lose his life, perhaps by taking another life.

That sinking, gut-hollow feeling a man gets when he's killed his first man, be he desperado or demon, inebriated fool or prodding braggart, was a feeling that Wickham didn't want Charlie to experience, if he could help it.

"We'll see, horse." The marshal patted his mount's neck and readjusted himself in the saddle. "We shall see. And sooner than later, I suspect." He glanced up toward the far-off bank of gray-black clouds, low and unforgiving—rolling toward them—on the northeast horizon.

"Storm across that valley. Those clouds will be moving in within a few hours, horse. Might mean snow. They sure as shootin' don't mean a light summer rain. Not in autumn in the Sierras." Many people had died horrible, needless deaths underestimating such a fast-moving blow.

Memories rushed back of that time years before when he'd been one man of two dozen sent into the Sierras to find a wagon train that had become lost. Flashes of grim memories flicked in his mind then, of seeing the tops of wagons, the sides of them where they'd tipped, or been flipped by incessant wind.

They'd had to root in the hard, wind-packed snow for survivors. All the rescuers doing the same thing—praying for survivors, shouting for help, digging down with their mittened hands, with rifle butts, boots, anything. And finding entire families huddled beneath their wagons, blankets wrapped tight around them, all blue-tinged skin, all rimed with packed snow crystals, all frozen stiff, solid as stone, clutching each other.

Wickham could never forget those looks of desperation. For weeks after, they'd haunted his dreams. He'd see them crack those films of snow, their eyelashes caked, but the eyes, frosted blue and blazing, would stare like sunlit glass right at him and he'd hear their voices as a chorus: "Why? Why? Why?"

He'd try to answer, but nothing would come out, and all the while the voices grew louder, the looks more desperate, and finally he'd awaken in a sweat, chest pounding, the woodstove long gone out, and his own breath misting in the cold cabin air.

No, sir, he'd not helped provision that boy well enough, and now it was up to him to make sure what he brought with him sustained the two of them and their mounts. For if the storm brewed up into what he suspected it would, tracking Haskell and the rest of his gang would be the least of their worries.

He sucked his teeth once, made a decision with finger-snap speed, and dug his rowels into his horse's belly. Time to stop tagging along like a wayward duckling and start playing catch-up, before it's too late.

Chapter 30

"What do you mean, Hoy? You got to come with me."

"Randy," said Hoy, his eyes rimmed red as if he'd been pelted in the face with lye. He stepped out onto the porch and closed the door behind him. "I can't leave my mama and sissy all alone, not now."

"But we got a chance—the last chance—to get the man who did this thing."

"But my brother . . . my twin brother, Hill, he's lying in there on the dining table, dead and never coming back." His pointing arm trembled and Randy Scoville noticed he still wore the shirt he'd cradled his brother against as the boy died.

But Deputy Scoville was not to be swayed. He leaned close, his whispered voice frenzied but not loud enough to be heard from inside—he hoped. Mrs. Tompkins was a hard woman to know. And now one of her boys was killed, a death she'd openly blamed on the deputy. He could hardly blame her, but this dilly-dallying was no way to get the job done.

"Look, Hoy, tell her you had to slip out for a bit. Or tell her the whole truth, I don't much care. What I do need is for you to join me on those two horses right over there. We're all loaded, provisioned up for the journey, and we'll trail the man who gunned down your brother. He'll be as good as dead if we get on out there right now."

The bloody-shirted young man stood before him, a man whose twin brother was one of the victims. Hoy sighed, shook his head, and nodded slowly. "Nothing for it, then, since you put it like that. But I don't know what to tell Mama."

"Then don't tell her anything. But show her what you are made of. Help me bring back your brother's killer. Besides, you won't be doing it to avenge your brother. You'll be doing it for everybody in this town who was affected by the mess that happened. You hearing me?"

The haggard young man nodded, looked once in through the dimly lit room containing what was left of his family. His mother and sister staring glassy-eyed at the body of his brother, Hill. He turned around, stepped down off the porch, strode to the second horse, and mounted up. Deputy Scoville was right beside him, atop his own horse.

"Where do we meet the rest of the posse?" said Hoy, toeing his boot into the right stirrup.

"I thought I made that plain, Hoy. There ain't no others. Just you and me. They all curled up like kicked kittens when I asked them. Not a one had the sand to ride with me. None but you, Hoy."

The lone twin looked at Scoville in the near dark of the street. Presently he nodded, nudged his horse into a fast walk. He ground a thumb and knuckles into his red, tired eyes. "Getting cold, Randy. I expect it'll snow soon."

"Already is in the mountains."

"Where we're headed?"

"Yep," said Deputy Scoville. "Just where we're headed."

They rode out of town as dusk settled in. A cold wind ruffled their coats. Neither man was yet dressed for the weather they'd find in the high mountains. But neither man seemed to care. Their faces wore grim, determined looks, anger brewing below the surface, as if at any moment they might erupt in unstoppable anger.

Chapter 31

Close to the top of the close range he'd been slowly making his way up and into, with its sawtooth jags jutting skyward near the top, Charlie paused, looking up at them. A gust caught him openmouthed and nearly froze his teeth, parted his flapping overshirt, the one missing all but a pair of buttons. It had been a waste of time to fight with the remaining two.

He'd ridden with his arms close together and his spare holey socks on his hands for mittens. They did little to keep his hands cold, but he reckoned they were better than nothing. He wished he had a wool cap with the earflaps, as he'd seen a number of men wear in various towns in the past during his travels. But he didn't. So that was that.

The gale smelled like snow, Charlie decided. And that was not a scent he'd sniffed for a while, but one that he was familiar with. One that once smelled was not easily forgotten. For it brought with it a slab of intention. It was backed by months of cold temperatures, too many clothes, worn in uncomfortable, bulky layers, and numb ears, fingers, and toes.

He'd be happy to be shed of such weather for good.

And yet he did like a bit of snow, especially about the end of the year, the time when folks with families cele- brated Christmas, held feasts, and prepared all manner of fancy foods and gifts for each other.

His mouth watered at the prospect of a long farm ta- ble groaning with shiny glazed hams, heaps of smoked sausages, breads steaming from the oven, their buttered tops glistening. And the vegetables and sweetmeats! Oh, he could only imagine such a feed. Mostly because the closest he'd ever come to such a thing was being invited one Thanksgiving Day to a neighboring farm three miles down the road as a boy.

His gran would never have let him go, but she was abed with the ague and must really have been feeling under the weather, because she had told him he could go, though with great reluctance. He suspected it was only because she thought she would have had to feed him, never mind that he often fed himself.

But she had only given him two hours to walk there, dine, and then return. He'd chewed up a good deal of that time in making sure she had everything she needed before he left. He'd gotten to go into the Johnstons' home, and all the smells were there, along with the entire family, and a few other neighbors. And they all had looked at him as if he had arrived from some foreign land you only read about in books.

Red-faced, Charlie had told them he walked down to wish them a happy Thanksgiving Day, but that his gran was under the weather and he had to be getting back.

Their faces had changed from looks of stern surprise to a roomful of kind smiles. Nothing they could say or do would dissuade him and force him to stay. He had known they all knew his gran, and there had been pity and amaze- ment in their eyes when they looked at him. It made his face purple all the more. After a fashion, they had all wished him a fine holiday and bade him good-bye. He had turned to leave, sneaking a last long look at the table before closing the woodshed door on it all.

He'd about made it down the end of the barn lane when Mrs. Johnston had shouted to him, "Charles! Charles Chilton?"

He'd stopped then. Nobody who knew him, which wasn't a whole lot of folks anyway, ever called him Charles. "Ma'am?" He scooped his old brown wool flat cap off his head. It had belonged to his father and he thought it might look nice when he went visiting, though it had been savaged by a moth a time or two.

She had thrust a brimming flour sack into his arms. "You'll need to eat some of this soon, as it's still hot. And I won't take no for an answer. I only wish you could stay here and enjoy the meal with us. Won't you reconsider? Paget will drive you home in the wagon."

"I'd like to, ma'am, but . . ." He'd turned red once more, a trait he hated.

"I understand, Charles. Believe me, I do. Now, you don't give it another thought. You run along and make sure you tuck in to these vittles right away."

"But your sack, the other things inside . . ."

"Nothing I need back, Charles. Unless you want to stop by for a visit sometime, I suggest you use them as you see fit."

"Yes, ma'am."

Still smiling, she had turned to go back to the house. "And, Charles."

"Yes, ma'am?"

"Happy Thanksgiving to you. And tell your gran the same."

"Yes, ma'am," he'd said, "I surely will."

"Oh, Charles, one more thing."

"What's that, ma'am?"

"Put your hat on before you catch a chill."

"Oh yes, ma'am."

It had been as close as he'd ever come to sitting in on a big family meal like that. But as he had walked home, devouring every last crumb and speck of food in that flour sack, he felt himself the luckiest boy in the world, the food was that good.

Now, alone on the cold mountainside, wind whistling over, around, and through him, Charlie was grateful for only one thing—the trail before him looked as though it would once again descend between two fingers of mountain range. And with that descent would come a lessening of the wind, he hoped. He also knew, though, that mountain valleys came with a dangerous peculiarity all their own. The cold always seemed to settle in them early and deep of an autumn season. And far below he spied a treed valley that he knew he'd have to traverse the length of to get to the Needle he felt sure lorded over the far end.

As long as Haskell was somewhere up ahead, and as long as Charlie was somehow gaining on him, he didn't care what sort of weather or terrain he had to endure. He would do it, come what may.

The next few hours unfolded as he'd expected. The weather turned much colder, the bank of clouds thickened and pressed closer to the already shivering earth, and Charlie's tension increased the closer he drew to the bottom of the valley.

As he descended, a sound, faint and bland at first, then sharper, more distinct and bold—and familiar— became clear. There before him was the reason for the thickly treed valley floor. He dismounted on the banks of a gushing, roiling river, wider than most rivers he'd had to cross on horseback, and thick and deep. How deep, especially in the dark, swirling center channel, was anyone's guess.

Was this the right route to Haskell's hideout? He didn't know anymore. He didn't recall the man saying a thing about a river, let alone one so big. But he looked up at that moment, and in a cleft in the peaks across the river before him, there looked to be a stone spire. Could it be the one Haskell had told them was called the Needle? Could be the very one, he thought. Especially considering that he'd seen no other such formation in two days of searching. The thought that he might truly be on the right trail was both a relief and a worry.

He'd have to cross that river, and if there was one thing he did not go out of his way to experience, it was the bone-chilling cold of water barely frozen at the edges. The afternoon light glowed gray on the rimed, jagged edges of ice formed along the banks.

Charlie had no doubt that this river would be frozen clear across with thick ice in another month, two at the most.

"Maybe if we explore downstream for a spell, eh, Nub? Could be there's a narrower place to cross." He tugged the reins and the horse lifted his head from cropping the tops off spindly riverbank shoots, still somewhat green. His curiosity took them another quarter mile down along the river, but the waterway itself grew more contentious-looking.

"I reckon that's the reason the trail is back up thattaway and not down here." The horse barely acknowledged his chatter, but followed along, head bowed. They turned in the riverbank mud and made their way back to the spot they'd first come up on the river, back at the trail.

It burbled, wide and cold. Charlie readied the gear atop Nub, lashing down the bedroll and his bag with extra gear. Aside from that, Charlie had very little that he could do in preparation for the savage flow he was about to plow on into. Never, he felt sure, was a man more ill-suited to a task than was he to the notion of fording a river.

He briefly toyed with the idea of taking off his boots. But that thought passed as soon as he bent down and ran his fingers in the flowage, waggled them, then pulled them out. It would be much too cold to bear. He expected he'd still come down with chilblains, but it would be worth it if it would get him across the river and back onto Haskell's trail.

Charlie pulled in what he was sure would be his last breath on earth—and the guess was verified as soon as his stovepipe boots filled with water that seeped through the cracks in the leather between the boot and sole. He didn't think it was possible to draw in a breath on top of another breath, but he did. The frigid water felt as if it were minutes from becoming ice. The cold seized his core as if a snowy hand had wrapped itself around his insides and squeezed.

Even Nub, usually a hardy brute not inclined to utter protest no matter the circumstance, winced and whinnied at the shock the water brought. "Come on," said Charlie, in gasps. "We can't stop now, Nub." Charlie led the way, tugging the reins and stepping slowly.

He found that if he slid his boots along in front of him, he felt more stable. The horse, he saw, had no troubles in finding solid footing. Then again, Charlie reasoned, Nub had four feet to his two.

The current raged, pushing into him with a steady pressure that sometimes was supplemented with a slamming of whitecapped waves. They pulsed downriver from the various obstructions nature saw fit to pepper the river with, mostly in the shape of boulders, misshapen and craggy, and for the most part, unseen.

The river had a voice too, and it grew louder the farther into the river he ventured. Soon enough, though he didn't dare look behind him to see how far he'd come, the river's voice roared, a gushing, thick-throated thing full of surprise and anger. It sounded like what he imagined the chants of a thousand angry Indian warriors might sound like.

Charlie tried to keep an eye on the far shore, certain that he'd heard such advice from somewhere. Something about how it helped with dizziness when crossing a river. He didn't feel dizzy yet, so maybe it was working. Trouble was, he had to rely solely on his feet to do the close-up work of inching forward. And that was why he didn't see the cluster of boulders dead ahead of him, the tops of which jutted slightly from the roiling, boiling surface.

His left boot angled into a crevice wide enough that the toe of his boot fit perfectly between two rocks. He inched his right foot forward and it stubbed into the side of an unseen boulder. His right knee buckled slightly, and green river water splashed his pant leg halfway up his thigh. He could right himself, he knew, if he could get that left foot upstream a bit more, provide some stability. But the boot had wedged tight.

His eyes widened, Nub kept splashing forward, hooves clomping, water surging upward with each step, not daring to give up his well-earned head of steam, and definitely not stopping to worry about the beginnings of some sort of odd flailing dance that Charlie had begun.

The big man felt Nub's reins slip from his hand. He wasn't worried about the horse, knew he was better off than Charlie at this point, but he also knew that Nub wouldn't go far once he made it across. Charlie's biggest worry was whether he would make it across the river himself.

Before venturing into the river, he'd taken the old socks off his hands that he'd used as paltry mittens, so he'd have a better grip should he need his hands. He windmilled his big arms, desperately trying to dislodge his left boot and at the same time trying to gain purchase with his right, but having no luck at all. Then he went down, like a big tree felled in the forest.

As he pitched forward Charlie felt as if it were all happening in a slowed-down fashion, as if someone were holding the clock's hands. He saw the rocks before him, the water parting, spraying upward as his legs cleaved the river's flow. He felt, rather than saw, the wrenching of his right knee as it slammed into the tallest of the river boulders.

Charlie's howl of pain was cut short as icy river water filled his face, snatching away his breath and instantly numbing him. His body slammed into the river, and he scrabbled frantically with his hands, managed to paw a few slick river rocks with one, nothing but water with the other. But there, beneath his left hand, he felt the bottom.

He pushed, but something held him down. It was his left boot, still lodged in the rocks. The weight of his body hadn't quite snapped his lower leg, but it darn sure tested the bone's limits. The pain, even in the cold water, bloomed hot and angry within his leg.

But he could pay it no heed at the moment, for his biggest concern was the fact that with one foot pinned, the other was splayed, bobbing with the downstream current. He was unable to drive it back down beneath the water, where he might jam it into the riverbed to gain a foothold. But he had no luck. The leg whipped back and forth in the current like a child's toy.

All this happened in a matter of seconds, and try as he might, Charlie wasn't able to push himself up out of the current enough to grab a mouthful of air. The current thrashed him as if he were in the midst of a bar fight with a pair of twin giants. Jolts of hot pain pulsed up and down his legs.

In his right, it radiated up from his knee. In his left, it burned and snapped from his ankle to his knee. He strained against the current and the wedged boot. But with each roll and push caused by his body as it obstructed the natural flow of the raging river, new pains bloomed.

Then, as quickly as it had begun, his boot popped free of its underwater death hold. Nearly unconscious, and nearly spent physically, Charlie knew he had to somehow flip himself over, felt sure he was facing downward in the water. Air, he needed air—he wasn't a dang fish! And with that unlikely and comical thought, both of Charlie's substantial fists punched forward from his chest.

That was the direction they needed to head, for his knuckles slammed into the river bottom and pushed hard. He felt the skin splitting, felt small bones, maybe his knuckles, popping and crunching into the stony river bottom. But he didn't care. Somehow deep inside, he knew it was his last shot at life.

When Charlie's head began to turn, followed by his big body—like a huge log slowly rolling over in the current, pinwheeling downstream—he felt the cold air on his face, spewed a gout of water from his mouth, alternately gagging and coughing as he sucked in air.

Charlie lay on his back, spinning in the middle of the river, a wide stretch of unruffled current. His arms floated outward by his sides as if he were a bird testing his wings. His legs hung limply. Too soon the currents conspired to upend him once again and he thrashed to gain his footing, but could not.

The river was too deep. His long, bulky legs churned beneath the roiling brown surface, groping for purchase on the bottom. But it was no use. And then all too soon he was sucked back into the rapids. They boiled all about him as if he were in the midst of a witch's mighty cauldron.

He spun, thrashing wildly, saw something dark approaching fast. Then that something slammed him in the head, as if it were a giant's fist landing a solid punch to his eye socket. He thought he heard himself groan, couldn't be sure as the river's anger rose to a roar all about him. He fought to pull in breaths of air, but his lips found only water.

He fought to keep the light of the sky—now water, now sky, over and over again—above him, the water below, but there was no one here like Pap to tell him how it should be done, no one to share the secrets gained from experience. No one. . . .

And soon the great river flipped Charlie Chilton over once more, his great bulk of a body rising from the water before slamming, facedown, striking rock after rock, caroming from one to the next until he was rendered motionless, save for the push and pull of the river's unending, ageless forces.

Chapter 32

Marshal Dodd Wickham thought for sure he'd have caught up with the overgrown galoot before now. Stood to reason he would have—the big young man, though he hadn't dallied terribly, was far from speedy. Whereas Wickham had doubled his pace, much to his Missy's consternation. She kicked up a fuss now and again as he'd urged her to move along faster than she liked.

Maybe he'd lost track of him? Not likely. The big man's sign was easy to read, boot prints deep and wide. His horse had looked to Wickham to be some sort of Percheron cross, big-hoofed and weighty. Just the mount for a man such as Charlie Chilton. It also meant together they left enough of a sizable imprint on the trail's dusty, packed surface that Wickham could follow quite easily compared with a number of rascals from the old days who'd decided to head on out on the trail in hopes of escape.

A couple, as he recalled, did make good on their escapes. But most, he'd caught. He smiled, remembering the good old days, the glory days for one such as he. He'd been the toast of many towns along the way. And as a result had been able to slide his boots under many a fine woman's springy bed.

A noise like a far-off roll of steady thunder broke his reverie. What was that? A storm? No, the snow clouds would open on them soon enough, but they would be silent. This was something different, a sound he'd heard much in his past. But what? He scanned the valley below and spied the rolling gray course between trees—a river.

He was not certain which one, but it didn't matter. He'd been told a long time ago that they all ended up in the same place. Something about the oceans. How the rivers stayed full was another matter. Something about snowmelt and being on top of the world. Again, it really did not matter to him.

His old dear and long-passed daddy had once told him, "Worry about the things you can do something about, boy. Else you'll wind with bloody insides and a head full of worms and mush and not be of use to anyone." Wickham recalled too how the old man had come to tell him that.

Young Dodd had experienced his first true love, and as he'd come to learn, in true love's fashion, that also meant he was due sooner or later for a true-love heartache. And that was what he got from Henrietta Bulgins. Now that he recalled, her face, and even her demeanor, sort of matched her name—all lumpy and unpleasant.

He came to learn months later, once he'd stopped mooning over her, that his faithless chum, Clarence Wiggins, had done him a mighty favor in taking her off his hands. Last he heard Clarence was a haggard whip of a man and Henrietta had become as big as a stable and had birthed a baker's dozen young Wigginses. No doubt they'd all gone on to do the same.

All those years later, Wickham shook his head and smiled as a stray gust whistled through his mustaches and chilled his teeth. His horse had picked her way down the scree slope toward the river, and from the looks of it, it was the same spot Charlie had chosen.

"Good lad," said Wickham, on seeing Charlie's tracks. He looked ahead, but the path wound to the right. He heard the river, though, and knew they were very close. The trail leveled off, then curved around the rocky corner and there was the river before them, in all its roiling, brash, rock-thumping glory. "That looks colder'n a grave digger's heart." The horse nodded once, as if in agreement.

The marshal dismounted, bent to examine the tracks. "Looks like he cut upstream." He low-walked forward, eyeballing the spongy, sandy riverbank. "Then came back — couldn't find a spot to cross, eh, Charlie?"

Wickham's mare, Missy, nickered. The marshal glanced up, saw her staring downstream across the river. A large, riderless horse was thundering up the far bank, nursing a hind leg, water sluicing from the saddle and dragging gear. He knew that big beast!

Wickham gained his feet, already wrapping a gloved hand around his pommel. "Charlie!" he shouted, cutting his eyes to the river. Downstream from the horse by a dozen yards, he saw what looked like a big ol' log flopping over in the current. But this log had arms, a big shaggy head, and wore a sopping wool overcoat.

Wickham quickly read the water, yanked the reins hard to the right, and sank spur. The mare responded with renewed vigor to match the old lawman's barking commands and raking rowels. Water sprayed and hooves clomped as the pair followed the river's near edge. If he could reach the slowly spinning man, who looked to Wickham as if he was unconscious or worse, Lord help him, then maybe he could cut left across the river at that point ahead where the rapids rose and the water was shallower. He had to try.

"Hang on, Charlie!" growled Marshal Wickham through clenched teeth. The river spray soaked him, lashed across his face, stinging with its coldness. He barely heard his horse's breathing over the roar of the river and stabbing, splashing hooves.

It was going to be close ... and he yanked hard again on the reins, cutting the horse to the left. The beast was undaunted by the quickly deepening river. "Charlie!" shouted the old man, fighting with one hand and his teeth with the rawhide thong he'd cinched down too tight around his lariat. When it seemed the water-swollen strip of hide would not give in, Wickham, with a final gnash of his teeth, was able to break the back of the tiny knot and work it apart. He shook out the loop as they reached Charlie, angling downstream with each second that passed.

The big body had hit the faster current sooner than Wickham expected and he had to thunder into deeper water, slowing the horse. Soon it was up to the horse's chest and then he felt the horse bob and go buoyant, and he knew they were no longer in contact with the stream-bed. He gripped the horse's barrel tight with his legs and focused on getting that loop around Charlie.

It wasn't looking good. The big man was facedown in the drink, but there was little Wickham could do at the moment about that. He stuffed the wet leather reins between his teeth and teased out the loop. Angling his horse with his knees and head, as much as reining with his mouth was effective, Wickham managed to work the horse, slower and more reluctant by the second, to their left and into deeper water.

The loop hit the water, slapped against Charlie's legs,

and Wickham jerked it . . . too quick. It slapped over Charlie, whose massive shoulders and head bobbed out of reach, turning all the while like a leaf thrown on stormy water.

One more retrieve back and a fresh toss, the last Wickham knew he could make before he'd have to thunder farther downstream to catch up with the big, floating body.

But this time the loop snagged Charlie's torso, and Wickham wasted no time in snugging it as tight as he could. He wanted to flip the big kid over, but there was no time. He had to get his own horse back to shallower water before they foundered much more.

As if sensing the best direction, his trusty mare bee-lined upstream at an angle. This took them through the rest of the deep, swift current, and for one moment he felt sure they were about to go belly up, but he trusted his Missy.

He felt more than heard the horse's hooves strike something below—no doubt a mammoth boulder lurking in the gray-green depths. But she righted herself and pressed on. Wickham tugged on the rope, tried to flip the bobbing Charlie over, but had no luck. He spurred his horse to move faster, to give it all she had, and the old girl did just that. In seconds he felt her frantic lashing legs strike something once more, but this time it wasn't something momentary, but the river bottom.

He worked his frozen legs as best he could, trying to spur her to gain that bank a dozen yards ahead. Now ten, seven, five . . . he tried to spur her again, but his legs were useless. Might as well have been lengths of wet stove wood for all the good they did. But the old girl gained the bank and kept scrabbling upward, wanting that high ground, wanting to leave the cold, strange river behind.

Once at the top of the ice-rimed bank, the horse staggered. Wickham smacked at her neck feebly. And she gave another lurch upward. It was enough to get Charlie up out of the water.

Wickham couldn't feel his legs, could barely dismount, but forced himself to move. He grabbed at his leg and with a handful of sopping trouser cloth, managed to yank his unfeeling leg out of the stirrup. Then he pushed against the saddle and dropped, sliding, belly in, to the ground. He landed with a thud on top of Charlie, and immediately worked to drag the boy so that his head faced down the bank, with his feet higher than his head.

It proved a big task, but Wickham managed it in a few seconds of wordless shouts and straining. Then he dropped to his knees and flipped the big brute onto his side. The man's face was the color of lilac flowers with a blackness creeping in beneath it all.

Charlie's eyes were closed, his lips pursed, and his face looked puffed, as if he were holding his breath. All this Wickham took in as he kept rolling the big brute, trying to balance him up onto his side. It took all the strength Wickham could muster, and then holding him there proved a whole other task.

But he did it, and managed to angle Charlie so that he was almost, but not quite, facedown again. He held him like that, propped against his own shoulder, while with his left arm he whomped on the young man's back. Then he reached to the front and pushed hard, punching as if he were pounding a big wad of dough, hoping that this effort might expel some of the river water the man had likely taken in.

"Charlie!" He slapped quickly at the big face. "Charlie! Curse you, boy, don't you die on me! I'll not be responsible for hauling your carcass back to town! Ain't got the strength for such a Herculean task! Charlie!" He slapped again.

Next he muckled on to Charlie's face, pinched either side of his mouth, in an effort to force Charlie's mouth open. It worked and stayed that way as he released and recommenced his pummeling of Charlie's gut, then whomping on his back.

He'd about run out of breath himself, and felt Charlie's big girth slowly slumping down toward him, threatening to crush his old bony frame, when he heard a cough. He held his breath, not sure if it had come from himself or . . . there it was again!

Wickham commenced to whomping and punching with renewed vigor and Charlie's coughs increased, terrible, deep-body retching sounds. Soon, with a great heave, Charlie vomited a great quantity of brown, brackish bile, half spraying it on the old lawman's face. Wickham lost his grip on Charlie, managed to roll backward in time, and Charlie flopped facedown once more on the riverbank mud, his great shaggy head a foot or so from the slopping, ice-and-mud-churned riverbank.

Dodd Wickham glanced at Charlie. With relief he saw the big man's back rising, falling, rising slowly, saw one big hand twitch, the fingers begin to flex and curl, raking mud and twigs.

Wickham raised himself up on his elbows, dragging a sopping cuff across his face with a grimace, his breath coming in ragged pulls. It had been a long time since he'd had to exert himself in such a manner. He saw movement to his left, up on the bank. It was Missy, his horse. It appeared she didn't know which leg to favor, so cold was she.

Her withers flinched uncontrollably. He felt bad for the old girl, but she was a trooper. He had faith she'd

shake it off, though he'd tend to her once he got his wind
back. She'd be okay if left alone, as long as she kept
walking, stumbling and shambling as she was. He barely
heard the other horse, Charlie's big mount, make its way
to them, but saw it out of the corner of his eye as he kept
a watch on Charlie.

The big horse looked shaky on his pins too, but was
still upright. And though trembling and with gear trailing
from him, Wickham suspected he'd make it through too.
The exhausted lawman watched Charlie try weakly to
get his arms up under himself, to push himself up like a
dazed grizzly who'd taken a mighty knock to the bean.

"Take her easy, boy. You been through the worst of it.
Take her easy and don't flop forward into that dang river
or I've a mind to let you go this time."

The only acknowledgment he got from Charlie that
the young man had heard him was a low guttural grum-
ble as he slowly pushed himself up onto his knees, his big
hands planted firmly in the oozing, freezing mud. He
swayed like that, a figure more grizzly than man, huffing
and chuffing and nearly growling, shaking his big head
slowly side to side.

"You don't sound so good," said Wickham, unscrew-
ing the top of his flask. Though possibly now more
dented than he remembered, it appeared not to have lost
any of its precious cargo. He took a pull, smacked his lips,
and lay back on the bank, his eyes closed, his breathing
leveling off. "You had me worried there, Charlie. My
word, don't do that to an old man, eh?"

Dodd Wickham flicked his eyes open and saw a shadow
fall over him. He squinted up and shouted, "No! Charlie,
no!" as a big fist drove downward at his face.

Chapter 33

Grady Haskell yanked once more on the lead line, the very line that attached him to a fortune in wonderful money, cold cash. He laughed at that one, for in this weather it surely was that—and only that sliver of momentary self-induced mirth kept him from spinning around and drilling that laggard plug between her foul walleyes. A homelier horse he'd never seen, and she came with a trudging gait to match.

"Step it up, Methuselah, or you'll be feeding crows and coyotes in very short order."

If the old girl had heard him, she gave no indication. Could be something was genuinely wrong with her, thought Haskell. Not a surprise, considering that she was Ace's horse. And he was as useless as his horse.

Speaking of useless, he thought, I should be coming onto Simp and Dutchy about any time now. Another reason he didn't dare risk a shot yet. Didn't want to tip them off that they were being followed. He'd rather give them the old surprise attack, if he could. All this dilly-dallying with the oafs had slowed him down by the better part of a day and he wanted to get to that cabin, rejigger his load, and wait out the posse.

He'd promised himself that if he ever made a big, big haul—and this surely counted in that category—he'd not spend his days glancing at shadowy places and strange faces and wondering. No, sir, he'd deal with them all in quick, short order. He'd snipe the do-gooders from Bakersfield as soon as they showed their heads, poking up like rabbits because they were sure the Almighty and the all-important Right were on their side.

Well, he had news for them. Nothing could be further from the truth. All he needed was a few good vantage points, and he recalled several, where he'd stashed the weapons he'd collected off the bodies of the fools he'd hired. Then he'd be set up as pretty as you please to deliver an almighty lead rain on the do-gooders.

He almost chuckled, but didn't want to reveal anything about his location, should they be closer than he suspected.

And dang if he wasn't. Not a quarter mile along the trail ahead, Haskell saw the unmistakable sign, then smelled it, of weakly veiled smoke from a small cook fire. Yep, had to be Simp. He was the only one fool enough to give in to such urges to make a fire. On the other hand, maybe he'd brewed up a few cups of fine coffee. Heck, thought Grady, even bad coffee would be better than the coffee he hadn't had in days now.

As he approached, he worked to keep his horse's steps slow and measured, kept his rifle drawn and laid across his lap, cocked and at the ready. And his left-side revolver was ready to be snatched free should Simp mistake him for a posse man.

As it turned out, Grady needn't have worried. The man, and it was indeed Simp, was asleep, curled up like a baby by his tiny campfire. He'd taken care to angle wide, frondlike branches of pines around the fire to help disperse the smoke. But it hadn't helped, now, had it, Simp?

Haskell smiled, a wide, cat-caught-a-mouse grin and swung down out of the saddle, his rifle held out and aimed forward. Simp might be dumb as a sack of horseshoes, but he was, Grady had to admit, a fair hand with a gun draw.

Grinning, Haskell approached the sleeping man. Still a few feet away, Grady paused, pooched out his bottom lip, and regarded the man, noted the dark staining of his lower legs and boots. Wetness. Hmm. He looked about the rest of the camp, then nodded, as if coming to a decision.

There was the man's horse, saddled and reins looped lightly, ready to be grabbed should a clean escape be necessary. The horse also had caked dust on its feet—a sign of recent wetness. And there were the two laden saddlebags, filled, no doubt, with Grady's money. Good, good, good . . .

"If I was to shoot you now, Simp, why you'd be . . . dead." Haskell's smile spread as he watched the dozing man's reaction to his unexpected words.

Simp's arms and legs stiffened and shot straight out, as if he were trying to jump in all directions at once. He clawed for his sidearm fast, almost out of instinct.

"Don't, don't. No, no, no . . ." Haskell shook his head. "That's not how it's going to play out."

The surprised man's eyes widened. "Boss . . . what's going on." He rested his hand on the butt of the revolver, but didn't lift it free of the polished cherry grips. He ran his other hand down his stubbled face, rubbed his eyes quickly with a thumb and knuckle.

"Howdy, Simp. Kindly take that hand off'n your pistol."

Simp complied, a newly roused curiosity and concern knitting his brow. "What . . . what you got that thing pointed at me for, boss?"

"Oh," Haskell sighed, his voice casual, his eyes still narrowed on the horizontal man. "You see, I know what a hand you are with your shooter, and there wasn't no way I could think of to wake you up safelike so that you wouldn't up and plug me full of holes." Haskell offered Simp a grin and a shrug. He tipped his hat back, and all the while kept his rifle trained on the man.

"Well, as you can see, I'm not about to shoot you. I'm all awake over here." He grinned, looked embarrassed. "Been trying to dry out. Got a mite damp crossing that river a ways back."

"Mm-hmm. I can see that, Simp." Haskell nodded, but didn't otherwise move.

Simp swallowed, ran a raspy tongue over his equally dry lips. "So you can go on ahead and lower that rifle of yours, all right?" His smile was a weak, thin thing.

"Oh, this here rifle?" Haskell wagged the black-barreled Henry.

Simp nodded, not taking his eyes from the man.

"I will gladly do that," said Haskell. "When you pinch that revolver out of your holster, nice as you please. Two fingers, then toss it this way."

"You can't be serious with me, boss. That ain't right. You know me. We're working together."

"Now, see, there's a couple of things wrong with what you said." Haskell canted his head and regarded Simp as he would a daft child. "First is that you assume because we are acquainted that I like you and trust you. Nothing could be further from the full truth. Next thing is that we are not working together. Never did. You worked for me."

Simp made to get up, but Haskell thrust the business end of the rifle at him and shook his head. "Not so quick. You need to toss that hog leg over this way."

Paused in midrise, Simp stared at the man.

"Get on with it," said Haskell, jerking the rifle again.

Simp made to speak, then with a hard sneer tossed the pistol as Haskell had instructed. It landed near Grady's feet, skidded, and kicked up a small spray of dust.

"Kind of feel naked now, don't you, Simp?"

The seated man said nothing, but stared at Haskell, trying to look angrier and less confused than he was. "What'd you mean when you said I used to work for you?"

"What it sounds like, Simp. The big deal has gone ahead as planned and you and the boys . . . well, let's say this was a onetime employment opportunity and now your services are no longer needed."

"Hey, anyway," said Simp, as if ignoring Haskell's utterances, "how'd you come to be snaking around behind me and not up the trail. When you left us early on you said you'd see us up ahead."

"In a manner of speaking, I have. But I had things to tend to here and there. Oh, by the way, Simp. Ace sends his fondest wishes for a speedy recovery. Said to tell you that he went through it and it wasn't nothing. Over in a finger snap and now everything's all right. You got any thoughts as to what he means by that?"

Simp looked up at Haskell as if he'd recited part of the Bible in Latin. "I have no idea what you're on about." He looked away, down at his feet. "Me and him, we never got on much anyway."

"That is a shame. He was such a . . . no, I can't even say he was all that interesting. Just annoying, mostly, if I have to be honest."

"What you mean . . . 'was'?"

Haskell stepped closer, leveling the snout of the rifle inches from Simp's pocked, trembling features. Though it was a cool day, tears of sweat bubbled from his brow, leached through his ratty beard.

"You're gonna shoot me, ain't you?" It was almost an accusation.

Haskell grinned wide. "Shoot you? Great hoppin' goats, boy, what sort of a boss do you take me for? Course I ain't gonna shoot you." He leaned close, fixed Simp with his eyes as a snake will a hare, and in a low, husky whisper, said, "Gonna gut you, boy."

As the words sank into Simp's brain, so did Grady Haskell's skinning knife sink deep into the poor sop's gut. He had time to widen his eyes and think about screaming. But by then it was far too late. Something inside him burst and it was as if a candle had been blown out. His eyes dulled, relaxed, and blood spooled from his sagged lips.

"Naw," said Haskell, still bent low, still grinning, still talking quietly to the newly dead man. "Shootin's much too loud. And besides, bullets cost money, and you ain't worth a nickel."

He worked the knife in a little deeper, wrenched it back and forth, then slid it free and wiped it on Simp's tatty frock coat. "Now, all that palaver has worked up a powerful thirst in me. And as I recall"—Grady parted the dead man's coat and pawed inside it, patted down the sagged body—"you have a taste for corn liquor. . . ." He smiled as he withdrew a corked glass pint bottle half-filled with honey-colored liquid. "I take it back, Simp." He popped the cork and tossed it away. "You are good for something after all."

He upended the bottle, gurgled it all back, smacked

his lips, ran his tongue around them, then tossed the bottle. It bounced off the man's head with a thunk.

Haskell smiled and sauntered on over to Simp's horse. After reassuring himself that the saddlebags contained his money, he rigged up a lead line from the horse to Ace's, then looked about the camp once more. His eyes settled on the little campfire, still quietly smoking. He considered it a moment, then walked to it, unbuttoned his fly, and drizzled until the fire steamed, giving up its embers to the dousing.

"You really ought to give more thought before you light a fire on the trail, Simp." He looked over at the dead man as he buttoned his fly. "You never know who might show up. Lots of bad men out there." His little joke brought a smile to his face and sustained him as he rode on out, heading for the Needle and beyond.

Chapter 34

Charlie felt a terrible coldness, a bone-deep chill that he felt sure would never leave him for all his days. *Ha, all my days,* he thought. *I am dead—have to be to feel like this.*

As the memories of what happened dribbled back to him—the trail, the river and its water, that cold, cold water—his thoughts curved back to the river and he realized he was not dead. Somehow he had survived. Was it even possible?

When he finally pried open his eyes, he felt like one of those frogs who emerges in the spring from being dug down deep in the pond muck all winter. But those frogs lived. So if they did, maybe he had too?

None of this made any sense to Charlie. He felt a wet, cold grittiness beneath him, on his face, his hands, tried to work his fingers to grip, to ball them into fists. Surely there was somebody to blame, somebody to deal with for all the misery he felt collapsing down on him.

And then there was—Haskell. Grady Haskell. That was the vicious brute who'd caused all this, for certain. He was the one Charlie wanted so badly. Even as he tried to force his eyes open, blinking them out from a long winter's layer of half-frozen mud—no, that wasn't right. You're not a frog, Charlie. . . .

No matter, he knew that as soon as he was able to get up out of the mud, stand for himself once again, he was going to track Haskell and that would be an end to it. And once he found him, Charlie vowed, he would show no mercy, vowed to peel the man apart like a soft apple.

He managed to get up onto his knees, forcing his eyes to stay open while he shook his head to dispel the fuzzy-headed feeling that lingered like a bad headache. Then he heard a voice behind him. He wasn't alone—someone else was there, sharing his riverbank. He knew that voice? Who was that? Who would be there with him? Only one man he could think of who knew he'd be there—Haskell. Had to be. It was as he'd feared; the man had been waiting for him, had seen him coming some-how and had decided to wait for Charlie. That meant Charlie was not only half-dead from his dunking, but unarmed and in the weaker position.

Charlie grinned. There had to be a way to make that work in his favor. Keep acting confused, he thought. Work your way on up to Haskell. Then lay into him sud-denlike. Make him pay for everything he's done.

As bad as Charlie felt, all he cared about was getting close enough to Haskell to kill him. He trusted that his bare hands would do the job. That was all that mattered to him at the moment. Not whether he would live through the attack, for he was convinced he would not. Haskell would slit him open like a caught fish. But surely I have enough of something left in me to get close, close enough to snap the man's neck, twist his head off like a flower. Only Haskell was no flower. He was a killer. And Charlie only wanted one shot at making the man pay for his crimes. Just one.

He rose on his knees, tried to steady himself with his hands planted firm in the mud. He felt himself swaying, bulled through it, forced himself up onto one knee, pushed off the mud, and stood slowly full height. His vision was a blurred thing. The sound of the river, so close he felt almost pulled back into it, as if he were somehow attacked by its loudness, tugged at him. He slowly turned.

Through crusted, muddied eyes he saw a figure stretched out on the bank above, lying there like the arrogant man he was. Haskell. Yammering something at him, telling him no doubt how he was going to kill him. Well, thought Charlie, let him talk. I will use that to my advantage.

He lumbered up the bank, but didn't have to wobble too far. For there was Haskell. There he was. Right in front of him. Now or never, Charlie, old fellow, he thought. And with all the meager strength he could amass, he drew the fingers of his right hand into a big, hard ball of bone and skin, and with his lips stretched back tight over his teeth, Charlie drove that fist straight downward.

"Charlie! No! What are you doing?"

But even that wasn't enough to stop him. He knew the man was a deceitful liar, a rogue of the first order. Someone who would lie and cheat and steal and kill to get what he wanted.

Charlie landed a good one, right on the jaw of that rascal. But even as he did so, the momentum from the mighty punch he threw kept him going, kept him pitching forward. His body followed that fist downward, as if he were a mighty tree falling in the forest. He had enough wits about him to tuck one shoulder under and roll with it. Come back up, Charlie, he told himself. Come up and swing wide. You're bound to hit something.

As he rolled with it, came on up again, pivoting on his left knee, he shook his head to clear the fuzziness. Had to get straight, had to see what he was up to. This was his chance to best the killer. He knew for certain that any second he'd be shot.

"Charlie!"

The bum was howling at him now, a thin, reedy voice. Why wasn't he shooting? Charlie spun, faced the man, not wanting to waste the opportunity he was given, wanting to grab the precious moments before the bullets began to fly. Charlie could almost feel them hitting him, driving into him, even before he heard them. Had he been shot? No, no, it was the man, hitting back.

Charlie kept right on lashing out, spun around, and caught sight of Haskell, only it didn't look like him. Must be the Devil's wearing a disguise, thought Charlie. Like one of those stage performers he'd seen back in that railroad town, touring the streets, drumming up business for that evening's performance. He recalled wanting to go, but there was no way he had the money to get in. This had been months before he'd met up with Pap and the boys anyway.

Charlie's thoughts were a jumbled, tumbled mess, his legs shot fire up and down them, and his head felt stuffed full of ticking and an achiness that wouldn't go away. The only thing he knew he needed to do was keep swinging his big fists. He'd catch sight of his tormenter again any second.

Then something hit him hard on the side of his aching head. Stars bloomed before his eyes and through a hollow ringing sound he heard shouts, someone shouting his name, "Charlie! Charlie!" and then he thought he heard the word marshal. But that didn't make any sense. What did it even mean?

And then he fell, not remembering to roll this time, piling into the soft riverbank earth. So cold, so tired, Charlie wanted nothing more than to lie there, head aching, body aching, maybe sink into the mud and be done with it all. All this living and fighting and killing and dying and wounding. Fight, fight, fight, it never seemed to end, just got worse and worse until finally you ended up a man floating down a river, someone who should have died, but then . . . someone saves you. Someone . . . saved you?

Who would do that? Not Haskell, surely. Man wouldn't have any reason to save anyone except himself. Not for the first time that day, a dark veil pulled down low over his eyes and he knew no more.

Chapter 35

"Hoy, you ought to give thought to putting that overcoat on. I didn't outfit us for cold weather so I could be impressed with myself."

Hoy Tompkins didn't respond to Randy Scoville, just kept riding, his head hanging like that of a whupped dog.

"I said—"

"I know what you said," Hoy finally responded. "I'll dress myself when I'm good and ready."

They rode a few moments more in silence. The snow, when it finally came, was a pelting, driving thing at first, pellets that stung the face so that the deputy had to scrunch his eyes to melt off the fringe of frosty snow that had gathered along his lashes. Then the snow eased into a less painful, but thicker mess. It accumulated with a speed Scoville found amazing. "Must be because we're up in the mountains," he said.

"Huh?"

"You ain't going to listen to a word I say, are you, Hoy?"

"In case you hadn't noticed, you don't say an awful lot that bears listening to."

Deputy Randy Scoville pulled up short, watched his

traveling companion's snow-covered shoulders and head as the man slowly walked on. Then he shouted, "What is that supposed to mean?" He knew what it meant. He was surprised that Hoy Tompkins had the sand to say it. Heck, both he and his brother, Hill, God rest 'im, were meek as mice, at least whenever Scoville was around. But that stinging assessment, a truth Scoville didn't like to admit, shocked him. "Must be the grief getting to him," said Scoville to himself.

He rode forward at a lope, calling to Hoy, "Hup there, fella. I don't wanna tell you again, but you got to put on that coat. You'll be useless to me otherwise." He rode up alongside his partner, glancing at him and keeping an eye on the boulders that crowded in along this stretch of the trail. It had been difficult dogging the escapee, but he felt confident they were on the right trail. The dang snow didn't help one bit, though.

Then his eye caught movement up-trail to the left, off into the rocks. It was a coyote working away at something, didn't seem to see them, so intent was it at its task.

"Hold up there, Hoy," whispered Scoville. He laid a hand on his companion's arm and the sullen man looked up, automatically tugging on the reins and bringing his horse to a stop.

"What?"

"Shhh, hush, now." Scoville nodded toward the coyote, but only the rump could be seen. He winked at Hoy through the thick snowfall and slid his rifle free of the boot. "Gonna have us some fun." He thumbed back the hammer slowly, brought the rifle to his shoulder, and sighted.

Hoy said, "You think it's wise to shoot now?"

Scoville's cheek muscles bunched. He squinted down along the barrel, tightened his finger on the trigger. Dang that Tompkins for being right. He wasn't so sure he liked this new side to Hoy. He liked him a whole lot better when he was with his brother. But those days were long gone.

He sighed, lowered the rifle. "Reckon I'll let him be. C'mon," he said, thumbing the hammer off cock and sliding the rifle back in the boot. "See what he's so all-fired busy with in them rocks yonder."

They heeled their horses forward. The coyote stood atop a tumble of smaller rocks, most no larger than a man's head, that looked as if they'd been wedged there by some slide from above, or else by human hands. The snow covered most of them so that they looked like a pile of dusted eggs. When they were within six feet of the coyote, he lifted his head and stared at them. A small splash of red gore hung from his mouth corner, and the lighter hair running along his black lips was streaked with a pink-red tinge.

"Go on!" shouted Hoy, waving his arms.

The thin doglike creature bared its teeth and growled.

"Get on out of there!"

Its storm-cloud-colored hide twitched and rippled and, as if by unseen strings, it danced upward among the higher rocks, then down again, following some path of its own. No doubt it wouldn't go far, for whatever it was snacking on was a prize it did not wish to give up easily.

"What you go and do that for?" said Scoville, grinning as they watched the critter depart.

"He was eating on something and I can't stomach the notion of killing and blood right about now."

"Then, mister," said Scoville advancing his horse so he could see what it was the coyote had been so all-fired interested in, "you ought not to have come on this posse ride."

"As I recall I didn't have much of a choice."

The deputy canted his head. "Hoy, I can't figure you today. Seems like you never talked to me this way before."

"I ain't never had a dead twin brother before neither." He dismounted. The snow reached halfway up his boots. He stamped them to get the circulation flowing. "You try it sometime. I tell you it's not a good feeling."

Scoville shook his head. "Ain't likely to happen," he said, climbing down out of the saddle. "I ain't even got a brother, let alone a twin."

Hoy rubbed his eyes with the heels of his hands, but he said nothing.

Deputy Scoville lightly slapped the ends of his reins across Hoy's raised arms, handed them to him, and clambered, slipping and sliding, on up the man-height tumble of rocks, his curiosity spurring him on. The reddened snow before him was a promising sight. Maybe the coyote had gotten a rock rabbit. Certainly not a fawn of some sort. Wrong time of year for that.

He toed a loose rock aside, and it tumbled backward into a crevice. When he looked down to where the rock had resided, he saw part of a man's lower face. The cheek had been chewed away to reveal frozen bone and muscle and the bare long gleam of teeth where they curved impossibly long from the gouged-away meat of the lower jaw.

"Oh, oh," he said, stumbling backward, shaking his head. He slipped and slid back down the rock, landing splay-footed back beside Hoy. The horses danced and backed away from him, but Hoy held firm to the reins.

"What is it?" he said.

"You don't wanna know." Scoville's grimace told it all.

"Yeah, I guess I do."

"Okay, then. It's a man. Who it is, I don't know. But somebody covered the man with rocks. Sure as shootin' he didn't do it himself." He winked, smiled. "Rocks ain't all that warm a blanket, eh, Hoy?"

"You have never been funny, Randy. Just want you to know that." Hoy handed the reins to the staring deputy and headed for the rock pile himself.

"Where you going?"

"To see what this is all about. Might be it's the man we're after. Might be we can get on back home with his body and be done with it."

Scoville shook his head. "Oh no, you don't. We're going to dig him up all right, like I had planned before you opened your yapper. But this don't change a thing. We've still got to go on and find whoever did this. 'Cause even if this is the man we're tracking, that big boy who, I think, Marshal Wickham let go from the prison, then we still got to drag the ringleader of the gang back to justice in Bakersfield. It's my sworn duty."

Hoy snorted, kept climbing, his hands sliding off the snow-slick rocks.

"Besides," Scoville went on, "I aim to drag Wickham back too. Something ain't right with that old man, and I can't put my finger on it. But the more I think about it, the more I think maybe he's in on all this, yessir." Scoville tied the horse's reins together and looped them over a stunty bush. It would do for a few minutes.

"Here, now, here, now," he said, scrambling past Hoy. "You got to make sure you don't taint the evidence."

For the first time in a couple of days, Hoy smiled. His longtime friend's natural annoying attitude never ceased to amaze him. There was no way he was going to get in the deputy's way. Let him have the road, the glory as he would no doubt call it. For Hoy's part, all he wanted to do was investigate the body, see who it might be. If it was indeed one of the men who had helped kill his brother, then he would let his emotions dictate his reaction.

His mother had always told him that still waters run deep, especially when she looked at him as opposed to his dear dead twin, Hill. He always took that to mean that she thought he was a smart fellow, and that he wasn't afraid to think for himself. He'd done precious little of that, especially when in the company of Randy Scoville. It had always had been that way. And for the time being he saw no reason to think otherwise, but he'd let him have his way for now. For a little while anyway.

"Help me with these rocks, Hoy. But don't look at the man's face. Oh, but he's a hard character. I don't recognize him. You can look if you like, but he's rough."

Hoy glanced at the man's face as they lifted free the rocks covering him. "I recognize him. He's not the man from the jail. The big one they caught, I mean. And he ain't the head of them all. Least not by the descriptions of him. He's one of the others, though. He's one of them, to be sure."

Scoville paused. "You sure, Hoy?" There was a light in is eye, a gleam that shone like tiny tinder fires.

"Yep," said Hoy, nodding, not slowing down on the rock removal. "We'll never get this done this way. Too cold and there's too many rocks on him."

"Well, what do you suggest, then?" Scoville shook his head as if he were addressing a child.

"How's about we throw a loop around him, yank him out of there with a horse?"

Scoville nodded. "Now you're talking. You said what I was about to say, but you interrupted me." He glanced at Hoy, then looked away quickly. Hoy was too busy cuff-ing aside a nest of smaller rocks lodged against the dead man's chest to respond. But Hoy did smirk.

Scoville's face burned hot in the white pelting snow. "Yeah, okay. I'll get the horse. You keep on tugging at them rocks. I daresay you'll make some headway one of these fine days. . . ." He chuckled, but it was not a convincing sound.

Behind him, Hoy's smirk faded as a fingertip poked the dead man's chest. It was stiff, cold, unyielding. As was his brother's body back home on the family dining table.

He straightened and sighed, closed his eyes a moment as the cold snow hit his face and melted against the warmth there. There would be no more tomorrows for his beloved Hill. But, Hoy vowed there would be an uncounted number of them for him.

And, he vowed, he would make certain that he spent each moment of each one tracking the vicious killers who laid his brother, his twin, low. And if he should lose his life in the process, so much the better. Even if he had to put up with Randy Scoville, old friend, old pain in the backside.

"Hey!"

Hoy opened his eyes and spun toward the voice of the very man he'd been thinking of. A frost-hard rope slapped him hard in the face.

"Wake up, dunderhead!" Scoville's bray carried off on a southerly wisp of breeze. Hoy pulled in a long, deep draft of breath, let it out slowly, and nodded. It would be a trial, but it was his burden to bear.

He scooped up the rope and looped it about the dead man's exposed torso.

It took them scant minutes to drag the dead man up, where he teetered, as if he were dithering about whether to leave his cozy rocky cocoon or allow himself to be

dragged back down to the trail. Then the dead man top-
pled, still bent, down the rocky slope to lie wedged on his
shoulder in the trail. His rescuers stared down at him for
a few silent moments.

Finally Scoville said, "He's been savaged with what I'd
guess was a knife."

"Golly, Randy, what makes you say that?"

"Fact that his gut's been opened up." He looked at
Hoy, narrowed his eyes. "You know so much, you should
search him," said Scoville, hands on his hips. "Might be
he's carrying more clues."

Hoy regarded him a moment. "Might be," he said, before bending to the task. He carefully pawed the dead
man, whose body was a stiff thing, bent in odd angles
from being stuffed into the rocky crevice.

Scoville wrinkled his nose and nodded. "Now, that's a
dead, dead man. Hoo-boy, but I tell you what, he don't
smell half as bad as he should. On account of the cold
and all. We should be thankful for that. You know what
I'm driving at, Hoy?"

Hoy stopped, looked up, one hand resting on his knee.
"I believe I do. It seems I have a recent history with the
dead. Which you seem to have forgotten."

"Oh." Scoville's face reddened. "Didn't mean to cause
hurt there. But what I was driving at was something
about when he was killed. You know, his gut being all
opened up like that and all. Might be I could apply the
training I've got to how he's been killed off." He stood,
rubbing fingers across his stubbled chin.

"Don't you think," said Hoy, "that you would see
more if you bent down and studied the man?" He tried
to keep a grin from escaping the corners of his mouth.

Scoville reluctantly nodded. "Mmm, yeah." He coughed,
kneeled, still several feet from the body, pointed toward

the dead man's belly. "Now, see there? That's a sure sign that something was wrong."

Hoy sighed. "Randy, he was gutted with a knife. Anyone can see that."

Scoville nodded. "Mmm, yeah. I was getting to that. But you are far too hasty to ever make a good lawman, I can tell you that."

Chapter 36

He neared the last steep cleft in the rocky trail, the cleft that would lead, hopefully before nightfall, to the old leaning miner's shack that Haskell knew to be there. At least he hoped it was still there. He could use the solidity of walls and a roof about him. And in this storm he would not be worried about sending up smoke from the old sheet-steel stove that had been in the corner of the cabin.

Might have to empty it of pack rat dung and send to hell the few critters who might have looked on the shack the same way Haskell did. Heck, he might even waste a bullet or two on their mangy little hides. Not as if he intended to go farther through the mountains until he'd done the same to the posse men who would surely be following anyway.

It took another two hours before the shack came into view. Seeing it was a relief for Grady. He'd half expected it would have blown down or had been burned—or worse, moved into—by some soul other than himself. He approached the tin-roofed structure slowly, halting his train of three horses on the near side of a last jutting jag of rock. From behind it he would be mostly unseen from whatever scanning eyes there might be within the shack.

Though there was no smoke rising from its leaning chimney pipe, Haskell knew that might not mean much at all. He leaned back against the rock, felt the chill and wetness of the snow. It had soaked into his boots, down his collar, through his old hat, and cold wetness had run down his face, caught in the stubble of his beard, and itched like dozens of little bugs.

Right now all he wanted to do was get in that shack, stir up a warming fire, and dry himself out. He wanted to be in good shape when the storm was over. If he knew much about posse men, and he'd had his share of scrapes with them, then he knew they rarely trekked toward their prey in the midst of a little blizzard such as they were now having.

He felt safe in this judgment. After watching the shack for a full two minutes, he saw no shadowy movement, no sign of breath rising from a window—the only one visible to him was a paltry window covered with the remnants of sacking tacked up on the inside. As Haskell recalled, that sacking had been there when he was here last, about two, two and a half years before. Had anyone been here since?

"Well, horse," said Haskell to the hangdog mount standing closest to him, "looks like we'll be sleeping pretty tonight." He looked at the horse. "Leastwise I will be. You, you sorry old soap sack, and your two compadres, will be outside. You better pray the snow lets up. I ain't got but a few handfuls of feed left for you all. But I daresay you can eat through the snow and find yourself something. Won't matter. I'm fixing to make a meal or three out of one of you anyway. Whichever of the three of you looks worst will be the one to go in the fry pan. The other two, I have use for. So you stay fit."

There were no tracks in the snow, leading to the shack, no depressions in it to indicate anyone or anything had ventured there at the least since the snow began the day before. Haskell cradled his rifle and leading the horses he strode purposefully to the shack.

He poked the snout of the rifle in through the flapping window cloth, parted it, and saw nothing inside save drifted snow, the stove, and the rough log bunk in the corner. The little lopsided table with the fancy turned legs still stood by the door. Grady smiled and led the horses around to the lee side of the shack. "Enjoy yourselves. I got housekeeping to get to."

Grady sighed, squinted into the slowing snow. The clouds still hung low, dark, shapeless masses that threatened more of the chilling white stuff. It took Grady twenty minutes to get the stove cleaned out. The stovepipe hadn't been clogged, and for that he was grateful. Must be my lucky week, he thought, a scratchy laugh bubbling up his throat. Another few minutes and he had the shanty as cleaned out of debris and snow as he was likely to do. He laid the rest of the gear—money bags first—on the rough bunk.

He set the coffeepot and fry pan, both filled with water, on the little stove top, to melt. He chewed slowly on a strip of jerked beef, parted the window rags once again with the rifle barrel, and gazed out. He saw only his own tracks. The trail beyond the little cabin could represent trouble, should someone somehow get beyond him and double back, or come at him from the northeasterly direction toward which the trail led. But he doubted it would happen.

It was more likely that any attacks would be from the

same direction he'd come. But one thing still bothered him, and that was Dutchy. In truth, Haskell had had his doubts about the man. He'd not seen eye to eye with him since he first met up with Pap and his gang. He'd also recognized that the man was not your average lazy thief. He was a man out for himself, for anything he could grab.

That was a trait Haskell himself knew only too well. He'd been surprised that it wasn't the big, sullen Indian who'd lived through it all, the one who'd been a pain in his backside, the one to cause him grief. But no, he'd been the first of the gang to die. At least he'd provided a welcome slowdown, distracting the crazies from that town long enough for him to plug Pap and then ride hot on out of there.

But now Dutchy was nowhere to be found. Before Haskell had split with them all on the trail, he'd told them he'd meet up with them, that he had to go on ahead and make sure things were as he expected on up the trail. And to prove he wasn't leaving them to fend for themselves in the dust, he was letting each continue to carry the money they'd all ferried from the bank.

Ace and Simp looked as though they'd bought it. And the fact that they were still heading toward the rendezvous point verified their foolish acceptance. But Dutchy, that man was a different piece of work altogether. He'd looked at Haskell with something like humor in those two dark eyes. Even as his mouth grinned and his head nodded, Haskell knew that Dutchy was on his own page of the book.

But to abandon them and make a run for it on his own? Not hardly. No, Haskell didn't buy that gambit one bit. And that was why he suspected Dutchy was fixing to ambush him, rebound, and set a trap for him. After all,

Chapter 37

The cool, steady snow pelting his face brought Charlie around, dragged him up out of his deep torpor. He tried to stretch his arms and legs, as was his custom when he awakened, but he hurt something fierce, and he couldn't move his limbs. He was leaned against a log; that much he was pretty certain of.

The fuzzy feeling in his head began to pull apart enough that he was able to recall snatches of all that had happened to him. Once again the river washed over him—this time in his mind, feeling that pain from the rocks wrenching his legs, the water slamming him this way, then that, filling his mouth.

Then he remembered being dragged . . . a rope up out of the river by someone . . . a horse? Then there was mud, lots of mud.

"Charlie? You okay now, boy?"

Someone called his name—Charlie forced his eyes open, tried to run a hand over his face, but something held his arm down.

"Charlie? Can you hear me?"

He tried to speak, felt as if he had gravel in his throat.

He swallowed and tried again. "Yeah, who's there? Who's that?"

"Charlie, it's me, Marshal Wickham. You in your right mind now?"

"Marshal . . . you found me. Oh, I'm coming around now, I suspect, but I tell you . . ." He swallowed again, ran his thick tongue around his dry mouth. "I reckon I've felt better. What in blue blazes happened to me?"

Wickham laughed. "That's a long story, Charlie. Time enough for all that once you've waked up enough to take a drink of water. You're dry as a cork, I'd wager."

Charlie nodded slowly, kept his eyes open. "You're right. I could use a cool drink. Thank you." He focused through the steady snow on the bright, dancing shape before him, past his feet. It was a campfire. It felt good enough by his feet—which he noticed weren't in their boots—but he wanted to crawl forward and put his face right by that fire. He tried to shut up again, but found he couldn't. "What's going on here, Marshal?"

Wickham brought a tin cup full of water. "That's a long story. Lemme untie your hands so you can drink."

"Who tied my hands?"

"I did," said Wickham as he worked the knots free. "You was trying to kill me, so I had to do what I had to do."

"What's that mean?"

The rope came free and Charlie slowly raised his hands before him, rubbed the wrists gently. He reached for the cup with one big paw, gulped it gratefully, then reached for his head with the other hand.

"Easy on your bean, there, son. You've taken a mighty wallop."

"I remember."

"You do?"

"Yep, the river. That was one hard ride."

The marshal slowly made his way down to Charlie's feet, began working on the ropes there.

"You tied my feet too?"

"Yep, as I said, you were a mite worked up."

The firelight reflected off the old man's face. Charlie saw a swollen nose and purpled cheek, and the eye above was half swelled shut. "Marshal, what on earth happened to you?"

The old man finished untying the rope, dragged it free from Charlie's ankles, and sighed. "You did, you big galoot."

Charlie sat up too fast, got a case of the dizzies, and held his head. "I . . . I did? Marshal, I don't know what you think, but I wouldn't do that to a man. Not unless he deserved it." He peered at the marshal.

"Relax, Charlie. You wasn't in your right mind. I had to yarn you out of the river and revive you by whomping on you to get you breathing again."

"That don't sound like something I'd beat on you for."

"Well, like I said, you weren't in your right mind."

Charlie sat in silence for a minute, then said, "You mind me asking how you got the better of me?"

Wickham laughed, then reached up and held his jaw. "Oh, that hurts. Charlie, seems to me you'd make a pretty good politician. I mean that as a compliment." He took a pull on his flask. "I did the only thing a man in my position—and condition—could do. I beaned you upside the head with a length of driftwood by the riverbank yonder."

Charlie looked into the dark. "So that's what that sound is. I thought maybe I was all fuzzed up in my head."

"No, we ain't made it all that far in the last day and a half, Charlie."

"Day and a half?" He said it too loudly, sat up too fast. His head throbbed like a cannon booming.

"Yep, but you needed the time to recover. I think you're better off for staying put."

"But Haskell," said Charlie. "He's . . ." Then he sagged back against the log. "Oh, he'll be up there, waiting for us at his little shack. I reckon we're not but a day or so from him."

"Charlie, Haskell's likely got a whole lot of stolen money and a couple of horses to lug it. He'll be long gone over the pass up there. Best thing we can do is head on back to Bakersfield. We've given it a good lick, but there isn't much more we can do."

Charlie spoke, his voice coming out bigger than he anticipated. "You do what you need to, Marshal Wickham, and I'll do the same. I'm heading on up into the mountains." He leaned forward. "Hey, how's Nub? He make it okay?" Charlie swiveled his head around, as if he could see through the snow and into the dense dark surrounding them.

"Relax yourself, boy. He's fine. Off yonder with my Missy, picketed and as well as I can make him. He has a sore back leg, but I think it's a bruise. He should heal up in fine shape. Heck of a horse, that one. Nub, you say?" Wickham chuckled. "Good name."

Charlie leaned back, closed his eyes. "He was a gift. From a good man, a good friend of mine."

Wickham nodded, said nothing.

Soon Charlie roused himself. "I tell you, I could eat a small elephant, Marshal. No offense, but you didn't send me packing with much food." Before the marshal could answer, Charlie said, "And while I'm talking on it, I reckon you trailed me awhile, huh?"

"Yep, since town."

"Then you saw what happened to Ace?"

"I saw what you did for him, if we're talking about that man on the trail. The one I assumed Haskell killed."

"That's what happened all right. Ain't no reason Haskell should have done that."

"No man deserves to be murdered."

"So where's the posse, Marshal?" Charlie wiped the snow off his face. "And why in blue blazes didn't you build a shelter?"

"Well, pardon me all to heck, Charlie Chilton!" The marshal sounded half ticked off. "I been a little busy tending to you and your ailing hide and then there's the matter of my own whomped-on head."

"Oh, Marshal Wickham. I'm sorry about that."

"You are a prize package, Charlie Chilton. But tell me more about why you think Haskell will be waiting on us, up ahead on the trail."

Charlie sighed. "Only if you tell me why you let me go free from the jail. And what you're really doing out here."

Chapter 38

Haskell sat upright, not knowing where he was. It was dark, cold, and he felt sort of numb—then that much at least came back to him—he'd polished off the last of the whiskey he'd had in his own saddlebags.

It wasn't enough to lay him low all the next day, but it was enough to dull him up for the next few hours of sleep. Which was something he should have known better than to do. Especially given his jitters over being eyeballed by Dutchy. He didn't think the man was lurking around, had been mostly convinced he wasn't, in fact, which was why he'd tucked in to the whiskey.

But there was a little bug, burrowed deep in the back of his brain somewhere, that kept on digging, making him think that he should be paying attention. And that was what woke him up. That and the sound of a disturbance somewhere close by.

"Coulda been a mouse," said Grady to the small, dark room. Where he was at was coming back to him, the miner's shack, above the little cluster of buildings, the remnants that had at one time been a mine camp. But Grady was glad there was only this one left. He didn't need other folks around. Never had and never would.

Instinct had driven him to snatch at his rifle, the worn stock cool in his hand. His other held the haft of his skinning knife. He held his breath. Focus, boy, he told himself. Something had awoken him. Something had made a noise, a scuffing sound that set his instincts to jangling as fast as a finger snap.

Had to be that rascal Dutchy. Ain't no way any posse could have gotten here this fast, even if they knew where to go—and the only one who could have told them was the big kid, Charlie boy. He'd have blabbed all right.

But Grady had sent the first batch of do-gooders back home to Bakersfield, crying into their hands with at least one dead man among them. They'd lick their wounds and the fool young lawman who'd been leading the charge would have a time whipping up lather enough for a new batch of posse members.

Haskell knew he had a couple of days on them—and that was before the storm. So who could it be? Likely it was Dutchy. He'd been a lippy one, and too uppity for his own good. Should have shot him when I had the chance. Right there in the bank when he'd started haranguing me about popping that old man. Too annoying by half.

Part of Haskell wanted Dutchy to show up. Might mean he was dumb enough after all, to wander in expecting his share of the loot. But more than likely he would be sniffing around for all of it.

There it was again! Grady tensed, eased his right leg down off the bunk. He shouldn't have slipped his boots off. Now his feet were cold, especially the big toes ticking through the holes in the ends of his socks. Ought to trim those nails, else they'd keep on and eventually work their way through his boots too.

Wouldn't matter once he got to some city where he could hole up. He'd have a Chinese whore trim his toes, feet, and tend to everything else that needed it. But first, it was time to gut whatever was roaming out there. Didn't sound like a mouse to him, sounded like a Dutchy. . . .

He gently shoved the seven bank bags off him—he'd used them as a partial blanket, and found it was true, cold cash that could keep a body warm—and slid the rest of the way off the bunk. He paused when a plank popped from his weight. He shoved upright and padded across the room to the window.

Earlier he'd managed to cover the thing with an old flannel shirt. It managed to keep much of the snow out, save for twin drifts along the floor where the wind whistled on through.

The stove had chewed up most of the wood he had managed to scavenge, but there was little point in keeping it going. Save for the coffee and beans he'd warmed, there was little heat in the paltry affair. He had initially thought to give it a day or so, make sure he wasn't being followed. But the cold was helping convince him that his plans might not have been the best to begin with.

There—had that been a shadow? Not hardly, not with all that cloud in the sky. Again he heard something. By the door this time? He bent low, cat-footed to it, and peered out through a gap between boards. Dark . . . the snow had slowed to a lighter flurry, and . . . there! A long shadow fled by!

Haskell poked the snout of the rifle hard between the boards, pried to make the gap wider, but he was too late. Whoever had made the shadow was gone from range. Haskell held still, heard nothing but his own breath and the wind beginning a soughing sound through the ragged top of the tin chimney pipe.

He tugged on the rifle. It was stuck, wedged tight between the boards. For the moment he forgot the intruder, the fleeting shadow that wanted his money. Grady tugged on the rifle, yanked harder. The door bucked back and forth on its strap hinges, sounding violent and out of place in the windy, dark canyon.

He paused, his teeth grinding, cursing himself for the noise, for jamming the rifle in there, for finishing the whiskey—he could have used a few swallows about now—for not having much tobacco left, for the cold night, for his foul plans. It was all building up to a big headache.

And then another sound, beyond his huffing and his under-the-breath growling, came with a fresh round of eerie soughing from the stovepipe. The new sound was a shade different, rose with it, reached a higher pitch, then split from it. And that was when Grady heard it for himself, the unmistakable sound of a man's chuckle, a dry, wry sound rising above the shack, spinning there in the breeze, then peeling apart and blowing away. But as soon as it vanished from his hearing, another round descended, seemed to swirl around the outside of the cabin.

Grady stood, wrenched free the rifle, snatched up his boots, tugged them on, and kicked open the door, bellowing, "Show yourself, you howling cur! Might as well, 'cause I am Grady Haskell and there ain't no escaping my wrath!"

The cackling laugh pinched out, but the wind kept right on building blustering snow into his eyes, pelting like cold sand. He held up his forearm, shielded his eyes, even though there was precious little to see save for snow, the shadows of the peaks surrounding him, and the bulk of the cabin to his back. And that was where the laugh came from once again. He spun, peered into the gloom of the single room, saw nothing.

From behind, a soft swishing sound as though someone was running through the granular snow. Grady spun again, completing a circle, snow pelting his face, catching in his eyelashes, his mustaches. There! A dark shape disappearing around the far corner of the shack.

It was not a large structure and Grady covered the span in three strides. Scowling, he looked down at his feet, bent low as she shuffled forward. The snow had drifted deeper on this side of the shack. Sure enough, there was a ragged trail, as though someone had run along before him.

"Come and get it, you dog!" Grady howled his seething rage into the wind's own snapping bite. All he received for his efforts was more laughter trailing to him from the far side of the shack. Grady bellowed wordless oaths, growled as he drove forward through the snow, stumbling and spitting snow.

Before he made a full circuit of the shack, he thought he saw movement far off to his right, where the land dipped low and away to a narrow wash, the site of many rummagings in the past by old dirt hounds looking for color among the rocky outcroppings of the jumbled landscape. And leading back to him from that far-off point of motion, a thin trail through the snow was visible.

In a flash, he realized what it meant. Already running around the last side of the shack, Grady let out a long, thin moan and lunged for the gaping doorway. Snow had been kicked in. Had to be more than he'd let in when he exited. . . .

But his main concern led him to the bunk, to the sacks of money. There had been seven when he left—the three he'd ridden off with, plus two each from Ace and Simp—and as he groped, his heart pounding, clawing its way up

out of his throat, he felt two, then two more, then ...
"No! No, no, no!"

Grady swept the bunk free, the four sacks thudding to
the floor, his blankets and saddlebags flopping down by
his feet. He kicked them, clawed at them, scrabbled on
the earthen floor, seeing almost nothing, but knowing,
after seconds of fruitless searching, the truth.

"Gaaaah!" His shouts as he bolted from the shack
drowned out the storm's whistling winds. He kept up the
shouts as he bolted, half tripping, half lunging down the
trail. Not easy to see, but plain enough for a dedicated,
haunted man, the footprints were spread far apart, made
by a man in a hasty retreat.

Haskell ran, falling every few feet, driving his knees
into hidden wedges of rock. The pain bloomed sharp and
searing, but he didn't care. It was all he could do to lift a
revolver and crank the hammer back. But he did.
"Dutchy!" *Blam*! "Dutchy, I will catch you!" *Blam*! "And
I will gut you!" *Blam*! *Blam*!

Soon he lost all sense of direction, realized he'd likely
strayed from the trail. Breath came in stuttering gasps.
He couldn't pull it in fast enough, and when he did, it
only trickled. His heart pounded like the fists of ten angry men against his chest, neck, and throat. Grady bent
over, rested his palms on his knees, and gasped, spittle
stringing from his mouth.

The snow swirled about him, and the entire time he
shouted, "Dutchy!" over and over. But soon he realized
he wasn't really shouting, rather chanting the name of
the cursed thief. He was sure there was humor in that
somehow. A thief who steals from thieves. But not now.
Now there was nothing funny in this.

When Haskell's breath had begun to dribble back

into his throat, a new thought seized him, stopped the breath in his throat. The money, the rest of the money.

He was barely aware of the desperate whimpering noises rising out of his mouth as he scrabbled in the snow, sometimes on his hands and knees, looking for his own trail back to the miner's shack. As he rummaged in the snow, following his own blustering false trails, a far-off sound stilled him for a moment—a cackling laugh.

He looked toward where he thought the sound might be coming from, a ridge across the ravine down which he'd stumbled, and, yes, there it was, a flare of light as if a match had been struck. A match for one purpose—to taunt him.

Haskell sagged into the snow, his teeth grinding into powder. As the laughter whirled away on the wind, he staggered to his feet and slowly made his way back up the hill down which he'd stumbled. Yes, of course, he thought. That's the direction. And he made his way back as fast as he was able.

The four remaining sacks were still there. And though he was too tired to rage, Grady managed to slowly put the mess back to rights once again. He retrieved his rifle from the floor and checked it over. Fine, just wet from the snow. Then he sat on the bunk, rifle across his lap, and gritted his teeth, listening to the storm and waiting for a second attack. Sure that Dutchy now felt he was an easy target.

Most of all, Grady Haskell stewed over the fact that Dutchy the thief now had three more bags of cash to add to his initial two, giving him five. That left Grady with only four. Only four, blast it!

Chapter 39

Despite Marshal Wickham's protests, Charlie insisted on pressing forward the next morning. "Lay around enough for the last couple of days, so you tell me. And I'm grateful for your help, I truly am. But I been wronged, Pap's been wronged, and most of all, there's a whole town of folks been wronged, some of them terribly. And all by one man." Charlie leaned against Nub. "I can't let that be."

"But, Charlie," said the marshal, still hunkered over the campfire, rubbing his hands together and shaking his head. "You're barely able to stand. Look at you, man."

"I got to try. Marshal, don't you ... don't you feel nothin' for them folks?" As soon as Charlie said it, he knew it stung the old man, who slowly looked up at him with wet eyes.

"Yeah, Charlie. I reckon so." He hung his head for a moment, then scratched his chin and pushed to his feet. "Okay, let's go." He ambled toward his gear and began stuffing it into the saddlebags, rolling his blankets. "I still say you're off your bean. There's no way Haskell will be anywhere but gone."

"Might be," said Charlie, "but at least then we'll know.

I ain't sure about you, but I can't abide the thought of knowing there was a chance and I didn't take it."

"Okay, okay, you made your point. Now stop yammering and let's get on the trail."

Within their first hour on the trail, the snow had dwindled to little more than a scant pelting nuisance. By the time nearly four hours passed, the low gray sky, which for two days had felt like a massive wet wool blanket pressing down on the world, had begun to show signs of fraying and splitting apart, revealing slices of lighter gray glowing through.

"In luck, eh, pard?"

It was the first time in an hour that either of them had spoken.

"How's that, Marshal?"

Wickham looked up, then back to Charlie, who was riding behind. "The weather. We're in for some honest-to-goodness sunlight, methinks."

Charlie looked up. "I reckon. Be a nice change to this gloominess." He was smiling when he looked back to the marshal. But his smile faded as he saw the man had stopped at a bend in the trail up ahead. It looked as if it was opening up, widening. "What's wrong?"

The marshal took a few seconds to respond, then said, "Charlie, you'd best gird your loins, son."

"What?" Charlie didn't know what that meant, but from the man's tone, it couldn't be a good thing. "What are you seeing there?"

Marshal Wickham looked back. "Charlie. I think we may have found another of your friends."

"Oh, Lord no."

The marshal nodded, beckoned the big man to ride up beside him.

The scene before them was odd. A man was laid out

on his back. Small drifts of snow had sculpted against his outstretched legs. At first glance it looked to Charlie as if Simp—for, from the coat and hat, the side of the face he could see, that was who it appeared to be—was stretched out, feet toward a campfire, taking a nap.

Surely the marshal was wrong. As Charlie recalled, ol' Simp was always a little dozey. But something prevented him from shouting, "Ho the camp!" And then he saw it, saw the scene for what it was. The fire wasn't smoking. The man's legs were akimbo. Blood stained his front.

"Aw, no. . . ." Charlie urged Nub forward.

"Charlie, hold up there!" The lawman had drawn a revolver and rode ahead of the big man, eyes scanning, neck swiveling. "Won't do to get ourselves killed, now, would it?"

But Charlie didn't hear him. He'd already dismounted and was making his way to Simp's side. But the man was stone cold.

Marshal Wickham came up beside him. "Ah, another one. Too bad, too bad." He bent, nosed the man's coat with the barrel of his gun. "Killed before the snow came." He stood, looked around the little clearing. "Dang snow, can't get a good set of tracks off fresh, untrod snow."

"Don't need tracks," said Charlie.

"How's that?"

Charlie nodded down the trail toward a long narrow cleft in the ragged hills flanking them. In the distance, rising from the center, stood a tall rock spire, nature-made, but unmistakable to anyone searching for something called the Needle.

"Huh," said Wickham. "That's where Haskell's headed, eh?"

"That's what he said. Said to head to the Needle. Said there was the remnants of a little mine camp. The shack he'd be at would be a ways beyond that, off by itself. Near a draw, I think he said."

Wickham nodded, said nothing.

Charlie began kicking snow off stones, prying them loose.

"Don't tell me . . ."

"Can't leave him this way, Marshal. It wouldn't be right."

Wickham sighed, nodded. "At least let's drag him over there to that crevice, see if we can't make our work a little easier."

They did, and then Wickham suggested Charlie go through the man's pockets in case there was something they might use to contact Simp's next of kin. Charlie's eyes widened.

"Charlie, if you don't want to, I'll do it. Ain't like I haven't dealt with the dead before."

"No, it's not that. It's that . . . I forgot to do that for Ace."

"Well, you said so yourself that the man didn't speak much of kin. It's likely he was alone in the world. You did the best a man could for him, Charlie. Take comfort in that."

Charlie nodded glumly, and they dragged Simp to the gully in the rocks. As they gently piled stones atop him, Wickham said, "How come he trusted you with all this information anyway, Charlie? You don't mind me saying so, for an innocent man—and I'm not doubting you one bit, mind you—you seem to hold a whole lot of rare information."

Charlie stood, stretched, and sighed. "I been asking myself that same question. I think he didn't know what to make of me. I told Pap all I could remember, not that it did much good."

"It must have, Charlie. He didn't join them."

"He wouldn't have anyway. I thought maybe I could get Pap away from them. But Pap, he up and told me to get gone."

Wickham nodded. "He was saving you, Charlie. Plain as the nose on my face. He was making sure you weren't part of the mess."

"I reckon. I did see Haskell one more time, though. That night, I left camp, and he followed me. We had words and I laid into him. Thought for sure he was going to shoot me, but he didn't. Now I see that his weapon of choice is a knife. We was close enough he could have used it on me."

"Providence was with you, Charlie. That's all I can say."

"If I knew what that meant, I might agree with you, Marshal."

Wickham smiled. "Let's finish up here, say a few words, and then we best get going. There's another storm boiling up and we want to close in on this rascal before he comes to his senses and decides to vamoose."

Chapter 40

"What you suppose got into them so they named this town Tickle?" said Marshal Wickham, holding a jagged-edged plank at an angle, reading the crudely carved inscription: . . . ELCOME TO TICKLE. He set it aside, decided not to burn it. "What sort of notion would come into a man's head to make him do such a thing?" Then a slow smile spread across Wickham's face. He snapped a finger and leaned forward. "Well, now, it occurs to me I might know what they named it after. A sporting girl! Had to be."

Charlie's face bloomed bright red.

The old lawman looked at him and smiled. "Aha! Weren't so dark out, I'd guess your face looks like a hammer-struck thumb, Charlie. I was you I'd spend a little more time with a sporting girl or two, wear off that modest edge you got built up since birth, I'd wager. A woman has a way of softening the edges of a man, taking the mean and irritable out of him, if'n the man allows for it."

Charlie cleared his throat, looked away. Finally he said, "I . . . I wouldn't know about such things, but I do know you remind me of a man I knew . . . man who said the same sorts of embarrassing things."

The marshal let it lie for a few quiet minutes, then said, "I'm guessing you mean that fella Pap you talked about."

"Yessir, I do. He was a good man, you know. I know all those folks back in Bakersfield think they know what they know, but they're flat wrong, that's all."

Wickham nodded. "I'm sure they are, Charlie. You tally up all the times a man thinks he's right, then isn't, in this life, you come up with a bigger number than when he's pure-dee right."

"Could be."

Wickham unscrewed the cap of his flask, took a last pull, and stared into the small, comforting fire. He, for one, was glad when they'd decided to call it a day and build a fire. After burying that poor fella Haskell gutted, why, it was all they could do to cover more ground. They'd made it another hour and a half before the storm came in hard and fast. It was a howler. That snow of the day before had been a mere tease.

He'd known women like that, not many, but it was enough to give him pause. They had to be close to Haskell, if as Charlie said the man would be waiting. But could he trust the boy's gut feeling? Why on earth would a man like Haskell, who'd left nothing but a trail of vicious, mindless slaughter in his wake, want to stay put and wait for the posse? Made no sense, but Charlie was convinced.

He sighed and leaned forward toward the cook fire at the front edge of the makeshift lean-to they'd constructed. There was an ample supply of downed and living pines that grew in thick patches hereabouts. They would not be investigating the trail anymore tonight. The weather had made sure of that. Well, the weather and the dead man Haskell had left behind.

As if reading his mind, Charlie said, "One more."

"How's that?"

"One more to go. Fella by the name of Dutchy. Like I said with the others, I don't see him hurting someone for money."

"I know, Charlie," said Wickham, leaning in to stir the nearly bubbling pot of beans. "But sometimes when a man gets all caught up in a heated moment, he doesn't think so good for himself. He starts to think about what he could do with all that money and then he sees all the people who are in his way, and sometimes he commences to shooting."

"But the boys . . ."

"Now, I'm not saying they would do such a thing, Charlie. I'm only telling you what I've seen in my years as a lawman."

They were both silent a moment longer. Then the marshal said, "Goes by the name of Dutchy, eh?"

"Yes, sir. I don't know why. He don't look Dutch to me. Not that I know what that is."

Wickham laughed, ran a finger under his eyes. "Charlie Chilton, if you don't beat all. I doubt even people who are Dutch know what it is they are."

Chapter 41

"And there's something else too, Charlie," said the marshal, ladling up a dripping spoonful of beans and juice. "That first man you found, the one you know."

"Yeah, Ace. I told you all I know about him."

"I know, I know, but look." The old man wagged the spoon at Charlie for emphasis. "What didn't you find when you found him?"

Charlie scrunched his eyes. "All due respect, but what sort of a question is that, Marshal?"

The marshal tapped the spoon against his hat brim. "Think, Charlie. Think." He resumed eating.

Charlie shrugged. "I dunno. I reckon he should have had a hat. He wore a gray one, I recollect."

"A hat? Charlie, the man was a bank robber and all you can come up with is a hat?"

Charlie snapped a finger and pointed at the marshal, smiling. "I got it, I got it. Money. He should have had money on him."

"Now you're cooking with lard. But how much? What'd it look like? And how did he get it out of town?"

Charlie's brow knitted again. "A horse, he had a horse."

"Yep, and where was it when you found him?"

Charlie shrugged. "I kind of figured it run off some-where."

"Not hardly, Charlie. Not up here and not for too far. Odds are it was taken."

"Taken? By who? Indians?"

"Charlie, were you born this thick or is this something you picked up on the trail?"

"No need to get all rough-and-tumble with me, Mar-shal. Some of us ain't natural-born lawmen, you know."

"Oh, I know Charlie, I know. I'm funnin' you." He leaned forward. "Look. It's plain to me as the nose on my face, so I'll tell you what I think. We know this Has-kell fella killed your friends, right? And he took the horses and he took the money those men had carried with them away from the bank heist. You see? Simple."

"What's he want with all those horses?"

"To carry the money for a while. One horse would tire out. Likely he'll bundle it all up and put it on a pack-horse, take one with him. He's been collecting them so far, though, you see?"

Then a fresh thought occurred to Charlie. "If he's only set on bringing a horse to ride and a packhorse, what'll he do with the others?"

"Knowing his kind as intimately I do, I'd say he'll likely kill them, bring some of the meat with him. Won't have to hunt that way."

Charlie gasped. "But he can't do that to a horse."

"He can, and if my money's still good in these parts, I'm betting he will do that."

A new thought made Charlie's skin creep. "Marshal?"

"Yes, Charlie?" The marshal paused, a spoonful of beans halfway to his mouth.

"Marshal, if he's killed Ace and Simp . . . well, it ain't looking too good for Dutchy, now, is it?"

"No, Charlie, no, I reckon it's not." The marshal sat quiet for a time, watching the fire. "And that's the start of it, I'm afraid."

"How's that, Marshal? Start of what?"

"You don't see what he's all about, do you, Charlie?" The old lawman set his tin plate down on a rock. It wobbled, and the spoon slid to the edge, rattled off. He didn't pay it a bit of attention.

"Ain't you gonna pick that up?" Charlie looked at the spoon. His gran had always hated a mess, always despised mistreatment of her cutlery.

"What?" Wickham looked down at the spoon by his boot. "Fine," He snatched it up and held on to it. "Look, Charlie, I'm talking about something important here and you're concerned with a spoon? Wake up, boy. This character, Haskell, he's playing for the pot. He won't be satisfied until he has it all, and has us all dead. I don't think for a moment that he's beelining for MacLaughlin Pass, which is the likeliest place for him to cross. No way. He's holed up at that old shack, waiting on us, like you said earlier."

"How's he know we're the ones coming for him?"

The marshal stretched his legs out, rubbed his knees. "Oh, I don't think he's seen us from on high, but he's assuming—and rightly so—that the goodly folks of Bakersfield won't let his deadly shenanigans go unpunished. He's counting on them sending a posse, or more likely a rope-stretching brigade, to track him. And he'd be right, as I say. But he won't know how many or how far off his rowels they'll be. But I also know scurvy-ridden dogs like him, and it's rare they leave anyone behind who might track them. No, Haskell will hole up and kill all comers."

"And that's us," said Charlie.

Wickham nodded. "Near as I can figure, we're it."

Charlie sipped his coffee, winced. It was piping hot and the bitter brew hurt his split lip. He blew across the top of the cup. "What about that posse?"

Before the marshal had a chance to answer, a strange voice cracked through the cold night air surrounding the little camp. "Yeah, you old goat, what about that posse?"

Marshal Wickham spun, his black duster flaring even as he stood, his hands reaching for his revolvers as he turned. But he was not fast enough.

A lithe, dark form strode into view and whacked the old man on the right side of his head, catching the ear and knocking Wickham's black hat off. It sailed a few yards away into the dark.

Charlie rolled backward off the log he was holding down, flinging his scalding coffee outward. But the stranger was too far away by a yard—the coffee did little more than arc in a spittle spray and cause the man to sidestep.

But the real damage had been done—Marshal Wickham stood bent over, groaning and holding his head.

"Marshal!" he hissed, scrabbling to get ahold of his knife. A sharp quick pain in his lower back stopped him short. He tried to turn, suppressing a groan, but another round followed, preventing him from doing much more than grabbing the log with one hand, clapping a big hand to his back with the other. He'd been kicked hard with a boot toe or a rifle butt—so there were two of them, at least.

"Get your hands up, you vicious killer!" said the voice behind Charlie. "I want to see your face as a bullet drives a third eyehole in your forehead."

The first stranger spoke. "Stop your ruckus there, Marshal. You know and I know I caught you fair and square in the act of colluding with a known killer. Sitting here all chummy with him, telling him your plans, swapping plans betwixt the two of you to make off with the loot, no doubt."

"Don't be an idiot, Randy Scoville. You know blamed well I—" The tall stranger delivered a kick to the marshal's breadbasket and the old man folded up like a dropped coat. His head hit inches from the little fire. The marshal groaned, tried to push himself to his knees, but he was not, from Charlie's perspective, doing a very good job of it

The stranger stepped close before Wickham could gather his wits and stripped the old lawman's revolvers from him. He tossed them behind him in the snow, then reached in again and ripped Wickham's belt knife free. The action spun the old man's body and he cried out in pain. It sounded to Charlie as if something bad had happened inside to the old man, as if the kick had damaged something vital. He'd be lucky if it had only cracked a couple of ribs.

"Now hush up, both of you criminals." The man Wickham had called Randy strode closer to the fire. Charlie could see him now. He wore a sheepskin coat, leather gloves, and one of those wool caps with the earflaps Charlie had so long admired. He also wore a star pinned to the coat, right there on the outside.

The man behind him delivered another hot, dull boot kick to Charlie's back. This one glanced off bone, and it forced a surprised groan from his mouth. "Gaaah!"

"What did I tell you, killer man? You shut up until I give you permission to die."

That was the man behind him, who now stepped over Charlie and into view. Even in the dark he could see the man was a haggard-looking mess. His face was puffy, eyes reddened. He wore no hat, and his darkish hair, long in places, stuck up as if it he'd been licked by a cow. His over-all appearance was that of a man who'd been on a drunken spree for a week and had no intention of letting up.

"Randy," gasped the marshal. "You got the wrong end of the stick."

The tall man spun on the marshal, rapped the snout of the rifle lightly against the old man's wizened cheek. "Oh, that's the way of it, is it? Listen hard, old man. I heard you plain as day talking about all those wonderful things you were going to do up in the hills, talking about how you got horses all awaiting to carry the loot, how you and the killer, big boy over here, are going to head over some pass to live a fine old life. We heard all that, me and Hoy, and you can't deny it."

"You heard wrong, Randy. You dumb son of a—"

The next blow was a hard, wracking one, again with the stock of the rifle, that caught the marshal in the chest. He sprawled backward, his elbows giving way as he collapsed. His head dropped to one side and his breathing became a labored thing.

Charlie struggled to his feet, lurched forward, bellowing, "Why don't you pick on me for a change!" His shins hit the log hard. He felt it happening and tried to raise one leg up over the log at the last second, but only managed to trip himself further. He lumbered as if time had slowed, falling over the log, then sprawling face-first beside the fire. Anger gripped him.

Despite the lancing pains in his back from the coward's kicks, he pushed himself up on all fours like a great bear, growling his anger. He tried to rise, spurred on by the sad sight of his new friend, Marshal Wickham, a sagged mess of an old man, struggling to breathe, sprawled on his back in the churned snow of the camp.

But Charlie's rage was a short-lived thing, for the second man, the one who looked so poorly, drove a rifle butt into the base of Charlie's neck, dropping him once more to the ground. The dim sights of the nighttime camp, the smells of the sputtering, smoky campfire, the sounds of agitated horses nickering and stomping all jumbled and pulsed together, wavering in and out, then pinching out altogether. He hoped, come what may, that Nub would be taken care of.

The last thing he was aware of before blackness and silence overcame him was the sound of laughter, two men guffawing as if they had done something mighty. But as the blackness hammered down on Charlie, he wished he could have told them how wrong they were.

"We got 'em, by Jove. We got 'em!"

"Ain't all of them, though."

"Why you so sour, Hoy? I told you, didn't I, that Wickham was in on it from the start? And that other one, well, who would escape from jail if he wasn't guilty as sin?" Deputy Scoville upended the whiskey bottle and gurgled back a long swallow. He handed it to his companion, Hoy, who followed suit.

A howl, man-made, erupted out of the snowy night somewhere ahead of them. Hoy paused in dragging his hand across his mouth. "What was that, Randy?"

"Coyote?" But Scoville's voice was small and weak.

"Told you," whispered Hoy, "we didn't get them all."

In seeming response, the howl erupted again, closer, and tapered off into a cackling laugh. Then the voice shouted, "I see that campfire! You all must be posse!"

"Oh," whispered the deputy. "What does that mean? Who do you suppose it is?" He looked left and right into the snowing night.

"Might as well shoot yourselves now," growled the voice, closer but moving fast, off to their left. They heard snow crunching, branches snapping. "'Cause I'm about to do what you don't!"

"It's the head of them all," whispered Hoy. "The boss of the thieves. The one who's done all the killing." He stood up, ran a coat sleeve across his face to clear away the snow. His wet hair hung down in his eyes like strips of rag. Hoy pushed his coat aside, up and over his revolver. "The one who killed my twin brother, Hill."

With that, Hoy stalked off in the direction from where they'd last heard the voice.

"Hoy! You can't do that! I'm the boss here. You stay put. It ain't prudent. . . ." Scoville watched his friend's black wool coat disappear into the swirling bluster of snow and night. "Hoy!" he shouted louder. But heard nothing.

His shouts roused Marshal Wickham, who groaned and blinked, scrunching his eyes as if to clear his vision. "Randy?" he said in a muffled voice. He tried to raise his arms, saw they were bound at the wrist, as were his ankles. Charlie lay beside him, a trickle of blood curling around his neck, down his shirt. But Wickham saw the big young man's chest rising, falling.

"Randy, son, you've made a terrible mistake."

Scoville walked over to him, looked down at him. "Shut yourself up, old man."

Wickham looked up at him, narrowed his eyes. "You're scared, aren't you? What's wrong?"

Scoville turned away. "Nothing of your concern. Hoy went out to kill a killer, is all."

"What?" Wickham looked around the camp. "Randy, Haskell's out there. He's a murderer. He's insane, Randy. Don't let Hoy go out there alone!"

"What do you mean?" The deputy glanced down at Wickham, then out toward where he'd last seen Hoy. "Hoy?" he said.

"Randy, untie me. I can help. But we got to work together on this. Haskell's a ruthless killer. I'm guessing you saw the men on the trail?"

Scoville nodded blankly.

"That was Haskell's handiwork. Unless you want Hoy to end up the same, you'll cut me loose. That'd be three against one."

"What about him?" Scoville nodded at Charlie.

"He's a kid, Randy. A big kid, but a kid. He doesn't know one end of a gun from another. Had nothing to do with any of it."

Wickham held up his bound wrists, shook them toward Scoville. But the deputy's look of confusion and fear gave way to narrowed eyes. He shook his head and sneered. "You're trickin' me, old man. You're trying to play me false again. No, uh-uh. You are a bad seed."

"Randy, don't be a fool! That boy is going to die out there at Haskell's hands and you—"

A quick, high-pitched scream sounded, then clipped off, only its echo continuing for scant seconds before disappearing in the wind.

"Hoy! Hoy?" Scoville threw down the whiskey bottle he'd taken from Wickham's saddlebags. "I'm comin'!" He ran toward the scream.

"Randy, no! Don't do it! It's what he wants!" Wickham heard the foolhardy youth's footsteps punching away into the night. "Randy!" Soon there was only the wind and blowing snow.

Then came a grunt from beside him. Dodd Wickham leaned over onto an elbow. "Charlie?" he whispered. "You okay, boy?" His own head thudded like a cannon fusillade, but he did his best to ignore it. Had to wake the boy. They had no time before Haskell found them.

It took what felt to Wickham like long, long minutes—too long—but finally Charlie Chilton came around. Wickham scooted over close and Charlie was able to untie his hands, though the boy was acting dull-witted. As he untied their feet, Wickham explained what had happened, telling Charlie who the two men were and why they were there.

Charlie nodded and rubbed his temples slowly.

"You're worrying me, Charlie. You took a mighty knock to the bean. Too many more of those and you'll be a blithering idiot."

"Don't know what one of them is, but I'd guess I wouldn't like it. I'll be all right soon enough."

Wickham snatched up the bottle of whiskey Randy had tossed aside. It was still a third full. He gulped a couple of swallows then offered it to Charlie.

The big man shook his head. "Never have had any yet," he said.

Wickham tossed it aside. "Good. Don't ever start, you hear me? It's bad news for the man who can't stop. Trust me on that score. Now grab a handful of snow. Rub it on your face, hard. Work it in like sand, and then eat a fresh handful. Trust me, Charlie. It'll help revive you, straighten out the kinks in your head." He grinned at Charlie. "I know because I have 'em too."

Charlie did as Marshal Wickham told him to, and it helped. He felt less mechanical, a little bit more himself. He ate more snow and it felt good, in and out. "What do we do, then?"

"Since Randy saw fit to run off and leave us, no matter his noble cause, we have to arm ourselves and get away from this firelight. Might be if we leave it Haskell will be attracted to it, like a moth to an oil lamp. We can only hope."

It took some minutes, but they scavenged Wickham's rifle and two revolvers, and then he rummaged in the snow and pulled out the shotgun Charlie had carried. "Here," Wickham said, jamming it into Charlie's hands. "You're going to have to learn to use this thing, and quick. If Randy's campsite rampage didn't upend everything in my bags, I have a dozen shells for this thing."

He found them and handed them to Charlie, who brushed him away. "I can load it. I'm not a child, Marshal Wickham."

"Well, Charlie, that's good to hear. Now let's stick together, walk quietly, and head in that direction yonder. It's opposite from where Randy headed."

"But what about him? Shouldn't we help him?"

"That's what we're doing," said Wickham. "If we walk right into Haskell, what good will we be to Randy?"

"You sure the other fella's dead?"

Bending low and wincing with each step, Wickham beckoned Charlie to follow him, deeper into the dark night, snow swirling about them. "If that scream wasn't the last thing that poor boy ever said, I'll eat my hat."

They walked in stop-start fashion for a dozen yards, each man suppressing pain from various wounds and afflictions accumulated over the previous several days. Neither felt much like trudging through the snowy sparse woods looking for a freshly killed man, another who might soon end up the same, and trying to evade the dripping knife of a murderous fiend who might or might not be watching them while they trudged. . . .

They walked a couple of man lengths apart, each keeping track of the other with a wide eye. Marshal Wickham periodically bent low, scanned the snow, shook his head. Within a few hundred yards of the camp, Charlie glanced back but could no longer see the weak fire they'd left behind in the small lean-to.

A strangled cry far off to their right froze them in their tracks.

"Randy!" growled the marshal. "Come on." He motioned to Charlie and they bolted toward the sound, each knowing that Haskell had probably done in the young man, each doubting that it had been the other way around.

They hadn't scramble-slid ten yards when they heard a shout.

"That all of ya? That all you got? I doubt you'd only send two men—make that boys!" A laugh cut through the zinging wind sounding like a saw blade dragged over rusted wire. "You keep on a-comin'. You know where to find ol' Grady!" The laugh trailed off, some distance from where they'd heard the cry.

"Hask—" Charlie began bellowing the killer's name, but Wickham clapped a long, cold hand over the big man's mouth.

"Don't let him know there's more of us, and don't let him know where we're at! It's our only hope!" Wickham hissed the words close to Charlie's ear.

Charlie nodded, but it was all he could do to keep rein on his animalistic rage. He wanted to twist off Haskell's head with his bare hands.

"Come on," whispered Wickham. "Time enough for him. We got to find the boys."

And it didn't take them long. Wickham was in the lead, walking slowly and scanning left, then right, when he held out an arm and made a low whimper. Charlie looked down and there they were.

The snow had yet to cover the slumped forms of the

two young men with more than a light dusting. Wickham had bent down, grabbed the shoulder of the top form. The body flopped to the side. It was Deputy Randy Scoville. From the looks of the scene, he'd been bent over the prone form of his friend Hoy when Haskell had come up behind him and stabbed him high in the back.

As soon as Charlie realized this, he dropped to one knee and scanned the snowy scene, holding the loaded shotgun outthrust and ready. Wickham said close to his ear, "They're done, Charlie. Both of 'em. Vicious brute stabbed them both bad. Let's go get Haskell."

Charlie welcomed the idea. No more was said. No more needed to be said ... for the time being. They resumed their former way of progressing—the old lawman in the lead, bent low and scouring the snow for tracks. Charlie followed close, hunched low and ready to squeeze the trigger on the shotgun. He kept the remaining shells divided between his two outer coat pockets, their reassuring weight bumping against his gut as they walked.

Marshal Wickham halted, straightened, nodded ahead to where the trees thinned at the top of a rise. "See what I see?"

Charlie squinted. "No ... wait. It's starting to get light."

"Yep," said the lawman. "Good for us. Bad for Haskell. We'll wait here a few minutes more. Hold your patience, Charlie. That bad seed isn't going anywhere soon."

It was all Charlie could do to stay low as the sun made its slow climb skyward, brightening the landscape surrounding them, the snowfall slowing at the same time. Despite the sad, brutal situation they found themselves in, Charlie thought the snow was such a pretty thing, like a gossamer blanket laid over everything. Too bad so much evil rummaged under it.

"It's time, Charlie. Let's climb up to the rise, see what's what."

They did, switchbacking and keeping an eye out for anything that might vaguely resemble a killer in waiting. As they topped the rise, both men flattened out in the snow. And for the second time, the old lawman nodded, said, "See what I see?"

And Charlie did—down the slope in the gulch below sat the little miner's shack that had to be the one Haskell had mentioned. But the most unusual bit of it all was the thread of smoke rising out of the shack's tin chimney pipe, up into the windless gray sky of early morning.

"What's he on about?" Wickham squinted at the shack. "Does he think he's done with the posse? Or maybe he figures he can snipe easier from inside at whoever else comes?"

Charlie shrugged, studied the lay of the land. Now it began to make sense to him. Stretching from the shack in a long curving fashion southward, the trail they had been following for days led down. That meant their camp for the night was not too far down there too. He thought of Nub, of Missy, Marshal Wickham's horse, and the horses of the two other men, Deputy Scoville and his friend. He hoped the morning would turn warm and sunny for the horses.

"Because there's smoke doesn't mean Haskell's in there." Wickham said it aloud, though it sounded to Charlie as if it had been a private thought that had somehow escaped through his mouth.

He nodded. "But what if he is?"

Wickham turned his head, half faced him. "Then we best find out."

"How?"

"Simplest way's the best, I find. And that means we take him as close to head-on as we can. I expect he'll be looking for trouble first from the trail down below. That's the direction we would have come from. But if we approach the shack from the northwest, to our left, we can maybe gain a little edge on the surprise. There's no window that side, the side facing the trail from the south. With any luck there won't be a window on the north side either."

Charlie nodded. "And it looks like there's plenty of rocks and a few trees to hide behind as we get closer."

"You're learning, Charlie Chilton. Now let's go back downslope, head north toward that copse. Good place for us to set off toward the cabin from."

It took them much of an hour to make their way to the stand of trees that bristled to the northwest of the shack, some four hundred yards away in the gulch. By then the sun had crested the ragged peaks around them and set the snowed landscape to glittering. It was pretty, but harsh and blinding, and had made their route a slow affair.

They made it to the trees and slumped with their backs to a couple of large ones, facing the shack. "He's down there, warm and snug, and we're up here shivering in the trees. I'd sorely love a little campfire right about now."

Wickham nodded. "Not a prayer, Charlie. We can't tip him off yet. Might be he doesn't know there's anyone left out here. Now, I think we should low-crawl toward the shack. You angle up and over, and then come down at it straight on from the north. I'll come at it from this side, the northwest. Then when we both get about thirty yards or so from it, I'll motion to you like this." He waved his left arm in a wide arc. "And then get set, because I'm going to open the ball."

"What's that mean?"

"Means I'm going to raise a ruckus. Likely I'll shout something to provoke him into action. With any luck he'll scamper on out his south-facing door and come around right into my sights."

"What'll you do then?" asked Charlie, blowing on his fingers.

Wickham recoiled as if the big young man had slapped him. "What do you think I'll do? I'll shoot the evil creature."

"Okay," said Charlie. "But what about me?"

"What do you mean?"

"Don't you think I deserve a chance to . . . to lay him low?"

Wickham smiled, shook his head. "Charlie. You aren't a killer. You ever shot a man, Charlie?"

The big man shook his head no.

"Well, I have. And it's not something you can let go of. Ever. You're a good person, Charlie. Don't let Haskell taint you any more than he has already. Now stop yammering at me and let's get going." Wickham cat-footed away from him, looked back, and said, "Keep your head low, Charlie Chilton. And do as I say and we'll make it out in good shape."

"Yes, sir." Charlie nodded. "You too." He watched Wickham go for a moment, not sure of anything, not convinced of anything. He crouched low and headed in his own direction.

Scant minutes later, they were still both in sight of each other, despite a few moments when they lost sight of each other behind boulders, scrub bushes, and stunted trees. Charlie looked toward the shack. Smoke still climbed up steady but thin out of the chimney. We don't even know if he's in there. Maybe he's long gone. And where are the man's horses? Should have three or four of them.

A far-off whinny, then another, were his unexpected responses—from the east, sounded like. Charlie strained to see up that rise behind the shack, raised himself up on one knee—had to be Haskell was keeping the horses in those trees to the east....

A *spang!* sound cracked the silent morning air. Rock chips spattered in Charlie's face. He dropped down, more out of instinct than strategy, and gritted his teeth, one hand held to the right side of his face. He pulled it away. The cold red palm was speckled with blood.

"I see you out there, you big galoot! I knowed you was coming! Ol' Grady knows everything, Charlie boy! Wanna know another thing I know?"

The cold air carried Grady's voice perfectly straight to Charlie's ears. Charlie shook his head, tears of rage stinging the tiny rock cuts on his face. Before he could stop himself, he shouted, "No! You shut up now, Haskell!"

"Charlie boy, I got you pinned. I can even see your big ol' ham legs, Charlie boy!" As if to prove his point, shots, one after another, drove all around Charlie, some digging into the earth, spraying snow and gravel in their paths, some spanging off the big rock behind which he was poorly hidden. One chewed a divot in the toe of his right boot.

Charlie let out a yelp and pulled his legs up as tight as he could to his body. He was pinned down. He tried not to make the sounds he was making, but he couldn't help it. And the lead kept raining.

There wasn't a thing he could do. It was a matter of time before one of Haskell's shots hit him. Then another, and another. . . . Think, Charlie, he told himself. Think of something smart. . . .

Then he heard another voice, a different voice. It was Marshal Wickham. The shots stopped. Charlie peered around the base of the big rock, saw Wickham rise like a black-coated ghost, standing tall in the snow. His coal-colored duster flared and his rifle was pointed, cocked, and ready to deliver.

"Haskell, you cowardly no-account dog spawn! Come on out of there while you still can! This is Marshal Dodd Wickham and my posse has you surrounded! Surrender now or die soon!"

Wickham didn't wait for a response. He cranked shot after shot into the flimsy little cabin. Splintered chunks of raw planking erupted like startled birds from the walls. Charlie propped himself up, sent a shotgun blast at his side of the shack, and was pleased when it tore a ragged hole straight through. He thought, for the briefest of moments, that he saw someone inside spin and drop out of sight.

Excited, Charlie looked to his right. "Marshal! Get down!"

But Wickham wasn't listening to Charlie Chilton. He was thumbing shells into his repeating rifle, even as Haskell recouped inside the shack and began firing back at the marshal. Charlie guessed that the man must be gauging distance, though it made little sense, since the distance was not all that far. But his bullets were chewing up furrows in the snow, ever closer to the lawman.

"Get down, Marshal!"

Marshal Wickham ignored his shouts and looked up, regarding each encroaching shot with a cool regard before glancing back down at his task at hand—refilling the rifle. Wickham was also grinning.

Something happened to Wickham's rifle, though, because he thumbed the hammer and jerked the lever hard a few times, trying to free some bit that had jammed. It would not comply. And then, as Charlie shouted again, one of Haskell's bullets drove into the lawman's left thigh, above the knee. The old man howled in agony, threw down the rifle, and clutched at the raw wound.

Blood sprayed the freshly churned snow. Time seemed to slow as Charlie watched Wickham fight to keep himself upright. Even as more of Haskell's shots laced the air around the old lawman, he shucked a revolver with his right hand and cranked the hammer back, sent a bullet at the cabin, then another. The shooting from the shack stopped, and as the snapping echoes of gunfire dwindled in the little ravine, Charlie heard unintelligible but angry oaths snarling from within the shack.

"I don't bleed. . . . I don't bleed!"

What did Haskell mean by that?

Then, like a rabbit, a boot appeared, retreated, reappeared in one of the holes in the west wall, kicking, sending fractured, bullet-pocked boards sagging outward.

"Ain't the way it was supposed to happen, dang you all!"

As Haskell ranted from inside the shack, Charlie jammed in another shell, snapped the shotgun closed, and hustled toward Marshal Wickham in a low run.

He'd covered half the distance when the marshal's gun cracked again. The man's face was a carved gray mask of pain and teeth-gritted satisfaction, even as a shot drove into his breadbasket, then another behind it higher up into his chest.

He snapped upright, spun in a half circle, and faced Charlie, his eyes wide, as if the lawman was about to tell him some great secret. Blood streamed out the sagging

left side of his mouth and even before he fell, Charlie
lunged two, three great strides toward the shack. Through
the hole in the wall Haskell had kicked wider a second
before, Charlie saw a face peer out, eyes wide, then disappear.

Charlie bellowed, "Haskell!" as he brought the shotgun to waist height. He didn't wait for a response, but
snapped his finger hard on the gun's trigger. It barked
smoke and flame, tearing the hole in the shack wall even
wider.

As he spun and bolted down the short rise to Marshal
Wickham, he tossed the shotgun aside, barely heard the
gagging, clotted sounds coming from within the shack.

"Marshal!" Charlie dropped to his knees five feet
from the old man, who lay stretched on his side in a blanket of churned red snow, eyes staring skyward.

"Marshal Wickham!" shouted Charlie, crawling the
few final feet. He gently laid the man on his back, held
his face in one hand. "Marshal? You hear me? It's Charlie Chilton, Marshal."

For a moment nothing happened. Charlie looked to
see if the man's chest showed signs of movement. It
didn't seem so, but then again the man wore a whole lot
of layers. Then Wickham's eyes snapped closed, opened
again, and a long breath escaped his lips. "Charlie," he
said in a relieved whisper. "Is he . . ."

"Yes, sir, I reckon he's done for. You done him in."

"Good, good. Charlie?"

"Yes, sir, rest easy. I'll get the horses and we'll make it
back to town in quick shape, you'll see."

"No, Charlie. Stop that. I'm too old to listen to lies."
He smiled weakly. "Charlie, drag me to that tree there. I
want to sit up."

"You sure that's—"

"Charlie, don't argue. I am the law, after all."

"Yes, sir."

As gently as he was able, Charlie curled his hands beneath the man's arms and dragged him backward through the snow the few yards toward a decent-sized pine. The lawman gritted his teeth and held his breath until they made it to the tree.

Chapter 42

•

"Charlie, listen to me. Come close."

The big young man leaned in. "Yes, sir? What can I get you? I'll build a fire. . . ."

"Charlie, listen." Wickham licked his bloody lips then spoke in a slow, measured manner, stopping and gritting his teeth now and again. "You don't need to prove anything. You got to promise me you won't tote my old carcass back there to Bakersfield. Them folks don't know a good thing when they got it anyway. My being there won't make a whit of difference."

But Charlie knew, from the way the man spoke on the trail, that Bakersfield, for all its faults, was the place the marshal considered home. That he had no one else, and nowhere else to go. "I can't promise that, sir. No, sir, can't do it."

"Confound it, boy, you . . . oh, I'm in no shape to argue with a man as big as you." He cracked a smile, offered one slight wry chuckle. "Dig out my flask, will you?"

Charlie patted the old man's coat, felt how thin Wickham was. He unscrewed the top, held it to the marshal's lips.

Wickham sipped, pulled a wide sour look. "No, no. I don't need it. Got no taste for it. Isn't that something, after all these years, when I could use it, I don't want it?" He chuckled. "Life is a funny thing, Charlie."

"I reckon it is, sir."

"I'm no sir to you, Charlie. I'm Dodd. Dodd Aloysius Wickham, God rest my sainted mother's soul for naming me such. Always gave me highfalutin airs." He coughed, got control of it, then said, "Now, look, Charlie, if you won't leave me be out here, where I belong, then for your own good, don't go back there. It's a fool's errand, Charlie. Those people want blood. Your blood, my blood, doesn't matter."

He grimaced, blew out a mouthful of air. "They'll take what they can get. You're already on the short list of bad men they got pinned to their walls. You go back there and you'll end up at best going through some sham trial, and then you'll be swinging by a rope. A darn big rope, judging from the size of you. But it'll be a rope, nonetheless, Charlie. There's no way it can end good."

Charlie said nothing, but his furrowed brow told Wickham the big man was at least considering what he'd said.

"Just go, get gone, Charlie. You've paid whatever debt you may have earned because of the crime."

A moment later, Charlie shook his head. "No, sir. I reckon I'll head back to Bakersfield, just the same."

"Confound it, boy, the judge will send you to prison."

"Maybe so. I reckon if that's what the law sees fit to do with me, then that's the way I'll head. I won't be talked out of it, won't be a man who runs from his duties, his obligations in life. Some of the choices I made weren't good, some not so bad, but I never ran from a one of them. Once a thing's decided, it's decided."

Marshal Wickham sighed, sank back against the tree, tired. As if the conversation had taken too much from him. His eyelids fluttered closed and his breathing grew shallower.

Charlie bent low over him. "Sir? Marshal?"

The dying man opened his eyes. His voice came soft, faint, but Charlie heard it. "Glad to know you, Charlie Chilton. You're a good man. Frustrating as all get out . . . but a good man."

"Well, I don't know. I reckon I'm trying."

Marshal Dodd Wickham seemed to relax then, and a soft smile spread on his face. He closed his eyes, and his breathing slowed to a thread, then stopped, and his wiry frame sagged slowly against the tree.

Charlie stood, still staring at the old man. A tight weight filled his chest, his throat. Why did it happen to these men, the good ones, the ones who seemed worth knowing? Why couldn't he have had more time with them? Why were there men like Grady Haskell in the world? Men who fouled all the good things, the nice things, for the rest of the people trying to do what they needed each day, week, month, year, just to be happy. That's not a lot to ask, he thought. Not much at all.

Chapter 43

Charlie's jaw tightened as he turned his gaze toward the shack, visible in the rock-knobbed draw. Haskell was still up there. Charlie hoped the man was alive, holed up like a sick animal, the sort of beast who needed to be put down lest he infect others, over and over again.

Charlie felt a new, hot anger burn in him, burn like a hot fire up a chimney, clean up from his guts to his throat, to his nose, and into his brainpan. Felt it fill him. He ground his teeth together, his cheek muscles bunching. He walked straight toward the little cabin they'd been firing at.

From this distance it looked unchanged, as if no one had moved inside. Part of him hoped Haskell was dead, good and dead. Part of him secretly wished the man was still very much alive so that he could put him down himself. Finish off the hydrophobic beast once and for all, come what may to himself.

He stared at the shredded cabin a moment more, then gathered air and bellowed, "You in there, Haskell?"

The response was slow, but it was there. And it was unmistakable. Haskell was still alive.

"That you, Charlie boy?"

The words were faint but loud enough that Charlie heard. And they ended with a wet cough, as if Haskell was trying to spit but couldn't. It didn't sound to Charlie as if the man was faking.

"Come what may," said Charlie to himself, and strode toward the bullet-riddled, splinter-boarded miner's shack, unarmed save for his Green River skinning knife. And that he left sheathed at his side.

He walked right up to the door and kicked it hard. It spasmed inward, bounced off the wall, and settled, hanging from its top hinge. Directly opposite, Grady Haskell lay propped against the wall, a revolver in his hand, drawn dead to rights on Charlie.

Grady's bloody hand shook, the pistol wagging as if the man had a palsy. Sweat stippled his blanched face, and a wide, crooked grin twitched at the corners. Finally his hand dropped, the revolver clunking to the floor. Grady's eyelids fluttered, and then he pulled in a deep breath and looked at Charlie and smiled.

Charlie saw a long, thin man with his guts a churned mess from a shotgun blast and numerous other wounds. The big young man crossed the small room and with a boot toe nudged the revolver from Haskell's grasp.

"No!" Haskell's bloody fingers groped feebly for the gun. He dragged the hand to his lap and cringed as some inner pain racked him.

Charlie scanned the room, took in two rifles, a knife, and four revolvers. As he slowly circled the little room, gathering them, he spoke. "A gut-shot man, so I've been told, Grady, takes a long, long time to die. And what's more ..." Charlie tossed the guns out the door. He turned, regarded the bloody man, and rubbed his chin as if he were about to launch into a particularly exciting engaging story. "I hear tell that the pain is one of the most, maybe even the most horrible, excruciating pains a man can possibly endure on this earth."

"Charlie," said Haskell, trying to grin despite his obvious pain. "You are a cruel sort of fella—you know that? Now give me that gun, Charlie boy. It's the least you can do for me. One bullet's all I need so's I can do for myself. I can't take much more of this...."

Charlie went on, ignoring the man's words. "Now, I'm not telling you anything you don't know, am I? You being a man of the world, and do correct me if I'm wrong, Grady, but you're also a killing man, right? A man who I'm sure has shot more than his fair share of people in his day. Right, Grady?" Charlie pulled a wide, false grin, as if the two men were sharing a big old laugh.

"You ... you're meaner than I had you pegged for, Charlie boy." Haskell grimaced as shards of hot pain needled into him from all sides. It felt as if he were being roasted alive and being eaten by fiendish stinging insects, all at once.

"Oh, Grady, you in some pain, huh ... *boy*?"

"Yeah. . . . Oh Lordy, but it hurts like the dickens, Charlie boy. . . . I can't hardly stand it." He pulled his left hand away from his gut and held it up. The hand was barely recognizable, so much blood spooled off it, as if it were a hand dipped in a vat of gore. "Oh, Charlie ... boy ... make it stop. I can't hardly stand it no more."

"Make it stop? Hmm, no, that's plumb interesting. Makes me wonder what that little girl back in Bakersfield—you know, the one you trampled with your horse in the street?—makes me wonder what she was saying to her family. . . ." Charlie's voice cracked, but he knew he had to go on, for her sake, for all their sakes.

"When her family was gathered around her bedside and the doctor said there wasn't nothing they could do for her, except for them to all stand there and watch that young thing die. A child, Grady, with so much promise, from good people who wanted nothing but good things for her."

Charlie's big bull nostrils flexed and he leaned in close. "You got me, mister? And all them people who loved that little girl had to watch her die, awake and confused and bleeding and in agony? Oh, Grady, I sincerely hope such agonies are visiting you now, tenfold. You hear me . . . *boy*?"

Charlie stood, paced in a circle around the little busted-down, shredded-board, shot-to-ruin cabin. Outside he heard a bird of some sort warbling out a random string of night notes, the call of a far-off coyote drifting high and away. All around them life was going on, and death too. He looked through the tattered rag in the window and pulled a draft of fresh air into his lungs.

Then he heard a dry, cackling sound, soft but there it was. It was Haskell. The man had been silent and Charlie half hoped he'd expired. The fiend was laughing, a quiet wheeze, but even as blood oozed out his nose and mouth, he laughed.

"You find it all so funny, don't you? You think that little girl's death is a funny thing? I didn't think it was possible, Grady Haskell, but you are even more lowdown than I ever could have imagined you'd be."

"I'm not laughing about the girl, Charlie boy. Though . . ." He coughed. ". . . I don't recall stomping a child—don't sound much like me. Likely she was in the way anyway. Wasn't me, it'd been somebody else. Children, in my experience, are often underfoot."

Charlie's blood boiled anew. He looked down at the wreck of a man—not much of a man to begin with—and though Charlie had no sympathy for the beast, he did hope Haskell would die soon so he wouldn't have to listen to any more of his foul chatter.

"No, Charlie boy . . . I was . . ." Another wave of pain coursed through Haskell. The man stiffened, convulsed, his blood-gloved hands clawing at his gut. He groaned low, too far gone for screams.

"Charlie. . . ."

Charlie turned his back on the man and strode out the door, his heavy weight springing the spent boards of the floor, creaking them as he walked out. He filled the doorway a moment, his back to the room.

Haskell croaked, "Charlie boy, Charlie . . . boy, don't leave me like this, don't . . . Charlie boy. . . ." The "please" dissolved into a long, gagging groan, wet with blood and the imminence of death.

Charlie stepped off the sill to the hard-packed earth and breathed deep of the cool night air. It seemed he could not get enough of it.

He balled his big hands into fists, tight, realized he still held a revolver in his right, and looked at it, then tossed it away into the scrub brush. He'd had enough of such things. Had enough of everything, it seemed.

Chapter 44

Early the next morning, Charlie loaded the bodies of the four men, the good and the bad, onto their horses, to begin the long trip back down to Bakersfield. Marshal Wickham had said he didn't need to, but that wasn't so. That town and everyone in it needed to know that their lawman, their marshal, was a good man, a devoted man dedicated to the cause of being a lawman. And that was a good and noble thing.

He would bring back the sadly crazy deputy and the man with him, the one who'd lost a brother. They had no doubt been driven by fear and anger and a lust for revenge, and all that emotion only got them killed.

Ace and Simp, he'd leave them where they lay. Might be he'd have to pile up more stones on them on his return journey, but that would be part of it all. A thing a man should do for his fellows.

Charlie would bring the corpse of Haskell back for himself, to prove that he wasn't one of them, to prove that Haskell was a man who could be caught and should be caught, someone who deserved to be brought to justice, alive or dead. Then he'd toss the sacks of money at their feet.

If the judge still decided Charlie deserved to be included in that group of criminals, then so be it. At least Charlie, if no one else, would know he'd done all he could with what he had.

Mostly, Charlie wanted to go back to Bakersfield to make sure that Pap was buried with the respect due him. Pap Morton had been no saint, but he was a good man, as good in his own way as Marshal Wickham. They were men Charlie hoped to be like one day. It might be a long day coming, but he had time. Precious little else to his name, but he had time.

As the full light of dawn burned through the last of the storm's stray clouds, Big Charlie Chilton, trailing four dead men draped over their saddles, headed on down out of the mountains toward town and an uncertain future that he hoped one day might show signs of promise.

Read on for an excerpt from

THE LAW AND THE LAWLESS

A Ralph Compton Novel by David Robbins.
Available in August 2015 from Signet in
paperback and e-book.

Cestus Calloway sauntered into the Alpine Bank and Trust company as if he owned it. Which was remarkable, the people in the bank would later tell a journalist for the *True Fissure*, since he was there to rob it.

Calloway wore his usual wide-brimmed, low-crowned hat, tilted up on the back of his head so that his brown curls spilled from under it. One lady would tell the newspaperman that it had given Calloway the look of the Greek Adonis. His handsome face was split in a smile and his blue eyes danced with amusement as he drew both of his Merwin Hulbert Army revolvers and held them out for all to see. "Ladies and gentlemen," he boomed in that grand way he had, "we're here to make a withdrawal."

By "we," Cestus had meant the eight members of his wild bunch. Five of them strode in after him, spreading out as they came so that they blocked the windows and doors. It was plain they had rehearsed what to do. As one bank customer would say to the reporter, "They moved like clockwork."

The *True Fissure* would be able to identify the five by the descriptions witnesses gave. The robbers were Mad

Dog Hanks, Bert Varrow, Ira Toomis, a man who was only ever known as Cockeye, and the Attica Kid.

The bank's patrons and the pair of tellers all froze. Mrs. Mabel Periwinkle blurted, "My word!" and then blushed as if embarrassed.

Behind the rail at his desk, the bank's president, Arthur Hunnecut, was the first to get over his surprise. Rising, he moved to the rail. "What is the meaning of this?" he demanded.

Calloway chuckled and ambled over, saying, "You're a mite slow between the ears, Art."

"I don't believe I've made your acquaintance, sir," Hunnecut said stuffily. "And I'll thank you to stop waving pistols around in my bank."

Gesturing at the customers, Calloway laughed and said, "Do you hear him, folks? I bet if we look in his ear hole we'll find a turtle in there."

Mrs. Periwinkle snorted and turned red again.

"Let me gun him," Mad Dog Hanks growled. He'd acquired his handle because he looked exactly like a mad mongrel about to take a bite out of someone. It didn't help his appearance any that he had large tufts of hair growing out of his ears.

Calloway glanced at him sharply. "What's the rule?"

Mad Dog scowled and said, "Well, damn."

"No swearing in my establishment," Arthur Hunnecut snapped. "Not with ladies present."

Calloway hooked the gate with the barrel of a six-shooter and opened it. "You're a marvel, Art, and that's no lie. Step out here while me and my boys clean your bank out."

"I'll be damned if I will," Hunnecut said.

The Attica Kid came over, his spurs jingling, and just like that his Colt Lightning was in his hand. The youngest of the outlaws, he always wore black, including a black vest. His eyes, as one person would describe them, were "cold green gems." Cocking the Lightning, he said, "You'll be dead if you don't."

"I'd listen to him, were I you," Calloway said.

Arthur Hunnecut blanched.

Over by the wall, Mad Dog Hanks grumbled, "Oh, sure. Me, I have to behave, but you let the Kid do whatever he wants."

Calloway shot him another sharp glance.

"Step out here, money man," the Attica Kid said, "or your missus will be wailin' over your grave."

Hunnecut stepped out.

"That's better," Calloway said, and clapped the banker on the back with a revolver. "Now let's get to it." He nodded at Bert Varrow and Ira Toomis, and the pair went to the tellers and held out burlap sacks.

"Tell your people, Art, to empty the drawers and the safe," Calloway commanded, "and be quick about it."

Arthur Hunnecut looked into the muzzle of the Attica Kid's Lightning and became whiter still. "You heard him."

Showing his teeth in a dazzling smile, Calloway moved to the middle of the room. "I'm truly sorry for inconveniencin' you folks. This won't take but a few minutes."

"Are you fixing to rob us, too?" a man in a suit and bowler asked.

"Rob you good folks?" Calloway said as if the notion horrified him. "May the good Lord strike me dead if I ever took from the likes of you."

"What do you know of the Lord?" Hunnecut said archly.

"I know He's not fond of money changers," Calloway said. To the man in the bowler he said, "You must be new in these parts or you'd know I only rob those who deserve it."

"What did I do to deserve this?" Hunnecut said.

"Do you mean besides the high interest you charge those who borrow from you? And besides those you've driven from their homes when they couldn't pay their mortgage?"

"Now see here," Hunnecut said. "That's a normal part of doing business. A bank isn't a charity, after all."

Calloway winked and smiled. "I am."

At the front window Cockeye stirred and called out, "There's a tin star comin' up the street toward McGiven and Larner."

"Who?" Hunnecut said.

"Pards of ours," Calloway replied, moving toward the window. "Watchin' our horses while we conduct our business."

"Is that what you call it?"

The Attica Kid pressed the muzzle of his Lightning against the banker's bulbous nose. "I'm tired of your sass. Give me cause and I'll splatter your brains."

"If he don't, I will," Mad Dog Hanks said.

Cestus Calloway looked out the front window, careful to hold his revolvers behind his back. "It's that new deputy they got. Mitchell, I think his name is. He's supposed to be out of town with the marshal."

"That's what I was told by that barkeep when I scouted out the town last night," Bert Varrow said. He was the only one of the outlaws who wore city clothes—and a derby, to boot. His Colt pocket pistol had pearl grips, and he wore a diamond stickpin.

"Either Deputy Mitchell didn't go or he came back early," Calloway guessed. Quickly moving to the front door, he poked his head out and said, "Send him in here, boys." He stepped to one side, his back to the wall, and waited. It wasn't half a minute before a shadow filled the doorway and in walked Deputy Mitchell.

The deputy wasn't any older than the Attica Kid, and he had red hair and freckles. "Mr. Hunnecut," he said, "a man outside said you wanted to see . . ." Belatedly, he stopped and stiffened. "What in the world?"

Calloway stepped up from behind him and tapped a Merwin Hulbert on Deputy Mitchell's arm. "Turtles all over the place."

"What?" Mitchell said, gaping at the Attica Kid and then at Mad Dog Hanks as if he couldn't believe his eyes.

"Undo your gun belt," Calloway said, "if you'd be so kind."

"What?" Deputy Mitchell said again.

"You need to catch up," Calloway told him. "The bank is bein' robbed."

"Some lawman you are," Arthur Hunnecut said. "I told the marshal you were too young for the job, but would he listen? No."

Deputy Mitchell's features hardened and he started to lower his right hand to his holster. "Now see here. . . ."

"Don't be stupid, boy," Calloway said, jamming his revolver into the deputy's ribs. "We can blow you to hell and back without half tryin'."

For a few moments it appeared that Mitchell would draw anyway, but then he frowned and deflated, remarking, "I'm not hankerin' to die."

"No one has to if I can help it," Calloway said good-naturedly. "And I usually can."

Deputy Mitchell's eyes widened. "Why, you're him, aren't you?" he said as he pried at his buckle.

"President Hayes?"

"No. You're Cestus Calloway. The one everyone talks

about. The Robin Hood of the Rockies, they call you." The deputy let his gun belt fall to the floor.

"I should thank that scribbler from the newspaper," Calloway said. "What was that book he talked about? *Ivanhoe*?"

"You are him, though?" Deputy Mitchell said in awe.

Calloway gave a mock bow. "Yes, 'tis I."

"Why, aren't you somethin'?" Mitchell said.

Arthur Hunnecut muttered under his breath.

The tellers were hurriedly stuffing money from the drawers into the burlap sacks under the watchful eyes and leveled six-shooters of Bert Varrow and Ira Toomis. Toomis, the oldest of the gang, had a cropped salt-and-pepper beard and a wad of tobacco bulging his cheek. Thrusting his revolver at them, he barked, "Hurry it up, you peckerwoods. We don't have all week."

"And get the money from the safe," Bert Varrow said.

"It's shut," a skinny teller nervously replied, "and only Mr. Hunnecut has the combination."

"Is that a fact?" Cestus Calloway said. He bobbed his chin at the banker. "You know what you have to do."

"Never," Hunnecut said.

"We're takin' it all, Art."

"I refuse. Do you hear me?" Hunnecut said. "The people of this community have put their trust in me and I won't disappoint them."

"Kid," Calloway said.

The Attica Kid's smile was as icy as a mountain glacier. "How's Martha? Should I go call on her now or wait until tonight when you're off with your friends at that club?"

"What?"

"Or maybe I should have a talk with Cornelia. I hear she likes to wear her hair in pigtails."

A tremor rippled through Arthur Hunnecut's entire body, and he had to try twice to speak. "How is it you know my wife's and daughter's names?"

"We do our homework, as Cestus likes to say," the Attica Kid said. Suddenly leaning in close, he said so only the banker heard, "Now open that damn safe, or so help me, I'll pay your missus and your girl a visit sometime when you're not around. And you don't want that."

"You wouldn't," Hunnecut gasped.

The Attica Kid stepped back. "When I was little, I used to drown kittens in a bucket for the fun of it. I broke the neck of a puppy just for somethin' to do. And when I was twelve, there was this boy who used to pick on me and tease me because I was smaller than him and he reckoned he could get away with it. One day he was doin' it and I took a rock and put out his eye and broke most of his teeth, besides. Later there was this gent who—"

Hunnecut help up a hand. "Enough. You've made your point abundantly clear. You're a hideous killer of women and children, and if I don't do as your lord and master wants, my wife and daughter will be added to your string."

"I couldn't have put it better my own self," the Attica Kid complimented him.

His brow dotted with beads of sweat, Arthur Hunnecut went through the gate and over to the Diebold safe. Bending, he quickly worked the combination and turned the handle. There was a loud click, and he pulled the door wide open. "Happy now, you scoundrels?"

The Attica Kid glanced at Cestus Calloway, and grinned and winked.

"The puppy was a nice touch," Calloway said.

In short order the safe was emptied and the tellers handed the bulging burlap sacks to Bert Varrow and Ira

Toomis. Varrow hefted his sack and whistled. "This will be some haul."

"Bring it here," Calloway said, shoving his revolvers into their double-loop holsters.

"Must you?" Varrow replied as he carried the sack over.

"You know the rule."

"Cestus and his damn rules," Mad Dog said.

Backing toward the door, Calloway beamed at the banker and his patrons. "We're obliged for your cooperation. Remember to tell everybody how decent we treated you, and that no one was hurt." He paused and flicked a finger at the deputy's gun belt on the floor. "Mad Dog, bring that with you. We don't want Deputy Mitchell gettin' ideas."

The outlaws filed out. The last to leave was the Attica Kid. Standing in the doorway, he twirled his Colt forward and backward and then into his holster, and patted it. "Do I need to tell you what happens if you poke your heads out?"

"When the marshal hears of this, we'll be after you," Deputy Mitchell said.

"You do that," the Attica Kid said. "And be sure to tell the marshal that Ben Larner can drop a buffalo at a thousand yards with that Sharps of his." Spurs jangling, he backed out.

By then Calloway was in the saddle and reining away from the hitch rail. Some of the people on Main Street had noticed the flurry of activity and stopped to stare. "Folks, this is your lucky day!" Calloway hollered. "The bank is givin' away money for free." Laughing, he reached into the sack, pulled out a fistful of bills, and cast them into the air.

The astonished onlookers gaped.

"Get it while you can!" Calloway yelled and, gigging his mount, he made off down the street. He threw another handful of money at several women who had come out of a millinery and more bills at a group of boys who were playing with a hoop. Then he let out a yip and, with a thunder of hooves, whopping, and hollering, the outlaws galloped off.

No one tried to stop them. No one fired a shot. It was, as the *True Fissure* would later report, "as slick as anything."